Scruffy

by

Zee 'C'

New Generation Publishing

Acknowledgement

For my late Mum who was the only person for many years in the early days of my writing to read and encourage me to carry on.

Scruffy meets Sam

Scruffy lay with his head on his paws. He was very unhappy. He had watched his best friend leave the kennels for his new home and now Scruffy was lonely and sad. He always hoped that today would be his day to be chosen but it never was!

He didn't even bother to look up when the outer door opened. After all, what was the point? If it was someone coming to choose a new dog to take home they wouldn't choose a scruffy, clumsy, untidy one like him now would they?

Suddenly Scruffy realised a young boy was looking at him but still he didn't bother to get up. He just sighed and stayed where he was.

Scruffy looked at the boy through a tangle of hair and the boy looked back through an equally long and tangled fringe. The boy's T-shirt had a muddy patch on the front and his jeans had a tear in them. When Scruffy caught sight of the boy's feet his eyes widened. They were huge. Scruffy wagged his tail slightly but didn't lift his head off his paws.

The boy turned to the woman behind him, knocking all of the leads off the wall at the same time.

"Oh Sam, do be careful," the woman exclaimed. "You're a walking disaster area!"

The boy ignored this remark and said "Mum can I have this one please" pointing at Scruffy.

"Are you sure? You haven't looked at the others yet."

"Yes I'm sure, even his name is right, Scruffy, just like me" he answered.

"Oh Sam, I'm not so sure," the woman replied, "He's well, so big and scruffy."

"Well maybe he is but that's why he's so right for me. Please Mum you promised I could choose because he will be my best friend and Scruffy is just so perfect. You won't need to worry about me being lonely or on my own when you have to work because Scruffy will be there with me."

"Well I know I promised, it's just that I didn't think you would choose one like this," answered his Mum.

"Why wouldn't I choose him? He looks just like me and I know we will have lots of adventures together."

Scruffy couldn't believe his ears. He must be dreaming. He must have heard this wrong! What was this boy, Sam, saying, he wanted to take him home and they would have adventures together! He closed his eyes, shook his head, opened them again. No, the boy was still there. This was too much for Scruffy. He jumped up, forgetting about his big feet and clumsy tail. He bounded over to the door, fell over his own feet, upset his water bowl and bounced off the door. The boy clapped his hands.

"Oh Mum, look he is so excited his feet are going in different directions and his tail is in danger of being wagged off."

"Oh dear, it looks as if I'm going to be living with two whirlwinds instead of just the one, however am I going to manage? It is a good job we have a big scruffy house in the country" she laughed.

Suddenly Scruffy sat down. What was he thinking of? He had been re-homed once before but the people complained he had grown too big, he left muddy paw prints on the floor and his tail was too long. Now what was a dog supposed to do? He had only been chasing a bee in the garden and the soil under the bush had been wet so his paws got muddy. As for growing too big, he couldn't stop that now could he? The problem with his tail, it got out of control sometimes, well most of the time if Scruffy was honest with himself, but fancy having books and ornaments where they could get knocked off. Why didn't the family put them out of reach of his tail?

Scruffy had tried to be good but still they brought him back to the kennels and he was very afraid the same thing would happen again.

"Look Mum," the boy said, "you've hurt his feelings now. He'll be great, just what we want. Will you please stop fussing! I've made up my mind! Scruffy is the dog I want and we are going to take him home with us today. He will be sad left here for any more nights and I'll miss him too. You go and fill in forms or whatever you have to do and I'll stay with Scruffy to keep him company until you come back. We have lots to talk about and we have to make plans about all the adventures we are going to have tomorrow, the next day and the day after that."

"Ok you win," laughed Sam's mum, "but goodness knows what will happen when you two get together."

"Oh Scruffy you're perfect and we will have such fun together. Don't worry about your big feet and shaggy tail. I often fall over, my feet get muddy too and I'm always knocking things over. Mum's really cool, she won't mind, I promise."

Scruffy couldn't believe his ears. This boy was admitting he fell over, knocked things down and left muddy footprints on the floor. The boy's mum had gone to fill in the forms and they were going to take him home.

Was this possible? Had his dreams really come true? Was he going to be part of a real family at last?

It certainly looked like it!

When Scruffy's kennel door was opened he ran out and jumped up at Sam trying to kiss him all over. His paws planted themselves on Sam's shoulders and his head knocked off Sam's baseball cap. Both boy and dog ended up on the floor in a tangle of legs and arms. Sam's mum just laughed.

"Well Sam it seems you've met your match. It's usually you knocking things over, this time you're underneath."

Grabbing Scruffy by the neck she tried to haul him off the boy. The T-shirt was even muddier and the jeans were sprouting a new tear but Sam was just laughing and trying to get up despite a great, hairy lump of dog sat on his chest.

"Scruffy, get off me you great lump" laughed Sam, "if you don't get off me we'll never get home."

Suddenly Scruffy realised it was really happening. He was going home with this boy and his mum. What bliss and the boy's mum seemed fun as well.

Scruffy was finally pulled off his best friend and a lead and collar put on.

"Now be a good dog Scruffy" the kennel maid reminded him. "Don't play too rough and remember your manners."

"With a master like my son that will never happen," Sam's Mum replied, "Sam doesn't know how to play gentle and certainly won't remind him to wipe his feet or do anything slowly. It's like living with a hurricane and I suspect him and Scruffy will be inseparable except when Sam's at school. Meanwhile we have all the school holidays in front of us."

"Oh don't look so worried, there is nothing left in our house that's breakable, Sam has seen to that and rag rugs and tiled floors don't show dirt. Come on you two let's get you home so you can go exploring and I can get some work done."

With a wave at the kennel maid and a promise from Sam's Mum to let her know what mischief the two rascals got up to Sam's Mum drove away from the kennels. Scruffy sat on the back seat with Sam's arm about his neck and wondered when he was going to wake up. He shook his head and knocked Sam's cap off again. No he was still in the car going to a new home, what bliss! He reached out and gave Sam a big wet sloppy kiss.

Shortly Sam's Mum turned off the main road down a country lane. After a while they pulled up outside a big farmhouse at the side of a thick dense forest. At the bottom of the garden there was a stream with a rickety bridge over it leading to open fields as far as you could see.

Sam began to scramble out of the car and Scruffy tried to get out at the same time and they got stuck in the car doorway.

4

Sam's Mum burst out laughing.

"Well I expected you too might get to be inseparable but I didn't expect you to get stuck in the car doorway on the very first day! Come on Scruffy, you wait until Sam gets out. Don't worry we won't leave you in the car."

Finally after a scramble of legs and arms boy and dog tumbled out of the car and raced up the path to the house.

Scruffy suddenly became scared. What would this house be like? Was he going to get into trouble with his big feet and swishy tail? Sam put his arms around his new friend.

"Don't worry so Scruffy, it's going to be okay. Let's just go in and I'll show you. There is nothing to break or spoil. I'll show you where everything is then we'll come back outside and we'll go for a walk and explore before tea."

The words walk and tea did wonders for Scruffy. He bounded up the path after Sam's Mum with Sam close on his heels. They burst into the kitchen almost knocking Sam's mother over.

"Hang on you two, not so fast. Sam get that bowl and put some water in it for Scruffy so he can have a drink and I'll make you some juice then out you go whilst I get on with some work. Scruffy, that's your bed next to the stove and you'll get breakfast and tea when Sam has his."

Scruffy lapped gratefully at his water, it was thirsty work finding a new owner. The hair round his face became wet and he dripped on the floor. He looked down and realised that it didn't matter. The stone floor would dry, the room was warm and cosy and when he looked at his bed in the corner 'Wow' it was just a huge pile of cushions and blankets that he could flop down on. He bounded over to try it out. Yes, it really was comfortable, just like it looked. He tried to wait patiently but couldn't so he tore across the kitchen to remind Sam about the walk. He knocked Sam's elbow, which spilled Sam's drink but no-one shouted at him.

"Okay Scruffy lets go and explore before tea," Sam said "see you later Mum."

The two raced out of the door on their very first adventure.

Scruffy Gets Lost

The pair raced off down the path towards the forest.

"Come on Scruffy," shouted Sam, "I'm going to show you the den in the forest that I've made. I often go there but it's lonely on my own. Now I've got you to share it with me it will be better. We can do all sorts, build tunnels, climb trees, follow animal tracks and lots of other things."

At that Sam ran on ahead and Scruffy followed in hot pursuit. They entered the forest through a gap in the fence. At first it wasn't bad but as they went deeper into the forest it became darker and darker. Scruffy wasn't too sure about this new place. The trees seemed to loom over him and he kept imagining things were going to jump out at him. He tried to keep close to Sam but kept tripping up over things sticking out of the ground. Sam didn't seem to have any bother although now they were in the forest Sam had slowed down and the pair just ambled along. Eventually Scruffy got used to the dark shapes and began to enjoy the walk. He realised the trees and bushes were exactly that, not menacing shapes that were going to jump out and attack him. He began to feel braver and didn't stay quite so close to Sam's heels. He even ventured off the path a bit to smell at tree stumps and flowers that were growing on the ground. He saw several bees and butterflies, which he had seen before, but the smells were different, exciting, so he strayed a bit further off the path.

"Don't get lost Scruffy," Sam said, "You don't know your way back home yet."

Scruffy heard Sam but was busy smelling such an interesting smell he just had to follow it. With his nose to the ground he followed the trail. The smell got stronger and Scruffy's tail wagged harder. How exciting. He wondered what it might be? It sort of smelt a bit like another dog but different. He came to a patch of grass. His eyes grew wide, what were these floppy eared animals eating the grass? Suddenly they bounded away and disappeared into the ground. Scruffy was bewildered, they looked soft and cuddly. Why had they run away and disappeared? He wasn't going to hurt them, he just wanted to play with them! He went to look in one of the holes they had disappeared down but he could only just get his nose in the entrance and couldn't see anything. He sat down to wait to see if they would come out again to play, the smell he had been following forgotten. Suddenly he heard Sam's voice.

"Scruffy, where are you?"

Scruffy gave a couple of barks but stayed watching the holes where the animals had gone. Sam's head, then body, appeared through the bushes.

"Oh there you are Scruffy. I thought I'd lost you! What are you doing? Oh I see you've found some rabbit burrows have you? Were they playing in the clearing when you arrived and you wondered what they were? They won't come out again until we go as they are frightened of us. We might as well leave them alone."

Sam gave Scruffy a cuddle and Scruffy went a peered in another hole but still he couldn't see or hear anything. He sat down to wait again but when Sam came and sat down beside him and told him that the rabbits were now in their underground homes and may not come out for hours, Scruffy decided to follow Sam back to the path and see if there were any more smells and trails he could follow.

Sam and Scruffy ambled along the path a bit further until Sam came to a tree.

"Just stay here a minute Scruffy. This is my favourite tree for climbing. I know you can't climb trees but you can watch me."

Within minutes Sam was halfway up the tree and had disappeared among the branches and leaves. Scruffy sat down to wait like Sam had told him to but suddenly he saw a bee land on a flower. He bounded over to investigate, the bee flew away but a butterfly landed on another bush so Scruffy went to see if the butterfly would play. Sadly it flew away but then Scruffy smelt the smell he had been following when he had found the rabbits. Did this mean that there were rabbits nearby? Scruffy placed his nose to the ground and followed the trail. He completely forgot about Sam up the tree. The smell followed the track for a while before disappearing into the forest. Deeper and deeper Scruffy plunged into the trees. He was so excited he couldn't wait to find out where the trail led. He never gave a thought to Sam, his new home or even where he was going. Excitement just led him on. He came to a stream and lost the smell. He decided to cross the stream and see if he could find the smell on the other side. He waded into the stream, oh it was very cold and as he got to the middle very deep. It came halfway up his body and nearly up to his chin. Scruffy had to lift his head up to keep it out of the water but continued to paddle to the other side. He pulled himself on to the bank and gave himself a shake. He was cold and wet and didn't know where he was. He couldn't remember even why he was here at all. The trail he had followed had petered out and he realised he was lost. He sat down on the bank and looked across the stream. It was no good he could not remember how he had got to the stream and he certainly didn't feel like going back into the cold, wet water. He wandered down the side of the bank but he was cold, wet and hungry and surrounded by big dark trees. He lay down and began to feel sorry for himself. He had found a nice new home and a special friend and had just thrown it all away. He didn't know how to get out of the forest let alone find the house. Anyway he was quite sure neither Sam nor his mother would forgive him for wandering off and not staying with Sam. A big fat tear gathered in Scruffy's eye and rolled down his muzzle. Another tear followed, then another and Scruffy finally gave in and howled in sadness, fright and loneliness.

Meanwhile Sam thought about how unfair he had been on Scruffy to just abandon him at the bottom of the tree while he sat up it. He had been begging his Mum for a dog for ages and now on the first day he had left him on his own. He had not even left him at home in his comfy bed but out here in the forest where Scruffy had never been before. Sam scrambled down the tree as quickly as he could to reassure Scruffy he would never be so mean again only to find Scruffy had gone.

Sam looked around but couldn't see any sign of him. He called Scruffy's name and listened, but all was still and quiet. Sam didn't dare go back and tell his mum he had lost Scruffy already! Why, oh why hadn't he stayed with his dog and looked after him? Sam knew the forest, as he had explored every part of it and never got lost, but he knew that Scruffy didn't, and could be anywhere, lost and alone. Sam tried to think what to do? Then he remembered that Scruffy had huge paws and was a big heavy dog so surely he would have left paw prints in the soft ground.

Sam looked around for clues. Yes, there was one near the flower, another near the bush. He then noticed the prints going off down the side of the track. Sam carefully followed the paw prints, constantly making sure he knew where he was. Once the prints went off the track into the forest, Sam made sure he marked the way he was going so he could find his way out again. He was fairly confident that he was walking towards the stream which eventually ran at the bottom of their garden but wasn't taking any chances in case he was wrong.

Sam suddenly realised he had someone else to be responsible for now and would change the way he acted. Sam stopped dead in his tracks as he thought about how he would feel if he never found Scruffy again. He would be devastated! Although he had only known Scruffy for a few hours he felt he had known him all his life.

This thought galvanised Sam into action and he set about his task with renewed energy, determined never to let Scruffy down again. The sun was setting and the shadows in the forest lengthening but Sam continued to follow Scruffy's paw prints. He emerged from the trees and yes his hunch had been right, there was the little stream that eventually ran along the bottom of the garden. Sam lost Scruffy's prints on the side of the stream and decided that Scruffy must have crossed the stream. Yes, he could just make out the damaged bank where something big, likely Scruffy, had scrambled out of the stream.

Now Sam had a dilemma. Did he cross the stream like Scruffy or waste time walking upstream and crossing at the rickety bridge that he knew was there? Sam looked down at his feet at the new trainers his Mum had bought just last week. He really should have changed them before coming out but had forgotten as usual. He began to walk towards the stream fully intending to just wade in and pick up Scruffy's trail from the other side when he heard a noise.

It was quite faint but sounded like a howl. Now Sam was quite aware that there were several foxes living in and around the forest but it didn't sound quite like a fox. Sam listened again, nothing, then suddenly, yes there it went again. It sounded so mournful and unhappy. Sam felt instinctively it was Scruffy. Sam knew that all animals, but especially dogs, had better hearing than humans so called out his name.

"Scruffy, Scruffy, where are you? I'm here, Sam is here looking for you. Scruffy, Scruffy."

Scruffy pricked up his ears, he thought he had heard Sam calling his name. Scruffy shook his head. No he was probably dreaming. He was sure Sam would not come looking for a bad dog like him. He would just have to stay here until he died.

Then Scruffy heard it again, yes he was sure it was Sam. He couldn't believe it! He stood up and gave 3 good big barks and tried to decide where Sam's voice was coming from. Sam heard the barks and realised that Scruffy, he was sure it was his bark, was upstream from him. If he walked towards the bridge calling Scruffy's name they should get closer. Sam began to run, the mud from the bank squelched in his trainers, the bottoms of his jeans became plastered in mud and somewhere he lost his hat but he didn't care he was just intent on finding Scruffy. Every time he called Scruffy's name the barks became louder. The bridge came into sight and so did Scruffy a bit further along.

As Sam saw Scruffy, Scruffy saw Sam. Both raced to meet each other and met in the centre of the bridge. They collided in a tangle of legs and arms and fell off the bridge straight into the water. As Sam tried to stand up Scruffy knocked him over again. Sam sat up in the middle of the stream, threw his arms around Scruffy and gave him a great big hug.

"Oh Scruffy, I'm so sorry I left you to climb that silly tree. I'll never do it again. I was so frightened I had lost you for good. Please say you love me still and will stay and live with me and Mum forever?"

Scruffy couldn't believe his ears. He was sat in the middle of a stream soaking wet, well so was Sam for that matter, and Sam was asking him, Scruffy, to forgive him. He shook his head. No, this was stuff dreams were made of. It didn't happen to big, scruffy, clumsy dogs like him. But, no, Sam was looking at him and telling him how much he loved him and wouldn't let him down again. This was too much for Scruffy. He launched himself at Sam to give him the biggest kiss he could manage but knocked Sam backwards into the water again. Spluttering Sam tried to sit up again and laughingly said,

"I guess that's my answer. You do forgive me and still love me. Get off you great oaf and we'll go and see what's for tea. Mum will be wondering where we are."

Just at that moment Sam's mother came round the bend in the stream and saw the pair sat in the middle of the stream.

"For goodness sake why are you sat in the middle of the stream? Oh I guess the pair of you were on the bridge and fell off. Well get up now and come home. Sam, you go and have a warm shower while I find some old towels to dry Scruffy with. Sam you may as well put your pyjamas on as there will be no more adventures for today. You can both spend the evening sat quietly over the fire, although I think that might be impossible for you two."

Sam laughed, "OK Mum, for once I think you might be right about a quiet night in front of the fire. Scruffy has worn me out."

"I don't believe it! So miracles can happen! If I have heard you right you have just agreed to a quiet night. Let's get home before you change your mind."

Sam's mum hauled Scruffy off Sam, then pulled Sam to his feet getting nearly as wet as them. Scruffy couldn't believe this family. Everyone was soaking wet but just laughing about it.

"Come on Scruffy, you've just joined the daftest family ever. I hope you can survive a constant mayhem because Sam and I never do anything conventionally but I think you were just made for us."

The three of them hurried down the path and Scruffy realised that he had been near the bottom of the garden and if he had looked up he would have seen the cottage roof.

"Yes Scruffy, I heard you barking from the house and came to look for you both but I didn't quite expect to see you sitting in the stream. Mind you, I guess I shouldn't have been surprised at anything from my son, and it would seem you too."

Sam chased off for his shower whilst his mum towelled Scruffy dry. She put Scruffy's food down, put more logs on the fire and served tea. After tea Scruffy and Sam laid in the floor in a tangled heap watching TV. Scruffy kept reaching over and giving Sam a kiss and Sam responded with a cuddle for Scruffy. At bedtime Scruffy settled in his brand new bed, in his brand new home and dreamed dreams of running, playing, getting wet, muddy and dirty with Sam constantly by his side.

A New Day

Scruffy woke up with a start! Where was he! Had he died and gone to heaven? He gingerly opened an eye. He was buried in a heap of tangled blankets and cushions in a lovely warm room. Where was his cold dog basket on a concrete floor in the kennels? He opened his other eye. Yes he could still see kitchen cupboards and a big warm stove next to his bed. Then he remembered! He had been brought to this new home yesterday. He remembered Sam and him getting lost in the forest. Scruffy bounded out of his bed and across the kitchen floor to have a drink. He listened. He couldn't hear a sound. He listened again and then he realised he could hear someone moving about above his head. Who was it? Should he bark? Was it someone going to harm his best friend Sam?

Scruffy wasn't going to stand here and let Sam be hurt. He bounded over to the door where Sam had gone through last night to go to bed. He knocked over his water bowl and water shot across the kitchen floor but Scruffy didn't even notice. He launched himself at the door, barking furiously. He jumped at the door almost rattling it off its hinges. Scruffy wasn't used to wooden doors he couldn't see through. His door at the kennels had been made of mesh.

Oh why wouldn't the stupid door get out of the way so he could rescue Sam! By now Scruffy was sure Sam was in mortal danger and it was his, Scruffy's, place to save him. Scruffy decided more force was needed to break down this stupid door so he shot across the kitchen to get a better run at it. He sent his food dish and empty water bowl crashing to the other side of the room but Scruffy didn't care. His sole intention was to do his duty and rescue Sam. From across the room he launched himself towards the door, sending the dishes flying again with a mighty clatter. He knocked over a chair and bounced off the table leg.

He was nearly at the door when it opened and Sam appeared. Unfortunately Scruffy couldn't stop and collided into Sam. Sam toppled backwards and Scruffy trampled over the top of Sam and collided with another person coming down the passage, knocking them flying too. Scruffy managed to stop at this point and found himself sat on top of the person.

Oh no! Now he was in trouble! He found himself sat right on top of Sam's mother's chest! By this time Sam had sat up and he was laughing so much he was almost crying.

"Oh Mum! What an early morning welcome for us. Bet you've never been rugby tackled by a dog before?"

Sam scrambled to his feet and hauled Scruffy off his Mum's chest.

That's it thought Scruffy it will be straight back in the car and a return to the kennels now for me! He hung his head in shame. His tail went between his legs and he looked mournfully, first at Sam and then at Sam's Mum. He blinked and looked again. Sam's mother was actually sat in the floor, bent double laughing, not crying as Scruffy had first thought. Scruffy gingerly walked up to Sam's Mum and nudged her arm as much as to say, are you okay?

"Oh Scruffy, you great big daft dog. I am okay, possibly a bit winded, but fine, please don't worry. I thought I'd experienced the worst whirlwinds that could possibly occur living with Sam but I really think life with you is going to be worse. What on earth were you trying to do?"

Scruffy nuzzled Sam's Mum a bit more to say sorry, before rushing back to Sam. Sam fondled Scruffy's ears and gave him a hug saying,

"It is okay Scruffy, you probably heard Mum and me getting dressed and wondered what the noise was. You see Mum I said we shouldn't shut Scruffy in the kitchen when we go to bed as he doesn't understand what he can hear

15

and probably got frightened. If the door hadn't been shut he could have come to see and not been scared."

"I don't think he was scared Sam," laughed his Mum. "I think he was trying to rescue us."

By that time Sam, his Mum and Scruffy had reached the kitchen.

"Looking at the state of the kitchen though Sam, it looks as if a hurricane has passed through!"

Scruffy looked at the kitchen. Oh dear!! There were cushions and blankets strewn about, water all over the floor where he had knocked over his bowl of water. He remembered doing that! Bits of food from his food dish up the wall, he didn't remember that happening, two chairs knocked over, one even had a broken leg! Crikey he didn't know how that happened and the table was all askew. Again Scruffy hung his head in shame. Had he really done all that damage? Surely not, it had to have been someone else. But no, there had only been him in the kitchen until now and everything was fine when Sam and his Mum went to bed. How could he have done so much damage? This was worse than at his last place. He had sealed his fate now. It would certainly be back to the kennels for him.

"Okay Sam, give me a hand to tidy up before I get us some breakfast. It's a good job it's the school holidays as we have plenty of time to get Scruffy settled before we have to rush around getting ready for school."

Sam began to pick up cushions and dog dishes whilst his Mum moved the table back into position and picked up the chairs. Scruffy couldn't believe it. No shouting and telling him what a bad dog he was. No cross words or grumbles. Scruffy bounded over to Sam and nudged his arm. The water bowl clattered to the ground.

"Good job I hadn't filled it yet Scruffy," laughed Sam. "Do you want to help tidy up the mess you've made? Okay go and get your food dish from the other side of the kitchen so I can put it where it should be while I fill your water bowl with water and try not to knock it over again. Hey Mum, do you think it might be better to put Scruffy's dishes over in the corner near the units where we would be less likely to knock them over?"

"Good idea Sam, with two clumsy oafs living here it might be better. You might be a bit less likely to fall over them in the corner. Can Scruffy manage to get his head in there though, you need to think about that?"

"Yes I think he will but I'll check. Oh good boy, you've brought your food dish. See Mum, he knows what I mean already. Now look Scruffy, if I put your dishes in this corner can you manage to eat and drink from them? I know you can't get your body in but that might be better as your feet seem to have a mind of their own like mine."

Scruffy looked quizzically at Sam before showing Sam he could get a drink but how could he eat any food when there wasn't any in the bowl?

"Sorry Scruffy. Mum can I put some biscuits in Scruffy's bowl before I get the mop to mop up the spilt water?"

"Yes, of course Sam. I'll just put this broken chair in the workshop until Steve has time to mend its broken leg. I don't know, it's the same chair you broke last week. The poor chair will think it's living in a mad house. Actually it is probably right; it is living in a mad house. It might decide to run away and find a better home."

"Oh you are funny, Mum," laughed Sam, "You know that chairs haven't any feelings."

"How do you know, young man, they are made from trees which are living things, so how do we know that tables and chairs haven't any feelings? Just because they don't talk to us we cannot say they don't feel. Mind you it is probably best if they can't run away in this house, we might never keep the furniture. Right order restored, let's get some breakfast now. Oh can you go down to the farm today as I need some eggs and butter. Take Scruffy, but don't let him scare the animals or Steve won't let me have the vegetables and things anymore and mend the various pieces of broken furniture that keeps occurring in this house. I have a feeling that twice as much is going to get broken now, so you had better warn Steve if you see him."

"Oh ace. I love going to the farm and I'm sure Scruffy will too," Sam replied. "And you know Steve would never stop us getting our stuff from there or stop mending things. You know Mum, when I think about it, he must like us too. He's always popping in to see us."

Sam's Mum blushed.

"Well I don't know about that but get that breakfast down you and outside while the sun is shining and I'll get on with some work. I must finish those illustrations by the end of next week. We might then manage to have a few days out before I need to start the next piece of work. Have a think about where you would like to go but remember you have to think of Scruffy too now."

"Great Mum. What about the seaside or perhaps we can go and see the steam trains? Scruffy could do both of them."

"Yes you're right both would work. If we go to a quiet beach it won't matter if the pair of you scatter sand everywhere. You used to do it on your own and now you've got Scruffy it will be more than twice as bad. The steam trains might be a bit frightening so you'll have to reassure Scruffy they won't hurt him. That might be better after Scruffy has lived with us a bit longer, but we will wait and see what we think nearer the time."

Scruffy couldn't believe his ears. Sam and his Mum were making plans and including him as though he would always be living here despite the mayhem he had caused this morning. Sam's Mum had just said about leaving the trip to steam trains, whatever they were, until later. Oh he would be so good from now on he would make sure he didn't get lost, spill anything or knock people over, if only he could stay here forever with Sam and his Mum.

He was a bit worried about this Steve guy and a farm. What was that, and Sam's Mum had said something about animals. What sort of animals? He, Scruffy, was an animal, so did that mean other dogs? Why would he scare dogs? He liked to play with other dogs. Oh it was such a mystery but he was sure Sam would teach all about it.

Scruffy jumped up from the floor where he had been lying while Sam was finishing his breakfast. He would show everyone how good he was. In his excitement he began to chase his tail in a circle but he bumped Sam's chair and knocked over another.

"Oh Scruffy, there isn't room in the kitchen to do that," laughed Sam, "You're too big. Let's get outside first. Tell you what, we'll go and play in the field before we go down to the farm. Is that okay Mum?"

"Yes that's fine. Why don't you take a football and see if Scruffy has any football skills?"

"Hey Mum, that's a great idea. We will go and play football until lunchtime then go to the farm this afternoon. That way Steve will be in the yard feeding up and he can meet Scruffy at the same time. I'm sure he'll love him same as you and me."

"I don't know about that Sam. Steve's not as daft as you and me."

"Actually Mum I think he is, but is just shy and doesn't know how to show what he is feeling. Maybe Scruffy and I can get him to have more fun rather than working all the time."

"Well the problem is Sam, farming is such a hard life and Steve is such a good farmer. Remember I grew up on a farm and know how hard my Mum and Dad had to work."

"Well I know that but Grandad and Granny always have time to spend with us when we visit," replied Sam.

"Yes I know that's because your Uncle Pete and Aunty Jan run the farm now so Granny and Grandad have more time. That reminds me I'd better phone them all and warn them that we'll be taking Scruffy when we go for Christmas this year so they can clear the way for two hurricanes."

"Gran and Grandad won't mind," laughed Sam, "And Uncle Pete will just break more glass panes in the greenhouse than usual."

"Actually, thinking back you are probably like your Uncle Pete was when he was a boy, as I remember him having a dog that was as bad as Scruffy but smaller."

"There you see Mum told you Scruffy was perfect for this family."

"Oh get out the pair of you. I still can't win an argument with you Sam," laughed his Mum. "Go and play in the field. I'll give you a shout at lunch time."

"Great Mum, come on Scruffy, let us find a football and have some fun."

Sam and Scruffy headed for the door.

"Sam don't you think it might be a good idea to put some shoes on first."

Sam and Scruffy looked at Sam's feet. He was still in his slippers.

"Oh heck, nearly forgot, thanks Mum. See you later."

Sam grabbed his trainers and tried to put them on but Scruffy was so excited he stood on Sam's feet, knocked his hands and generally got in the way.

"Scruffy move out of the way and let me get my shoes on or else we'll never get out. Please don't worry, I'm not going to leave you or lose you or anything like that. We are best mates."

Scruffy gave Sam one last sloppy, wet kiss before he let Sam off the floor and the pair raced across the kitchen and out of the back door. Sam's Mum shook her head and laughed. She wasn't sure what she had done agreeing to Scruffy but she knew their life would never be the same again.

Sam and Scruffy shot out of the back door and raced across the garden, scooping up a football lying near the car. They went to the other side of the yard and Sam climbed over the gate. Scruffy hurled himself after Sam and tried to jump the gate but didn't get high enough and ran into the top half.

"Oh sorry, Scruffy. I always climb the gate but hang on, I'll open it for you."

As Sam scrambled down the other side Scruffy tried again, this time getting enough height to clear the gate. The trouble was he misjudged where Sam was and hit Sam in the chest. Sam didn't stand a chance and yet again, down went Sam with Scruffy landing on top of him.

"Oh Scruffy, I seem to spend my time with you sat on top of me. I know you love me but you will have to try harder not to keep knocking me over. Get off! Now where did the ball go?"

Scruffy saw the ball and was so eager to help Sam he bounded over. Problem was, as usual, his feet didn't obey his head and he knocked the ball flying with his feet. The ball shot over the field.

"Oh well done Scruffy, that was a good kick"

Sam raced across to the ball. Scruffy raced towards the ball and got there first. This time he managed to keep his feet out of the way and tried to pick up the ball in his mouth. Unfortunately the ball was too big and he just nosed it out of the way. Sam raced up and kicked the ball. Scruffy raced after it with Sam in hot pursuit. This time when Scruffy knocked the ball, it rose off the ground, straight into Sam. Off Sam went again, across the field, towards the other side.

Oh how exciting, thought Scruffy, intent on keeping up with Sam. Just at that moment Sam turned around with the ball at his feet. Scruffy couldn't stop so the ball got tangled in his legs and Scruffy found himself hurtling across the field with the ball sort of joining in.

"Oh great tackle Scruffy," Sam shouted and raced towards Scruffy. Suddenly Scruffy stopped running to look back at Sam and Sam collided into his bottom. The ball shot out from between Scruffy's legs across the field.

"Come on Scruffy. See who can get to the ball first," shouted Sam.

Boy and dog raced across the field. They both got to the ball together and a tussle between them began. Finally Scruffy won and knocked the ball with his nose and off they went again.

Eventually they became tired. They flopped down on the grass to regain their breath. Scruffy's tongue lolled out, he had bits of grass and twigs stuck to his coat and looked scruffier than ever. There was a fresh tear in Sam's jeans, a great muddy patch on his T-shirt, his hair stuck up in all directions but both dog and boy grinned at each other.

"Oh Scruffy, you're a great football player. Just wait until my Uncle Pete meets you. We'll have a great time but I think Grandad's greenhouse glass might be in severe danger."

After a rest, a few cuddles and lots of secret plans, most of which Scruffy didn't understand but trusted Sam they would be great fun, the pair began a new game of football.

This time Sam found some sticks which he stuck in the ground saying they were 'the goal' whatever that meant. Sam then tried to teach Scruffy that he had to knock the ball between the sticks but Scruffy kept grabbing the sticks and running off with them, Sam wrestled Scruffy to the ground to get the sticks resulting in lots more cuddles, sloppy wet kisses and more debris on Sam's clothes and Scruffy's coat.

All too soon they heard Sam's Mum calling that it was lunch time and they trooped back to the house. This time Sam opened the gate, a fact Scruffy was glad of, as he hadn't the energy to jump it. They arrived back at the house, Sam dropping the ball in the yard before opening the back door. As the pair emerged into the kitchen Sam's Mum turned from the sink.

"Oh my goodness just look at the pair of you," she laughed. "I don't need to ask if you've had a good time. Well Sam how are Scruffy's football skills?"

"Not bad at dribbling and kicking the ball. But hopeless at scoring goals, especially as he kept stealing the sticks marking the goal posts. I think we will have to practice a lot in that area."

"Well your Uncle Pete says you're the best player he knows so you'll just have to teach him. Meanwhile go and wash your hands before you sit up to the table. Scruffy you go and have a rest on your bed after a drink while Sam has his lunch.

Scruffy ambled over to his bowl and had a drink. He nosed about and found a few stray biscuits from breakfast before flopping down on his bed. He didn't dare go to sleep though in case Sam escaped without him. He certainly wasn't going to miss one minute of the fun and excitement that his life had become.

Briefly he thought about the other dogs in the kennels and prayed hard that they would find their 'Sam' to take them home and love them just like he had.

After what seemed such a long time to Scruffy, Sam finished his lunch.

"Come on Scruff, let's get your lead on and we'll see how good you can be walking through the village."

Scruffy jumped out of his bed and skidded across the kitchen floor legs going in all directions. He bumped into a chair then the table leg before landing in a heap in front of Sam.

"Oh Scruffy, you will have to curb your excitement or else you are going to end up with a burst nose. Now sit and let me put your lead on and please walk beside me when we are out. I want everyone to see how well behaved you can be."

"Scruffy, well behaved. Now that's a laugh," chuckled Sam's Mum. "It's like asking you to be tidy."

"Oh Mum, how can you say that. Anyway what is the point in being tidy. It is just boring whereas it will be dangerous if Scruffy misbehaves while we are walking down the village."

"You always have a logical answer don't you Sam. Oh go on the pair of you and get my things from the farm while I finish off some work."

"Okay, see you later Mum," answered Sam.

As the pair walked down the path in a sedately manner Sam's Mum wondered how long it would last. She just hoped she didn't get a call saying they were causing mayhem. Shrugging her shoulders she headed back to her work room.

The Farm

Sam and Scruffy headed out of the garden down the road, Sam constantly reminding Scruffy to be a good boy. Scruffy got a bit fed up after a while. Surely Sam trusted him to be on his best behaviour. He wouldn't hurt Sam. No Sam had rescued him from the kennels so no way was he going back there. Life was so exciting now. Soon Sam and Scruffy reached the main road. Scruffy remembered this was the way they had come yesterday. Gosh had it really only been yesterday. Scruffy felt he had known them forever.

"Now this is where we really have to watch our behaviour Scruffy," Sam told him. "There are lots of cars and lorries about and if you pull on the lead you'll pull me over and I might get hurt."

Scruffy looked up at Sam. How could Sam even think he would hurt him? He loved Sam. Just then a great big lorry thundered past. Poor Scruffy leapt about three feet in the air bumping into Sam's legs. Sam ended up sprawled on the pavement. Luckily he kept hold of the lead and quickly Scruffy remembered to behave so stood quietly while Sam scrambled to his feet.

"Oh, Scruffy. Why did you jump so much? It was only a wagon going by on the road. It was nowhere near us."

The pair carried on down the street without incident until Scruffy looked round and saw a great big monster trundling down the road. His eyes widened then he shot in front of Sam to get away from the monster. Sam ended up tangled in the lead.

"It's okay Scruffy," Sam said. "It's only a combine harvester going to cut the corn. It won't hurt you but I suppose it looks huge to you if you haven't seen one before. Hang on while I untangle us."

Scruffy managed to stay still but kept a close eye on the monster.

"OK Scruffy, let's try again. You will have to stop being frightened of strange machines. You are now living in the country and the farmers use all sorts of strange machinery to do their job."

The pair ambled on a bit further until Scruffy got distracted by a cat sat on a wall. He didn't realise he had gone one side of the post box and Sam the other until his lead became tight. As Sam tried to go round the post box Scruffy tried to follow Sam and yet again the pair were in a muddle. Sam was laughing so much he couldn't tell Scruffy what to do. Eventually Sam spluttered

"Stop Scruffy. Stand still until I can sort us out."

Scruffy suddenly remembered he was supposed to be good and stood still. Sam was running round the box so quickly that he ran into Scruffy's bottom and fell over the top of him. Yet again the pair ended up on the ground.

"Oh Scruffy, we are never going to get to the farm at this rate if every few minutes we end up in a tangle. We have to do better than this as we come back from the farm as I'll be carrying eggs."

Scruffy scrambled to his feet and hung his head in shame.

"Oh don't look like that I'm not angry. I'm as much to blame as you. I'm still learning to walk with you on the lead. Now come on cheer up and let's try again."

Both boy and dog concentrated hard and finally reached the end of the village main street. Sam turned down a lane. On one side of the lane there were brown stalks waving in the wind and on the other side, Scruffy's side to be honest, was some white woolly things that moved. Scruffy pressed close to Sam's legs.

"It is okay Scruffy they are sheep but they can't get out. Look they are behind the fence."

Scruffy wasn't too sure. What if they jumped over the fence? What would they do to him, or worse still to Sam? Would he, Scruffy, be able to defend Sam? Well he would have a jolly good try but these objects looked fierce with hard curly bits on their heads. While Scruffy and Sam were talking, one of these things that Sam had called 'sheep', came over to the fence. This was too much for Scruffy. With a yelp of pure terror he shot behind Sam, knocking Sam off balance towards the fence. Unfortunately this time Sam let go of Scruffy's lead and Scruffy shot to the other side of the lane but then he was too close to the brown wavy things so he shot off down the lane.

"Scruffy, stop, you bad dog, stand still!" Sam called sharply. Scruffy realised Sam was cross so skidded to a stop, turned around and ran back to Sam. He hurled himself at Sam and yet again the two of them found themselves in a heap on the lane. Scruffy was so sorry about being naughty he stood on Sam's chest trying to give him a kiss to say he was sorry.

"Scruffy get off me will you. Yes I know you are sorry and didn't mean to run off and I'm not really angry I just had to shout at you to make you stop. Now move yourself and let me get up."

Needless to say by this time Sam's T-shirt was very dirty and his jeans had a new tear in the knee but neither of them saw the damage or cared about it. Eventually Sam scrambled to his feet, gathered up Scruffy's lead and proceeded to walk down the lane until they came to a gate.

"Now Scruffy we are going into the farmyard and there will be lots of strange animals and noises. Please don't be frightened. There is nothing that will hurt you I promise."

Scruffy wasn't so sure. He had already seen moving woolly creatures so he wondered what else might come hurtling round the corner.

"Come on Scruffy, let's go and see Nellie the goat. She will be having babies soon and I can't wait to see them and play with them."

Scruffy wasn't too happy about this. Did that mean Sam was going to get rid of him, Scruffy, if he had other things to play with? He dropped his head and shoved his tail between his legs and looked at Sam sadly.

"Oh you great softy. I'll still play with you. The baby goats will play with us both. It's you and me now all the time. I'm never going to leave you out."

Scruffy perked up and tried to show Sam he was ready to play now.

"No we aren't playing here until you've met all the animals and aren't frightened of them. Come on over here."

Sam and Scruffy made their way over to a gate where a great white beast stood with its front feet up on the gate.

"Hi Nellie," Sam said. "This is Scruffy. He has come to live with me and Mum. Say hello nicely and don't frighten him as he is feeling a bit scared. Come here Scruffy and let Nellie have a look at you."

Scruffy held back. He wasn't too sure of this great beast. Slowly he edged forward and couldn't believe his eyes when Sam started rubbing its head. He edged a bit closer, then closer still until his nose was pressed against the bars of the gate. Nellie suddenly looked down and saw Scruffy. Thinking this might be someone else who would rub her head she reached down and came nose to nose with Scruffy. She blew down her nose and with a yelp and flurry of legs and tail Scruffy shot behind Sam.

"It's okay Scruffy," said Sam. "Nellie was only saying hello. She won't hurt you."

Scruffy wasn't too sure so he stayed a fair distance away behind Sam and eyed the beast up. Nellie climbed back up the gate and Sam continued to rub her head so Scruffy slowly crept towards the gate and stood still. Nellie was enjoying herself too much to bother with this great scruffy thing that ran away when she got close, so Scruffy was able to stand close to the gate and watch his hero, Sam. How brave was this master of his and how clever he was too. Presently Sam stopped stroking Nellie and the pair wandered off to see the other animals. Scruffy heard a strange noise, sort of grunting and scuffling sounds. Now where was it coming from? It appeared to be coming from behind the wall. Scruffy crept up to the wall.

Yes it was definitely coming from behind the wall but what was it?

"That's a good idea Scruffy we'll go and see Bertha and her babies."

Sam went round the corner of the wall with Scruffy tight at his heels. There was another gate but when Scruffy looked through there was a great fat lump laid on the floor with lots of little wriggling things around her.

"This is Bertha Scruffy, she is a pig and these are her babies. Look some are having a feed off her that's why she is laid down."

Suddenly Bertha opened an eye. She had heard Sam's voice, who she loved as he often brought her apples, so she scrambled to her feet. The babies squealed in anger at having their food supply stopped. Bertha ambled over to the gate her floppy ears covering her eyes. Scruffy thought this was great. His ears flopped forward but this thing's ears, what had Sam said she was, oh yes a pig, her ears were massive.

"Sorry Bertha I haven't been in the orchard yet so I haven't any apples for you. I've brought Scruffy to meet you all. He is my very own friend and lives with us so don't frighten him."

Bertha tried to get her nose through the bars of the gate but she couldn't and as Sam hadn't brought any apples she ambled over to her trough to see if she had left any breakfast.

"Bye Bertha. Scruffy and I will go into the orchard before I leave the farm and bring you a couple of apples."

Bertha just snorted a reply and continued to investigate her trough while her babies ran around her legs. Scruffy watched fascinated by these squealing little black things which didn't have any fur on. Scruffy wondered how they kept warm.

"Come on Scruffy let's go and see what else we can find" Sam said.

With one last look through the gate at the pigs Scruffy trotted off after Sam. He wasn't really paying attention until he suddenly looked up at a hissing sound coming from behind a fence. Scruffy's eyes widened. Now what on earth was this thing with a long neck and great big wings? Sam laughed at Scruffy's bewildered expression.

"It's okay Scruffy that's just the gander protecting his wives and he can't get out. Just as well because geese can be pretty nasty. Just keep walking by and he'll stop hissing."

Scruffy wasn't too sure about this thing. Was it all white animals, which were frightening? He thought he'd give this field a wide berth and shot to the other side of Sam, bumping into Sam as usual but Sam was ready this time and kept his feet firmly planted on the ground while he moved the lead to his other hand. Sam and Scruffy carried on round a corner of the farmyard until they came to a big building.

"Right Scruffy" Sam instructed, "this is the barn with the calves in. Now they probably look big to you but they aren't as big as the cows. You won't see the cows until winter when Steve brings them in from the fields. Calves are baby cows so they will be feeling very scared of you. Please don't frighten them. We will slowly go up to their pens then stand still. Eventually they will come over and look at us. But we must stay completely still. If we are lucky one or two might give us a lick if you put your nose on the bar of the gate near my hand."

Scruffy looked through his tangled fringe at these huge animals. They were at least three times bigger than him and here was Sam saying they were babies. Scruffy couldn't imagine how big these so called cows were going to be and he was mighty glad they were away in fields as he certainly didn't want to encounter one today. Sam slowly walked up to the gate and sure enough the calves ran away as far as they could to the back of the building. Sam hunched down so he was the same height as Scruffy and placed his hand not holding the lead through the gate. Without moving he encouraged Scruffy to take a step closer. Scruffy took a tiny step, then another. The calves stayed where they were. Scruffy took another step then another until he was level with Sam.

"Good boy" Sam said quietly, "Now put your nose on the bar of the gate next to my hand. Beware, calves' tongues are rough so if one licks your nose it will feel strange."

Scruffy wasn't sure about one of these great beasts licking his nose but he so wanted to please Sam, he was prepared to suffer it just for Sam. Slowly first one then another calf began to walk towards Sam and Scruffy. How Scruffy managed to keep still he didn't know, but somehow felt it was important to Sam that he did. Closer and closer the calves came. Scruffy's eyes were like huge saucers. When the leader reached Sam and Scruffy, Scruffy shut his eyes so he couldn't see as he was sure this big beast would hurt his best friend. Suddenly Scruffy felt a rough, wet tongue go right over his nose and up his face over his eyes. With a huge yelp Scruffy shot backwards falling over his feet and bumped into something hard. Scruffy quickly looked over his shoulder to see a pair of legs directly behind him. This was too much for Scruffy. He hurled himself at Sam knocking Sam over, the calves shot to the back of the pen and there was a loud shout of laughter. Scruffy was sat on Sam's arm and looked up above the legs. There was a man standing there shaking with laughter. Scruffy was beginning to get fed up with all these people laughing at him so he lay down with his head on his paws. Now this wouldn't have been so bad if he hadn't been laid on Sam.

"Scruffy will you get up and let me get up. I warned you their tongues were rough so why did you yelp? Now you've frightened them."

"Who have we here then Sam?" a voice enquired.

"Oh, hi Steve. This is Scruffy my dog, my best friend. I was just showing him round the animals but he has had so many shocks I think he is ready to give up," laughed Sam. "I think a kiss from a calf was the last straw."

"Is he always this quiet?" Steve asked.

"No Mum says she is living with two whirlwinds. We only brought Scruffy home yesterday and already he has broken a chair, got lost in the forest, given us a dunking in the stream, knocked Mum over and well I've lost count of how many times he has knocked me over."

"In that case give me Scruffy's lead and get yourself up from the barn floor and we will go over to the farmhouse, where I'm sure my mother will be able to find a drink and a biscuit for you both."

"Oh ace Steve. I think Scruffy might have seen enough for now although I promised Bertha some apples before I go and I wanted Scruffy to see Ned."

"Well let's have a drink then we'll go and see Ned although he is going to seem massive to Scruffy you know."

"I know but Scruffy trusts me that I won't let anything hurt him. He has already seen a combine harvester and lorries as we walked down the village."

"I can see you two are going to be inseparable. Did you say Scruffy broke a chair this morning?"

"Yes the same one I bust last week."

"Oh dear, the poor chair. I'd better come over later and see what I can do. Did your Mum send you for anything special today?" asked Steve.

"Yes she wants eggs and butter. I think that was all," answered Sam.

"What about milk or vegetables? I can walk back with you if you like. I don't think eggs will survive you two somehow."

Sam laughed.

"No they maybe won't today. I think poor Scruffy wonders what he's going to encounter next."

By this time Steve, Sam and Scruffy were crossing the yard towards the house. Scruffy skittered to a halt. What on earth were these great big birds doing here? Now Scruffy had seen birds before but these didn't look the same and what was that big brightly coloured one doing strutting around.

"Oh dear," laughed Sam. "It is okay Scruffy these are hens and that's the cockerel. This is what lays the eggs we've come to collect."

Just then another set of alien creatures came waddling round the edge of a wall. This proved too much for Scruffy. With his tail between his legs he set off towards the house and the open door he had just spied. He took Steve by surprise and Steve dropped the lead. Scruffy went hurtling through the door with Sam in hot pursuit. Steve just stood and laughed. Steve's Mum was sat at the kitchen table peeling apples when a great hairy beast shot through the door to the other side of the kitchen landing up against the wall with a thud.

"What on earth ...." began Steve's Mum when Sam followed through the door. Sam managed to stop before he hit the wall but fell over Scruffy and they ended up tangled together. Steve followed and explained to his Mum.

"Mum meet Scruffy, Sam's new dog who has just met hens and ducks and decided to head for cover."

"Oh I see."

Steve's Mum looked at boy and dog trying to untangle themselves and get up off the floor.

"Poor Diane. I can see a lot of furniture getting broken with those two, can't you?"

"Yes" answered Steve. "They have already broken a chair and Scruffy has only been with them a day!"

"But they will have so much fun too. Do you remember Max when you were about the same age as Sam?"

"Oh yes. I'd forgotten the mischief we used to get up to until just now. Oh we had such great times together. Mum, I promised Sam and Scruffy a drink and a biscuit before we walk back to Di's. She wants eggs and I don't think they will survive with this pair, do you?"

"No" laughed his Mum "I think you had better make sure Di has an intact supply of eggs and milk. Butter might get there in one piece but I'm not sure! Vegetables should survive."

"I think you might be right" laughed Steve.

Steve's Mum produced a drink and a biscuit for Sam and a bowl of water and some dog biscuits for Scruffy. Scruffy flopped down beside Sam's chair. He wasn't too sure now about this place that Sam seemed to find such fun. He had never had so many shocks in his life and Sam still wanted to see someone named Ned who this man called Steve said was going to be huge to Scruffy. Scruffy didn't think anything could be bigger than what they had met already without it being a monster.

"What have you done so far then?" asked Steve's Mum.

Just then another man came through the open door.

"Hello young Sam. Have you come to get something for your Mum or just to see us? It'll be school holidays now so no doubt you'll be getting up to mischief just like this lad of mine used to. If you get bored I'm sure I can find a job or two that will keep you out of your poor Mum's hair."

"Cool" replied Sam, "but I've got Scruffy here to keep me company and we are going to have lots of adventures."

At the mention of adventures Scruffy's ears pricked up and he jumped up from his place beside Sam. He knocked Sam's arm just as Sam was going to take a bite of his biscuit. The biscuit shot in the air and landed on the floor. Scruffy shot across the floor to get Sam's biscuit just as Steve bent down to pick it up. Crash!! Two heads banged together. Steve was knocked backwards ending in a heap and Scruffy lost his footing ending in a heap under Sam's chair which proceeded to tip over, Sam underneath it. Luckily the chair was made of sterner stuff than those at Sam's house so survived the onslaught of dog and boy. Scruffy looked round. He couldn't believe it! All the adults were laughing so much tears were streaming down their faces and Sam was trying to get himself untangled from dog and chair.

"Well Sam, I guess this is Scruffy" said the man.

"Yes this is Scruffy Mr B" said Sam.

"Well Steve it looks like history is repeating itself. Do you remember you and Max?" said the man.

"Yes Mum has just reminded me" laughed Steve. "Sam said Scruffy had already knocked over him and Di loads of times so I guess I'm in good company. But from now on I think I'll make sure I deliver eggs and stuff to Di otherwise I don't think she'll ever get anything. Well not in any shape she can use anyway."

"I think you could be right son" laughed his Dad.

Scruffy sat and hung his head in shame. Now these other people had seen him at his worst too. Oh it just couldn't get any worse. Surely this would mean his new life was over.

"Scruffy stop looking so sad" scolded Sam. "How many times have I told you not to worry? I promise no matter what you do neither Mum or I will send you away. I don't even think Steve or his Mum or Dad are cross with you either. Hopefully when you get used to us all you'll stop worrying and just enjoy yourself."

"It's okay Scruffy" said Steve still sitting on the kitchen floor. "Come here and I'll give you a big hug to show you that you'll always be welcome here with Sam, although Dad, you may have to rethink that offer of jobs for Sam unless the job is in a field."

"Well I thought that now Sam is getting bigger and after hauling Scruffy around will get even stronger they could help in the hay fields and things."

"Oh yes please" squeaked Sam "I'll make sure Scruffy behaves himself."

"Don't make promises you might not be able to keep," Steve said

"It's okay Steve your father and I can remember another boy and his dog and I don't think that young boy has turned out too bad."

"I guess not but I have a feeling Di could probably do with some support with these two living with her."

"I think Di is probably quite able to cope. She once told me Sam reminds her of her brother Pete."

"Yes Mum keeps telling me I'm just like my Uncle Pete. Mum thinks Grandad's greenhouse could take a battering though when we go for Christmas."

"Even with just you two it could be in danger but with Pete to help I think the greenhouse is in mortal danger" laughed Steve. "Now you two, are you ready to go and see Ned and get some apples for Bertha before we head off back to your house. Mum, Di wants some eggs and butter but can you get her a few vegetables as well. I might invite myself to tea one night. I believe there is already a chair needing mending but within a day or two there could be several other things."

"Right I'll sort Di's things and you three go and see what Scruffy makes of Ned. Ned will just stand there and blow down his nose but I have a feeling Scruffy could have nightmares for the rest of the night" laughed Steve's Mum.

Steve, Sam and Scruffy trooped out of the farmhouse kitchen, Sam holding tight to Scruffy's lead. They crossed the farmyard over to where the ducks had come from a few minutes earlier. They went through a gate and to Scruffy's surprise there was a big pond in front of him with lots of birds swimming on it. Now if there was one thing Scruffy couldn't resist it was water. With a huge tug on the lead he set off towards the pond Sam in hot pursuit. The swimming birds flew off in all directions frightening poor Scruffy to death. Unfortunately as usual, Scruffy couldn't stop in time and plunged headfirst into the pond. Oh where was the bottom? One minute he had been on firm ground, now nothing. It wasn't like the stream he and Sam had fallen into last night. Luckily Scruffy knew how to swim but his legs became tangled in the rushes growing on the side. Sam had managed to stop on the bank and Steve was close behind him.

"Look Sam. It is okay. Scruffy knows how to swim. Scruffy turn round now and come back to Sam and me a bit further down. Sam let go of the lead and we will go down to the edge where there are no rushes then we can haul Scruffy out of the water. I think it will take a joint effort."

Scruffy hadn't intended falling into the water he just wanted to get close but now he was cold and his coat felt heavy.

"Come on Scruffy, come down here to Steve and I" shouted Sam.

Scruffy followed the sound of his master's voice. Suddenly he saw Sam and lunged himself at the grassy bank. Both Steve and Sam were there and they grabbed his collar. The lead had become tangled in the rushes but Steve was able to free it so Scruffy could reach dry land again. Scruffy shook himself, soaking poor Sam from head to foot.

"Oh Scruffy that's the second night in a row you've soaked me" grumbled Sam, "and you've even wet Steve too."

Scruffy shook his hair off his face. Oh dear Sam was right. Sam was dripping wet and Steve's trouser legs were quite wet too.

"I think we'll leave visiting Ned for another day" laughed Steve, "and Bertha can manage without apples for once. Let's get your Mum's stuff Sam from the house and I'll quickly change my wet trousers and then we'll head for your house. The sooner you get out of them wet clothes the better.

"Yes I think it may be another warm shower for me just like last night. Oh Scruffy, what are we going to do? That's two nights in a row we've ended up soaked."

"Why what happened last night" Steve asked?

"Oh Scruffy and I fell off the bridge over the stream near our house. You know the one I mean."

"Yes I know. So what happened?"

"Well we sort of collided in the middle and both fell in. Mum found us like that."

"Oh, your poor Mum! She must be wondering how she is going to cope every day" answered Steve.

"Actually I don't think Mum minds too much. You know how much fun she is. She just shakes her head and laughs" replied Sam

"Yes I could imagine that. Right you and Scruffy stay here I'll be back in two seconds and we'll cross the fields from here. Scruffy you wait here with Sam and please try to be a good boy for at least a few minutes."

Scruffy hung his head in shame. What had he done now? Sam and him were soaking wet and Steve was like Sam's Mum had been last night. But yet again everyone was just laughing, no one was getting cross. Scruffy just couldn't understand these people. It didn't seem to matter what he did no one got upset or anything.

"It's okay Scruffy" Sam said, "I told you no one minds about accidents or anything and what's even more exciting is that Steve understands too, as he used to have a dog and they got into scrapes as well. I'm so glad you came to live with us and now here comes Steve so let's head home to Mum. Watch, she'll just laugh especially when she finds out Steve is just like Uncle Pete. I wonder if Steve plays football. Hey Steve, did you and your dog, what was his name, oh yes, Max, play football together?"

"Oh definitely and like your Uncle Pete constantly broke windows and things. That's why my Mum and Dad understand you and Scruffy. I'm sure your Gran and Grandad will too."

"Yes Mum says they'll be fine but she is going to warn them before we get there at Christmas. I can't wait to tell Uncle Pete all that's happened in the last two days since Scruffy came to live with me. Would you like to join me and Scruffy in game of football sometime?"

"Do you know Sam, I think that would be great, maybe some weekend when I have a bit less to do on the farm."

"Well talk to Mum because she said we might be able to go away for a few days when she finishes the work she is doing. I don't know how much she still has to do, she didn't say, but she will be able to tell you when she plans to go away."

"Great idea, I'll find out her plans when we get back to your house. A few days away will do your Mum good too. Although with you two together it certainly won't be relaxing" laughed Steve.

"No I don't suppose it will" answered Sam with a smile.

By this time they were almost at Sam's house. Sam's Mum was looking out of the door and threw her hands up in the air when she saw the bedraggled pair.

"Oh now what have you two been doing?" she exclaimed.

"It's okay Di, don't panic, Scruffy fell in the pond and Sam and I had to drag him out then he shook himself soaking Sam mainly, but I caught some of it too. No damage done but I've taken charge of the eggs and butter and things."

"Oh thanks Steve. Right Sam upstairs, warm shower and pyjamas again then I'll sort tea. You young man" she warned Scruffy, "it's a good towel dry and in your bed until you dry off. What about you Steve, do you need to rush off or can you stay for tea? I've a casserole in the oven because I thought these two might be hungry. They have had a busy day but there's quite enough for unexpected guests."

"That would be great Di. Shall I take a look at a broken chair a little bird told me about? Give me that towel and I will deal with the wet dog while you see to your son."

"Oh thanks Steve for being so understanding."

"Not at all, as my Mum and Dad have just reminded me I had a daft dog called Max when I was Sam's age and between us we broke just about every window, gate and door around the farm but we had so much fun. Sam, Scruffy and I are going to play football and all types of things when I have time too."

"Oh no" groaned Sam's Mum laughing, "not three of you and I've just had my brother Pete on the phone saying him and Jan might try to get down for a few days at half term and that's sure to be even more disasters."

"Sounds like fun. I'll not be too busy then either so we'll have to show Sam and Scruffy how to get up to mischief" laughed Steve.

"Oh no, you don't. Sam and Scruffy can wreck havoc alone without you two giving them ideas" she answered leaving Steve to dry Scruffy.

Scruffy just couldn't believe his ears. Were all these people as mad as hatters? He sure hoped so! Scruffy bounded over to his bed, burrowed into it and within minutes was snoring his head off having the most fantastic dream of chasing footballs with Sam, Steve and this other guy called Pete. He was sure he had died and gone to heaven. He didn't even wake up when Sam, his Mum and Steve came into the kitchen.

"Mum when I've had my tea can I go and read until bedtime because I'm so tired. Looking after Scruffy has tired me out but it was so much fun too."

"I don't believe it" Sam's Mum exclaimed. "My son is tired."

"I'm not surprised and look at Scruffy he's completely zonked out."

"Why so he is. Looks like Sam was right. Scruffy is just perfect."

Scruffy just tweaked an ear in his sleep. If he had been awake he would have agreed with everyone that they were just perfect for him too.

Preparing for Camping

One morning Sam's mother told Sam she had finished the piece of work she had been working on so they could take Scruffy away for a few days camping.

"Ace," Sam exclaimed, "hear that Scruffy we're going camping. That will be fun, won't it?

Scruffy pricked up his ears at the word 'fun'. He was learning now that when Sam said something would be fun it meant an adventure. Actually what camping meant he wasn't sure but he trusted Sam and his Mum that he would enjoy it whatever it was.

"Do you need me to do anything Mum?" Sam asked.

"Well you could get all the camping stuff from the garage while I look out the sleeping bags" his Mum answered. "Then I'll make a start on sorting food out. You could make up a bag of dog biscuits for Scruffy and a couple of his blankets ready for a bed. I suggest you and him share a tent as he might be lonely in the car during the night. Get some old towels too to take with us in case Scruffy gets wet during the day and hasn't dried out at bedtime."

"Ok Mum I'll make a start on getting stuff together so it's ready for you to pack the car."

"Good boy Sam. Take Scruffy with you he might be interested in poking about in the garage while you find the camping gear."

Scruffy jumped up. It didn't matter what Sam or his Mum thought, Scruffy had no intention of missing a moment of this new adventure.

"Come on then Scruffy I see you are ready for action," laughed Sam. "Shall I sort out the cricket bat and things too as you said we could go to the beach Mum?"

"Yes that would be a good idea as well as a football and frisbee."

"Brilliant Mum I never thought about the frisbee but the beach might be a good place to play with that as there are no windows or anything close by" answered Sam. "Okay Scruffy let us go. We have lots to do."

Sam pulled open the garage door and surveyed the chaos inside.

"Well Scruffy, where do you think the tents, cooker, lamps, gas and things might be among this lot then?"

As Scruffy hadn't a clue what any of the things looked like he wasn't sure if he could help but he began poking his nose among the various boxes that littered the floor. His nose twitched, there was a funny animal sort of smell. It wasn't one he had smelt before but he was sure it was an animal. He poked a bit deeper. Suddenly he felt his nose tickle and he sneezed. It was such a big sneeze his head shot up and hit the shelf above him. Boxes tumbled down on top of him spilling their contents all around. Sam looked up from the other side of the garage.

"Oh well done Scruffy you've found the box with the pans and things in. You are clever I was looking in the wrong place."

Scruffy wasn't sure what he had found as it had suddenly gone dark and he couldn't see. Also his head felt funny as though something was pressing down on it. He sat back on his haunches and shook his head. Whatever was on his head wobbled a bit but didn't move. Scruffy got up and turned around. Still the thing didn't move. He spun round the other way and hit a cupboard. The door flew open and tents, ropes and lots of other things cascaded down on poor Scruffy. It went even darker. Now there were things completely enveloping him and he couldn't hear anything either. With a yelp Scruffy tried to break free but just became even more tangled up. The more he fought to get free the more things seemed to be raining down on him. He didn't care about this new adventure he just wanted to get as far away as possible from the garage. Suddenly he felt some of the stuff moving off his back. He wriggled a bit and some more fell off. He wriggled the other way and a great lump fell away. Suddenly the thing on his head was taken off and he could see and hear again. Sam was stood laughing holding out the offending article.

"Oh Scruffy, you ended up with a pan over your head so you couldn't see or hear then you bumped into the cupboard and all the tents came tumbling out on top of you. You are clever, you have found most of what we were looking for all at one go!"

Scruffy wasn't too sure about this camping event if it included all the things that had fallen on him.

"Also you clever boy you have found the old cargo net I used to use to make a den. We can take it into the wood when we come back and see what we can make. Come on Scruffy get up now there is nothing on top of you. We need to sort through this stuff an put it outside the garage door ready for Mum to pack the car and tidy away the things we don't want to take. We still need to find the stove and lamps and gas but I imagine they will be somewhere in this corner where everything else was."

Gingerly Scruffy got to his feet wondering if more stuff would rain down on him if he moved. With great care he backed out from the tangled heap of pots, pans and tents and when he was sure he was safe he scampered across to the other side of the garage. Let Sam do the sorting he was staying well away from that end of the garage. He was in such a hurry to get out of the way keeping his eyes firmly peeled on the cupboard in case anything else jumped out and got him he failed to realise he was heading for more trouble at the other side. Going backwards without looking where you are heading often spells disaster and that was what was about to happen to Scruffy! As he got further from the tumbling corner, as he had mentally called it to himself, the faster he went backwards. Suddenly he crashed into Sam's old bike which rolled forwards and crashed into a shelf of old plant pots, discarded toys and boxes of nuts and screws. With a new yelp Scruffy leapt forward and crashed into the opposite corner which had tins of paint and old covers stacked in. Scruffy got tangled again in the covers with paint tins raining down on him.

With a blood curdling howl he got free and headed straight for the open door of the garage. Unfortunately Sam's Mum was just coming to investigate all the crashing and commotion that she had heard and Scruffy ploughed straight into her knocking her off her feet! With his tail between his legs he headed for the open kitchen door where he leapt on to his bed and put his head under the covers. He had seen enough of the garage to last a lifetime and if Sam and his Mum thought that he, Scruffy, was going on a camping trip they were sadly mistaken as he was staying right here where he was safe!

Meanwhile Sam had hauled his Mum to her feet and they were making their way back to the house both laughing about Scruffy's mad dash out of the garage and into the house Sam explaining to his Mum all that had happened to cause the mayhem.

"At least I've found all we need as Scruffy unearthed the cricket bat, old football and a selection of Frisbees and other balls when he knocked over the plant pots. Also the swing ball game fell off the shelf which I had forgotten about," Sam said.

"Good," his Mum laughed, "but let's go and reassure Scruffy he is not in trouble and make sure he didn't get hurt before we tidy the garage and pack the car."

"Good idea Mum," Sam answered, "poor Scruffy must think he is in real trouble as he knocked so many things over and some things broke but in fact the things that broke were old and useless anyway. I think when we get back Mum I'll sort out the garage for you and make a pile of rubbish for you to take to the refuse place. That way we can put all the camping gear together and it will make it easier to get away and not forget anything."

"I beg your pardon," his Mum laughed. "Am I hearing this right? Is my son actually volunteering to tidy stuff up and be more organised? What is the world coming to? I never thought I would live to see the day!"

"Ok Mum, quit being sarcastic, I just thought it might help us" Sam answered.

43

"Oh Sam it would be a great help but why now? I mean why have you suddenly decided tidying things up and being organised is a good idea?"

"Well when I saw everything falling on Scruffy I suddenly realised that he could have been hurt. I know it was funny when he was sat with a pan on his head but it really could have hurt him and then when I saw all the paint tins and flower pots raining down on him I was really scared. He really could have been injured if any of the tins had been full or if any of the pots had had jagged edges."

"Oh Sam," his Mum replied, "you really love that scruffy mutt don't you and that is a real grown up thought! Yes I suppose he could have been hurt real bad but I don't think he was, just very scared. You have to realise that so much is new and strange to him. I don't suppose he has ever seen or done anything like this before. You said he was poking around on the floor then sneezed. I guess he got dust from the floor up his nose or there even could be mice in here."

"Yes it could have been either of those things I suppose Mum, and like you say, I don't think he was hurt, but he could have been."

By that time Sam and his Mum had reached the kitchen where they were greeted by the sight of Scruffy with his head buried in his bed. Sam ran over and touched Scruffy on his bottom which was sticking out. With another howl Scruffy shot backwards.

"It is okay Scruffy, it's only me," Sam said. "Come out now and let me have a look at you and make sure you aren't hurt. It is okay you aren't in trouble or anything and quite safe here in the kitchen. Come on now it's only me and Mum here."

Scruffy carefully emerged from his blankets checking from side to side that there were no objects about to fall on him. When he was clear of the blankets and he could see he was just in the kitchen with Sam and his Mum he shook himself and leaned over to Sam. Sam fondled his ears reassuring him that he was safe. Scruffy reached out and gave Sam a tentative kiss as much as to say sorry.

"I know you're sorry Scruffy. It is okay no damage done, just let me check to make sure you aren't hurt first then we'll have a cuddle. Mum can you manage now outside if Scruffy and me sort out my clothes and bedding and food for Scruffy?"

"Yes Sam, I can pack the car with the stuff from the garage. Oh by the way I found an old sleeping bag we don't use anymore and I thought it would be warm for Scruffy to use along with a couple of his blankets. I also found a double carry mat so Scruffy and you can share that so the cold and damp doesn't strike up and make him cold. Also it will reassure him to be close to you during the night as there will be lots of strange noises in the forest that he will hear during the night."

"Good idea Mum that sounds ace. Right come on Scruffy lets fold a couple of your blankets and sort out your food first. Mum is it okay if Scruffy comes upstairs with me just this once as he has had such a frightening time?"

"Yes okay Sam, well presented, but just as a special treat today you understand. Off you go the pair of you," his Mum laughed as she made her way back outside to pack the car with the camping gear.

"Come on Scruffy" urged Sam, "the sooner we get packed the sooner we can be on our way. Oh I know this is going to be the best camping trip ever."

Scruffy wasn't too sure, it certainly hadn't started off well with things falling on top of him and scaring him half to death. But still that was over now and Sam was urging him to follow him through the door that Sam went through every night. Scruffy was intrigued to see what was through there as he had never been allowed beyond the door except that first morning when he knocked Sam and his Mum over in the passage. He bounded over to Sam ready for this new adventure.

"Okay Scruffy, can you wait two minutes while I find a tin or box to put some biscuits in for you as we can't take the huge bag which is in the pantry and I need to fold the blankets ready for Mum."

Scruffy sat down and watched while Sam rummaged in a cupboard.

"Ha, just the thing" exclaimed Sam, "perfect size for about three days biscuits."

Sam filled the tin and put the lid on, placed three tins of dog food on top of the tin and picked up a couple of thick blankets and folded them neatly.

"Hang on a minute Scruffy I'll just take this out to Mum then we can head upstairs."

Scruffy had no intention of moving. He was happy to watch Sam and wait until Sam told him to come. Scruffy was learning that if it was safe Sam would always include him in whatever he was doing. He trusted Sam now to look after him and he was learning that Sam and his Mum would never send him back to the kennels no matter what he did so he tried very hard to be good but sometimes life was so exciting he forgot.

Sam came back into the kitchen from taking the blankets and food to his Mum and headed for the 'forbidden' door as Scruffy called it.

"Come on Scruffy let us go and pack me some clothes" Sam said.

Scruffy bounded through the door as Sam opened it and down the passage. At the end of the passage he came to some steps. He looked up and they seemed to go on forever. Now Scruffy had encountered 1 step at a time before but couldn't imagine how he was going to get up all of them. He stood with his front paws on the bottom step but his back paws were still halfway down the passage. He reached up and placed his front paws on the second step. He looked back. Well his back paws were nearer the bottom step but still not close enough. He looked forwards again. Now how did he reach the next step without falling backwards? By this time Sam had reached Scruffy.

"Well now Scruffy you are going to have to learn to climb stairs if you want to come upstairs with me as I certainly can't carry you. Right I think you will have to jump on to the next step with your front paws and at the same time jump up with your back paws on to the bottom step."

Scruffy jumped on to step three with his front paws but missed the bottom step with his back paws and went thump on to his stomach. He slid backwards so he was upright again.

"Well Scruffy that didn't work did it? You had better try again."

Scruffy tried again, this time he managed to hit both steps together but then he was stuck. He daren't go forwards as he was scared but if he went backwards he wasn't reaching Sam who was now sat halfway up on a step encouraging Scruffy to come to him. Scruffy froze now what did he do? He was stuck. He tentatively put one paw on the next step then stood still.

"Well done Scruffy now put a back foot on the step above. No not that foot it would be better to move the opposite one."

Scruffy looked up at Sam wondering what he was talking about. He was confused now. Which foot did Sam mean and where was he supposed to put it. He cocked his head to one side as much as to say what now? He was stood with two back feet on the floor, one front paw on step two and one on step three. He tried to put his back foot on to the next step but wobbled over and ended up crashing to the bottom again in a big heap. He lay there for a minute before getting up and shaking himself. He looked up at Sam wondering how on earth he was going to reach him let alone get to the top of all these steps.

"Okay Scruffy try again you had the right idea only like I was trying to tell you, you need to move the opposite back foot to the front one you moved or you will wobble sideways like you just did."

Scruffy couldn't believe this was so difficult. Sam seemed to make it look so easy.

Sam came back down the stairs a bit so he was closer to encourage Scruffy. Scruffy put first one paw on the bottom step and then the other front paw on the first step. He looked at his back legs they were still on the floor. He moved the front paw off the bottom step to join its mate on the first step. So far so good he had 2 feet back on the first step and his back paws still on firm ground on the floor. He looked up at Sam.

"Come on Scruffy or we will never get upstairs to get the jobs done and be late setting off camping at this rate. We have to get the camp set up well before dark and at this rate it will be night before you get upstairs."

Scruffy didn't want Sam to be angry with him so he concentrated hard. He moved one front paw to the next step then automatically moved the opposite back paw on to the bottom step. He seemed stable enough and didn't feel wobbly. Now what next? Ah if he moved his other front paw to join its mate and at the same time brought his other back foot up he should be okay. Tentatively he tried, yes he was one step nearer Sam.

"Well done Scruffy now repeat exactly what you did before and you will get to me."

Scruffy thought hard, how did he do it before? Yes that was it move a front paw and the opposite back paw up a step then bring the other two to join them. Yes that worked, a bit slow, but he was another step nearer. He looked up and could now see that these steps stopped further up. That gave him the courage to try to get up there quicker. He quickly moved to the next step then he tried moving a back paw and front together. Wow he was closer still!! Sam had moved backwards up the steps as his friend managed each step and was now sitting at the top. Suddenly Scruffy got it together and managed to move all four feet together. Once the momentum set in he bounded up the stairs to the top in a great rush and knocked over Sam who was sat at the top. He couldn't stop and trampled over the top of his best friend before skidding to a stop. Oh no what had he done now? He rushed back to Sam just as Sam was sitting up and knocked him down again.

"Okay Scruffy," laughed Sam. "Enough now stand still and let me get up and then you can explore up here but be good and don't jump on the beds."

Scruffy sat down on his haunches with his head cocked to one side to wait for instructions from his master. He glanced down the stairs and though wow is that how high I climbed? Then he had another thought how do I get down again?

Scruffy shook his head no doubt Sam would show him. After all didn't he have the best master he could ever have? Sam and his Mum hadn't let him down yet ever and he didn't think they ever would. By now Sam had scrambled to his feet and the pair wandered off down the passage. Sam showed Scruffy the door to his Mum's bedroom at the end of the corridor and opened a door next to it saying this was the bathroom. Scruffy looked in and saw some strange pieces of furniture! He saw what looked like a large sink which was sat in the floor. He tentatively went through the door and peered over the edge. Yes it was a huge sink because there were the taps. He looked up at Sam as if to say what is this? Sam laughed.

"That Scruffy is a bath. See here are the taps and up here," he pointed to the wall high above Scruffy's head, "is the shower. If you get very dirty I'll bring you up here to give you a bath."

Scruffy wasn't entirely sure what a bath was but by the tone of Sam's voice he didn't think it would be very nice. He vowed he wasn't going to get dirty so Sam didn't need to give him a bath. He saw a small sink then he spied a very strange piece of furniture. Yes this looked very weird. It was a seat or kind of chair but with a hole in. What on earth was that for? After a few moments he plucked up the courage to go and look at it more closely.

"That's a toilet Scruffy not something for you to use" said Sam.

Scruffy was a bit perplexed by this. He went to the toilet outside something he had been taught as a puppy so why didn't Sam go to the toilet outside? Scruffy had never really thought about it but now he did he realised he had never seen Sam go to the toilet outside so this must be the reason. Sam actually used this strange looking chair. He went and peered into it. That was strange there was water in the bottom of it too. Scruffy thought this was a bit unfair he had to go to the toilet outside. It wasn't a chore when the sun was shining but he hated to go when it was wet and cold especially in the dark and it was even worse when it was raining, cold and windy as sometimes it nearly blew him over when he was balancing on 3 legs. Now Sam was telling him that he, Sam, could stay in the warmth whereas Scruffy had to go outside. Now that was just plain unfair! Weren't him and Sam partners in everything they did so why couldn't he use the toilet inside?

"Now Scruffy, don't start getting ideas. No, you can't use this toilet you still have to go outside! You are a dog so you go outside I am a boy that is the difference. End of discussion now let's go and get my stuff packed or else Mum will be ready to go and I won't have any clothes."

Sam walked out of the bathroom and down the passage way and with one last look at this indoor toilet that was Sam's, and probably his mum's too and followed Sam down the corridor. Sam opened the door and what a mess! There were clothes strewn about all over the floor and chair. There was a pile of books on the floor at the side of the bed and various bits of toys on top of the drawers. All the drawers were half open with clothes spilling out of them. In the middle of the room was a big bed but with bedclothes all in a tangle. Scruffy's eyes grew large. Sam's bed seemed to be a larger version of his. He ran over to it and jumped up on to it and burrowed under the covers like he did his own. Unfortunately he just pushed them off the side of the bed and was left sprawled in the middle. He looked over the edge at the pile of blankets etc in the floor and then jumped down on top of them. Sam joined in and the pair began a tussle with the bedclothes to see who could steal them from the other. The packing of clothes for the trip was quickly forgotten in the fun of a new game. Sam threw the bed clothes up on to the bed and Scruffy hurled himself on top of them. Sam followed and tried to stop Scruffy pushing them off the bed back on to the floor. The result was a tangle of arms, legs and bedclothes. Eventually Scruffy managed to get his nose under the bedclothes and with a huge effort hauled them over the side. Unfortunately he pushed Sam off too so he jumped down on top of the blankets to save Sam. He couldn't find him so he burrowed under them like he did his own blankets in his bed. Sam, bedclothes and Scruffy all bumbled across the floor knocking the pile of books down until they hit the chest of drawers. Wham! The drawers rocked, items flew off the top and eventually crash, the drawers fell over. At this point dog and boy could not be distinguished from bedclothes. Suddenly they heard Sam's Mum,

"Just what is going on here? I thought you were packing your clothes Sam? I don't see much packing getting done. In fact I can't see neither you nor Scruffy at the moment just a heap of moving blankets! Sounds as if Scruffy has recovered from his fright in the garage Sam! Sam come out, where are you in this muddle?"

Sam poked his head out from the heap of bedclothes and then Scruffy's head came out next to him.

"Okay you two quit larking about and Sam get this bedroom tidied. I will go downstairs and get a bin bag to put all the broken toys and bits of paper in. Please put all clean clothes back in the drawers and dirty ones in your laundry bin. Right Scruffy, out you come! Sam give me a hand to sort out the bed then Scruffy can lay quietly, if that's possible, on the bed while you tidy up and get packing. I'll drop the bag for the rubbish in on my way to pack my clothes."

"Ok Mum sorry we were just having a bit of fun and forgot what we should have been doing," Sam said.

"Yes I know I'm not cross it's what I expected to happen but maybe now you understand why I won't let you have Scruffy sleeping with you as you would never remember to sleep."

"Don't be daft Mum," laughed Sam. "Eventually we would fall asleep but not necessarily in the bed!"

"Well I'd rather we stick to our normal arrangement thank you," replied his Mum, "you upstairs in your bed and Scruffy downstairs in his. Now get out of that heap of bedclothes and help me make the bed then sort out this bedroom double quick or we will be putting the tents up in the dark and the little woodland people will have to go hungry tonight."

"Mum, now what are you talking about? 'Little woodland people', who or what are they?" asked Sam.

"Exactly what I called them. Well I suppose you could call them forest fairies or pixies and maybe some elves although they tend to be more mischievous and pinch noes and toes and twist guy ropes and things. Fairies and pixies are nicer they just get on with their day to day living, or should I say night to night living, gathering food and tidying up before having fun dancing and making music."

Sam looked over at his Mum. Was she joking and having fun or did she really believe in the stories she had told him when he was little? He wasn't sure.

"Mum are you being serious, do you really believe in fairies and things? I know when I was little you used to tell me made up stories about them and the magic they wove but you haven't mentioned them since I grew up."

"Of course I believe in them. Do you think I could draw them for the books I illustrate if didn't believe they existed? I don't talk about them to you as you seem to have forgotten about kind, funny people, it's all about aliens and monsters with you now," replied his Mum, "but why don't you listen closely tonight when we are in the forest and it's all quiet and see what you can hear? If you listen carefully enough you might be lucky enough to hear the tinkling of tiny bells or a quick knock when the fairies go to visit their friends or the faint rustle of their tiny brushes as they sweep up."

"Okay you win Mum," laughed Sam, "I would have said the knock or pop is when the gorse pods pop, the tinkling is water in the stream and the rustle is the wind rustling in the leaves but I'll listen tonight providing Scruffy and I don't fall asleep straight away. Now I'll help you with the bed then tidy up as I can't find clothes to pack until I do. Okay Mum I'm starting to see your point, if I kept it tidy all the time I would have been able to sort my clothes and pack straight away but on the other hand think of all the fun Scruffy and I would have missed!"

"Honestly Sam," his Mum laughed. "You have a logic answer for everything, just no imagination, but I suppose you're right you and Scruffy do have fun. Okay let us get this bed made and sorted and then we are ready to go. We will call at the farm on our way out just to let Steve and his parents know we are away so they can keep an eye on the cottage too."

Scruffy looked around him. There was chaos everywhere. In fact it looked pretty much like the kitchen did on that first morning but as usual Sam's mum just took it in her stride. There were no angry looks, cross words or even sigh of resignation, just a practical acceptance. Scruffy kept out of the way and Sam and his Mum quickly made the bed.

"Right Scruffy you get on the bed and supervise Sam. Make sure he picks up everything off the floor. Rubbish in the bin, books on the shelves and clothes either in the drawers or neatly, and I said neatly mind, on the bed ready to put in his back pack. Can you do that Scruffy please?" asked Sam's Mum.

Scruffy jumped on the bed and sat up straight. He was so proud to be asked to do such a responsible job as supervise Sam. Oh he would show Sam's Mum how good he could be, just wait and see!

"Woof" said Scruffy.

"Oh Mum look how proud Scruffy looks to be given a job, he is as pleased as punch. Right Mum I promise we will both be good now and get on with our jobs. If you like I'll run downstairs and get a bin bag for the rubbish unless you need something from downstairs too."

"No I don't think I do thank you. I'll make sure I get towels and toothbrushes and things. Did you find any old towels for Scruffy?"

"No Mum I'm sorry I forgot the towels but I did put food and blankets out for you to put in the car."

"That is okay Sam I saw them and packed them in the car and I'll find some old towels. I'm sure we have some more than the one downstairs. We probably need about 3 for Scruffy as knowing you two you will end up in the stream as well as the sea. You seem to both have a fatal attraction for water. Right you run down and get a bin bag Sam, you stay right where you are Scruffy, Sam will soon be back and I'll go and sort towels out. Oh don't forget your swimming shorts and an old tee shirt you can use on the beach. Do you remember if you found buckets and spades when you were in the garage?"

"Yes Mum I found them and put them with the Frisbees and cricket bat as I thought they would be best on the beach. I also found the swingball game and I thought it would be fun for us to play with in the forest as we wouldn't lose the ball like in cricket and of course the football is fine in the forest too" replied Sam.

"Good thinking Sam. Okay shoot and let us get this show on the road. Stay there Scruffy Sam will be back in a minute. You can lay down if you want but don't mess up the bed."

With that instruction, Sam shot out of the bedroom and clattered down the stairs. His Mum chuckled and left boy and dog to get on with their jobs whilst she did her own. Scruffy was such a character and seemed good for Sam. Sam was certainly starting to think more about how his actions affected other people and take a bit more responsibility, which was good, but also they had so much fun together. She secretly couldn't wait to take Scruffy to her Mum and Dad's house as it would be like turning the clock back for them. Pete, her brother, used to have a constant companion in one of their retired sheepdogs although as he was a much older dog maybe they didn't get up to quite as much mischief! He still helped Pete cause considerable damage to their Dad's greenhouse and on one occasion the kitchen window got broke much to their Mum's shock as she was washing up when the ball landed in her washing up bowl along with a shower of glass. Sam's Mum smiled and wondered what Pete would make of Scruffy when he and Jan came over to see them at half-term. She felt sure it would be love at first sight and bring out even more of the little boy in her young brother. Jan had confessed on the telephone last night that she was expecting a baby, their first, so it might be a good learning curve for the future for her, as she might possibly be coping with broken windows, a messy house and other things sometime in the future.

Jan was an only child and had not been brought up on a farm and had never even had any pets as a young girl herself this might be tough on her but so far she had coped well in her new role. She was slowly taking over more and more of her mother-in-law's duties around the farm but she might find it difficult in spring when she was faced with baby lambs, chickens, ducks and geese in the farmhouse kitchen as well as a new baby of her own. It was good that Pete's parents were close by to offer advice and support when both Pete and Jan needed it as Jan's parents were really no help to their daughter at all in her new life. In fact Sam's Mum felt that Jan's Mum would probably struggle to cope with her grandchild growing up surrounded by animals as she was used to a sterile town house. Jan, though to her credit, appeared to really love the unpredictable life of a farmer's wife and Pete was doing a good job of teaching her and supporting her as she grew into her role but it would still be a bit difficult for her and him on occasions.

Although Pete had grown up on the farm and worked alongside his dad, like Steve here did all his life, he hadn't been used to making decisions and running the farm like he was doing now. His Dad still did the paperwork and went up to the farm everyday but now Jan was giving up work she was going to take over most of her father-in-law's remaining chores and Pete and her were going to run the farm. This had been the plan since Pete and Jan got married and Pete's parents had now moved out of the farmhouse into the small cottage in the village that Pete and Jan used to live in ready for their retirement. In fact they were planning on having a holiday and Sam's Mum hoped that they would soon be able to come and stay with her and Sam which would be nice for both Sam and his Grandad as they had a strong relationship which would be further enhanced by Sam being able to show his Grandad around the area.

In fact thinking about it when she had her next gap in her work schedule she would suggest it to them as she knew that her Mum would want to be on hand as Jan's pregnancy advanced and the weather could be so unpredictable in winter. Obviously not half term, but maybe after half term, as Jan and Pete were going to make the most of this last chance for a short break that Pete's parents had offered them while his parents held the fort at the farm before assuming full responsibility for the rest of their lives. Sam's Mum accepted that this would be the last time they, Jan and Pete, would be able to come over for more than a day but as she had also been raised on a farm she knew how tying the work and life could be. Never the less she wouldn't have traded her growing up years for any other because the freedom and fun that she was able to have was the greatest thing ever. In fact most of her friends thought so too and there was never a shortage of willing volunteers to take up the offer of a weekend or few days spent on the farm during her growing up years. Her Mum and Dad were always happy to have a houseful of young people and Pete and her had been actively encouraged to bring their friends whenever they wanted. Sam's Mum was disappointed that Sam had never really expressed a wish to bring his friends to stay but she guessed that this was probably because they lived in the village and most had grandparents, if not parents, who were farmers. Thinking about it both her and Pete didn't have friends to stay until they went to senior school so maybe Sam would too.

It would be nice if they could also come again in the spring, say the Easter holidays so Sam, Scruffy and her could introduce them to this area. As Jan's baby was due at the end of January early February she would be ready by then for her and Pete to spend some time on their own coping with daily tasks around the farm and with a new baby. They would have finished lambing and Pete wouldn't be sowing the crops as Easter was too early this year so it would be a good time to spend a nice long time with her parents. She had missed them as neither had been in a position to spend much time together for many years. She would raise the suggestion of both a few days after half-term, maybe her Dad could help Sam and Scruffy build a bonfire and they could have a bonfire night party, and a longer stay at Easter. After her, Sam and Scruffy got home she would suggest it to her mother but right now she needed to think about items to pack for three nights away in a tent.

If they got a move on Sam and Scruffy could spend some time this afternoon exploring the forest then tomorrow could be spent on the beach as the weather forecast was good. They could have a ride on the train and a picnic in their favourite place on the moors the following day before packing up and coming home. Everyone should be warm enough, it was still summer after all, but she would throw in a couple of thick jumpers and get Sam to take his fleece just in case it was a bit cool at night.

Sam's Mum had, by this time, reached her own bedroom and could hear Sam telling Scruffy all about the sounds of the forest, the little stream no doubt both would fall in, the sand on the beach, the sea, ice creams, fish and chips eaten out of the paper of course, and the steam train. Well this would be an adventure that all could share Sam, Scruffy and her. If she were honest she was looking forward to it immensely. She was sure she could play swing ball and football, dig in the sand, paddle in the sea, explore rock pools under the excuse she was supervising her 'children'. Right she thought let the adventure begin.

Scruffy goes camping

Sam's mum quickly selected underwear, socks, trousers and T-shirts and packed them into her bag. She suddenly thought she had better pack a spare pair of trousers, socks and T- shirt than she would normally take as she was sure with Scruffy now part of the family there would be many more opportunities to get wet for both her and Sam. She selected a couple of warm tops to go over her T-shirts in case it was a bit chilly when they went to the seaside and added an old pair of trainers. A quick visit to the bathroom to collect her own and Sam's toothbrushes and a couple of towels and she was finished. Collecting her walking boots and fleece jacket as she left the house, locking the door and leaving the key under the boot scraper as normal she headed for the car.

"Oh are you sitting in the back Sam?" she asked when she realised the passenger seat had Sam's bag on.

"Yes I thought it would be better for Scruffy until he gets used to travelling in the car especially on long journeys," answered Sam.

"Yes probably. I will just pop to the farm and let Steve and his parents know we are going away on the way out then our first big adventure with Scruffy can begin," Sam's mum replied.

"Great we are ready, aren't we Scruffy?" laughed Sam.

Sam's mum slung her own bag onto the passenger seat and jumped into the driver's seat. As they were going down the lane they met Steve coming up. Sam's mum wound down her car window when she drew level and said,

"We were just coming up to the house to say we are away camping until Friday and ask you to keep an eye on the house."

"Well I was just coming to see if Sam and Scruffy wanted to come and help get the straw in from out of the fields at the end of the week after we finish combine harvesting, probably about Friday if the weather stays fine," answered Steve. "When are you back?"

"Depends on the weather but probably late Friday afternoon. Actually that sounds good if Sam and Scruffy came up to the farm on Saturday as it will give me chance to get the car unpacked and all the washing done as I have a big commission I need to start on Monday morning. It is all the illustrations for a series of initially 12 books but more might follow if these are successful. It's about a fairy and all her adventures. I need to concentrate hard as I need to keep to the basic design I submitted but have subtle changes so the pictures, as well as the stories, are a bit different to keep the readers interested."

"Sounds good you will really enjoy doing that I know," answered Steve. "There is no better illustrator that I know who can draw and paint fairies and elves generally, but fitting the pictures around a story will be right up your street. There will be plenty of work to keep Sam and Scruffy busy up at the farm next week until Sam goes back to school so you can concentrate on your work knowing we have them both safe. Mum will love having Sam to feed with me and Dad at lunchtime too so you don't even need to break off to prepare lunch."

"That would be a great help. Thank you so much, are you sure about this though? They can be a bit of a handful," laughed Sam's Mum.

"Completely sure Di. Dad and I will tire them out keeping them busy and Mum will love having Sam. She keeps hinting she wants grandchildren to spoil so this will be the next best thing. Off you go and have a break then head down and get on with the commission when you come back. I'll get Mum to prepare a casserole and pop it into the Aga for when you come home on Friday to save you cooking."

"Oh Steve that would be great. Why don't you come and share it with us and then Sam can tell you all about our camping trip."

"Sounds an excellent plan. See you Friday teatime. Have a great time."

With a wave Steve drove off down the lane to turn round and Sam's mum carried on towards the main road.

As they travelled along the road Sam kept up a conversation telling Scruffy all about the forest that they camped in and the various noises that they would hear especially at night. He also told him about the steam train that travelled up the valley. Eventually Sam ran out of things to tell Scruffy and apart from the odd comment like 'those are cows, those are pigs' or 'look at that tractor, they are combine harvesting that field of corn' silence reigned supreme in the car. At one point Sam's Mum asked if Sam wanted some music on but Sam said him and Scruffy were quite happy as they were and when Sam's mum sneaked a look at them she could see Scruffy laid out full length on the seat with his head on Sam's knee and Sam was just watching the landscape slide past the window.

Eventually they turned off the main road and Sam sat up straighter.

"Scruffy you can wake up now we are nearly there. It's only about 5 minutes and then we will cross the railway line at the station and enter the forest properly."

At the sound of Sam's voice Scruffy sat up to look out of the window.

"Oh look Mum the highland cows have a couple of baby calves. Look Scruffy, look at the highland cows."

Scruffy looked out of the car window to see what Sam was pointing to and nearly fell off the seat because looking back at him right at the side of the road was the biggest, scruffiest animal that Scruffy had ever seen. On top of that long shaggy coat were two of the biggest horns that looked so scary that Scruffy shrank back away from the window as close to Sam as he could possibly get.

"It's okay Scruffy they can't get us when we are in the car and in any case they wouldn't bother us if we weren't in the car as they are more frightened of us than we are them."

Scruffy wasn't so sure so he was quite pleased that he was in the car and they were on the outside. Suddenly he had a scary thought. Sam had said they just crossed something called railway lines and they were in the forest where they were camping. Did that mean these great big beasts could roam around where they wanted and would they be roaming about where they were going to be camping? Sam had explained that they would be sleeping in a tent and had showed him a picture on the label of what a tent looked like and it didn't look as if it would keep these beasts out if they wanted to walk or eat the grass that Sam, himself and Sam's mum were camping on. Almost as though Sam could read Scruffy's mind he reassured him by saying,

"It's okay Scruffy we go across something called a cattle grid before we cross the railway line and the cows can't cross the cattle grid as it is just bars across a deep hole and although you can't see it there is a fence stopping them from getting on the railway line. We actually camp at the other side of the railway line so we are quite safe from the highland cows or the sheep that you can see grazing here on the moor. Right, here we are, crossing the cattle grid, feel the shuddering of the car and there the station signal box. Now the car will judder a bit as we cross the railway tracks, yes here we go, and now as you can see we are right in the forest like the one near our house that you got lost in the first day only this forest is much bigger so you had better not wander off on your own. If I lose you in this forest I will never find you as even I don't know this forest very well except just around the clearing where we camp. Mum and I have walked down the road and there is a beautiful clear stream just at the side of the road I have played in but I haven't explored much further than that as I don't want to get lost."

The car wound round a bend a bit further on before Sam's mum pulled off the road onto a large flat piece of grass surrounded on three sides by very tall trees and lots of bushes. Sam's mum swung the car round so it formed another barrier on the open side of the clearing before stopping the car and turning off the engine.

"Okay Sam and Scruffy, here we are. Sam leave Scruffy in the car for a minute while we unload the tents and get set up then when all the tents are up you can let Scruffy help you sort out your sleeping arrangements while I set up the cooking area. Then I'll sort my tent out while you two go off and explore then I'll start tea."

"Sounds like a good plan to me," replied Sam. "Right Scruffy you sit here in the car while I help Mum with the tents. It is best this way as you would only get under my feet. Nothing you can do yet but you can sit and watch us through the car window."

Sam jumped out of the car and went to the back of the car and his mum joined him. They quickly unpacked the car boot.

"Leave the swing ball, frisbee and cricket stuff on the side for the moment," directed Sam's mum. "Let us get all three tents erected one for you and Scruffy to sleep in, one for me to sleep in and the other to store food in and cook and wash up in. I suggest we put the cooking tent in the middle between our sleeping tents then we can build a fire pit in front of the tents between them and the car. That way the trees will shelter all the tents but we still have space to sit round the fire."

"Yes that sounds good Mum, I tell you what Scruffy and I will go and look for stones and wood after we have sorted our tent while you make tea. That way the fire can be lit before we eat and we can sit around it to eat our tea. Gives me and Scruffy something to do while we explore."

"Okay Sam, right let us get these tents up. Come on we will pitch yours first then mine opposite. Can you remember how to do it this year, you have watched me plenty of times?"

"Yes I think so, well I'll give it a try anyway. If I get stuck I'll give you a shout. You go and make a start on your tent then we can work together on the cooking one."

"Okay Sam have a go on your own. It will be easier to pitch the cooking tent together as it is much bigger."

Sam took his tent to the space he had decided would be best and his Mum took her tent to the other side. Soon both tents were erected and between them they quickly erected the cooking tent. Sam got both sleeping bags from the car dropping his Mum's inside her tent and then taking his own to his tent. His Mum unpacked and set up the table to put the stove on and carried all the food across. Lastly she located the box with the pots, pans and cutlery in and placed it inside the tent. Meanwhile Sam had found the folding chairs and placed them near the cooking tent then went back to the car to collect his bag, blankets and sleeping bag for Scruffy and Scruffy. Scruffy had been watching all the activity trusting now that Sam would collect him when he was ready.

"Okay Scruffy, out you come and I'll show you inside the tent. Listen it will be a bit of a tight squeeze with both of us in the tent so you will have to listen and move where I tell you to go while I get your bed made then lie on that while I sort my sleeping bag and clothes out."

Scruffy jumped out of the car and ran over to a tent.

"No Scruffy that's Mum's tent. Here this is our tent."

Scruffy raced across to the other tent and poked his nose through the opening. He stood in shocked silence. How was he and Sam going to fit in this tiny place? He turned round to look at Sam.

"Yes I know it doesn't look very big Scruffy but we only sleep in here and therefore it doesn't need to be very big. Also we will both stay much warmer if we are cuddled tightly together. Now move, either go inside and let me follow you or let me in and you follow me."

Scruffy hung back so Sam crawled in through the opening.

"Come on Scruffy get yourself inside. Yes that's right, you will have to crawl in like I have to. Right you stay at that side of the tent while I sort your bed out."

Scruffy wasn't too good at staying still as he was too interested in what Sam was doing so he crept a bit closer then closer still. Sam laid a rubber mat down first then spread a blanket on top then came a strange sort of bag. Sam unzipped the side and laid it on the blanket before putting another couple of blankets on the inside of the opened bag.

"There you go Scruffy, you can try your bed out now."

Scruffy jumped up and banged into the roof of the tent.

"No Scruffy, you can't bound about when we are in the tent. Shuffle over here on your tummy and get snuggled on your bed while I get my bed made."

Scruffy did as Sam said and shuffled over to his bed. He crawled on to it but no that didn't feel right so he stood up to turn around. Whack, he hit the roof of the tent again.

"Scruffy what have I just told you? You can't stand up in the tent. If you want to turn around you have to shuffle round on your tummy."

Scruffy lay back down again and shuffled round into a different position. No that didn't feel right either. He twisted and turned a bit more but he didn't seem to be able to get comfortable.

"It's okay Scruffy it will feel a bit strange but by the time we come to bed tonight you will be so tired you won't notice the hard ground. Right that's my bed sorted and my bag of clothes tidy so we will go out now and see if Mum needs a hand. If not we have to go and find some stones to build a fire pit before heading off to find some dry wood to burn on our camp fire. Come on, remember we have to crawl in and out of the tent"

Scruffy and Sam left the tent and Sam zipped the door shut.

"Do you need a hand Mum or can me and Scruffy go and look for stones, wood, twigs and dry grass to build a fire?"

"No I'm fine Sam, I've nearly got the cooking tent sorted so I'll go and sort my tent out in a minute then get some tea for us all sorted. Is pasta okay for tonight?"

"Yes that's fine. Right Scruffy and I will take charge of the camp fire then."

"Okay remember to build it in the centre of the clearing. We don't want to set any trees or bushes on fire. Do you think there is enough room or shall I move the car?"

"No I don't think you need move the car Mum. I'm sure there is enough room away from the tents and the car to build a small fire. After all we don't need a huge one."

"No as you say we only need a small one. Right you and Scruffy work on the fire while I sort myself out."

"Will do Mum, see you soon. Come on Scruffy we have work to do."

Scruffy bounded over to Sam to see what they were going to do next. He wasn't sure what building a camp fire entailed, or even for that matter, what a camp fire was but he was sure it would be exciting anyway. Everything Sam and him did was exciting! Sam's mum watched the pair as they wandered out of the clearing. She was quite proud of how Sam appeared to have grown up and become more responsible in the last few weeks since they had got Scruffy. She watched Sam take control of Scruffy as they left the clearing, telling him about what they were looking for now and what they would need later. Sam's mum had expected Sam to get his tent sorted then chase straight out with Scruffy to explore as he would have done only a few months ago, but this time he not only helped set up all the tents but then took control of collecting and building the camp fire. Yes he took Scruffy with him to collect everything he needed but even this was done responsibly. Sam's mum shook her head in disbelief before disappearing into her own tent. It looked as if this was going to be a very different camping trip to the one she had imagined.

Meanwhile Sam and Scruffy had arrived at another clearing just on from the one where they had parked up, and yes as Sam had hoped, there was a heap of stones which he suspected someone else had collected to use to build a fire pit. Although they were not small stones they were not too big that Sam couldn't carry them one at a time. He picked up his first stone and set off out of the clearing. Suddenly he realised Scruffy wasn't following him. He turned around to call Scruffy but realised Scruffy wasn't there.

"Scruffy where are you? Come on Scruffy, where are you? I told you to stay close and not get lost. Hurry up these stones are heavy."

Sam put the stone he was holding down and went back into the clearing. Just then Scruffy came bounding out of the bushes and trotted over to Sam.

"Oh there you are Scruffy. Where have you been? I told you to stay close and not wander off as you could easily become lost in this forest. Oh well never mind, come on, we have these stones to carry into the clearing where we are parked to make a fire pit surround."

Sam turned to pick up his stone again but Scruffy went back into the clearing further but didn't completely disappear just stood at the edge as much as to say 'Come and look here Sam'

Sam left his stone where it was and went to see what Scruffy had found. Scruffy was stood at the beginning of a path that led into the bushes.

"What have you found Scruffy? A path well that is good maybe we can explore it later. Meanwhile let us get the stuff we need for the camp fire first."

Sam turned away from the entrance to the path but Scruffy just stood there and then he said 'Woof' and waited. Because Sam didn't respond he said 'Woof' again and set off down his path then came back to see if Sam was following him.

"Okay Scruffy I can see you are not going to come with me until I explore this path you have found so let us go and see where it takes us."

Scruffy bounded on ahead down the path he had found with Sam trailing behind. Suddenly the path opened out and Sam was astonished to find himself next to his tent that he had just put up.

"Oh you clever dog you had found a short cut between the two clearings. That is great as it means I don't have to carry those stones so far. Also I noticed lots of broken twigs on the edge of the path to start the fire too. Hi Mum, Scruffy has found a short cut between our clearing and the next where there is some big stones that other people have used to make a fire so we are just going to carry them round."

"Oh well done you two you are working well as a team I see, I am very impressed. Okay off you go. Was there any logs around did you notice, as we will need some bigger bits of wood to burn once the fire takes hold?"

"Well I didn't notice any near the stones but there is lots of varying sizes of twigs on the side of the path linking these two clearings. I'll have a good look round the clearing before Scruffy and I venture further afield if there isn't something suitable."

"Good plan Sam although if other people have also had a camp fire they might have already burnt all the wood nearby. Anyhow bring the stones round and collect a heap of twigs and then if there isn't any wood nearby I'll join you and Scruffy on a 'log hunt' not a 'bear hunt' like we used to sing round the camp fire when you were younger."

"Oh I had forgotten that camp fire song we used to sing," laughed Sam. "Right Scruffy back we go to the other clearing and get those stones moved first."

Scruffy happily trailed Sam back along the path back to the other clearing feeling extremely proud that he had been able to find the path between the clearings and both Sam and his Mum had told him he was clever. Scruffy thought he would burst with pride no one had ever told him he was clever before.

Sam quickly moved the stones now he had a short cut and then him and Scruffy collected several armfuls of twigs and placed them next to the stones.

"Right Scruffy let us go back and see if we can find some bigger logs to put on the fire when it is burning strongly."

Sam and Scruffy returned to the clearing and Sam went round the outside of the clearing to see if there was anything they could use to burn. At the other side of the clearing almost directly opposite the path joining the two clearings was another path much more overgrown though. Sam gingerly poked a way through the undergrowth until he found exactly what he was looking for. A tree had obviously fallen down and scattered around it was some large branches and even a few larger splinters of trunk.

"Brilliant Scruffy, here we are, a gold mine of wood, enough for us for all the time we are staying. Come on Scruffy you can help me pull these bigger pieces out of the grass."

Scruffy quickly joined his master and between them they pulled and tugged on the branches that had become overgrown in grass.

"Scruffy we will stay here and pull them all out and make a pile before transferring them to our campsite."

When Sam decided they had enough wood on their pile he picked up an armful and set off back down the path. When he looked back he was surprised to see Scruffy following him with the biggest branch trailing on behind him.

"Oh you clever boy are you helping too? My that is a huge piece of stick you have there it will help keep the fire going for ages. Can you manage? I can't really help you as my arms are full but you are doing real well up to press."

Scruffy tugged and pulled the stick as best he could, only problem was it kept getting tangled in the plants and bushes at the side of the path but eventually Sam and him emerged into the clearing.

"Now Scruffy we just have to manage the next path and we can drop our load. I think one more trip will be enough for tonight. We can always collect more tomorrow for tomorrow night if we need it."

Walking down the path between the clearings wasn't so bad as it seemed a much more used path so wasn't as overgrown but Scruffy, with his long stick still kept getting caught in the bushes at the side of the path. Eventually they made it into the clearing where they were camping just as Sam's mum emerged from the cooking tent.

"Look Mum," shouted Sam. "Scruffy is helping this time with the sticks and branches. He has brought his load just like I did."

"Well done Scruffy as I said before you are a clever dog and an equal part of the team. Sam, tea will be ready in about 10 minutes. Does that work for you two? Are you both going for another load?"

"Yes Mum. We think one more load will see us through tonight and then we can collect more tomorrow evening if we need some. Depends how long we stay up tonight but we often don't stay up late the first night. We always seem to crash early that night, it is usually the other nights we sit for longer round the fire."

"Yes you are right Sam we always have a little camp fire tonight but usually a bigger one tomorrow night. Right off you and Scruffy go and bring back one more load ready for tonight and then it will be tea time."

"Brilliant Mum that has worked out real well. Come on Scruffy one more load then we can chill after tea and plan what we are going to do tomorrow. Is it the seaside tomorrow mum for us all?"

"Yes it is supposed to be a nice day tomorrow so we will spend the day at the seaside then I thought we could take a picnic and you and Scruffy can have fun at the castle before we go for a train ride on Thursday. I thought we could stop off in the first village and have a walk and look at the shops then walk along the path to the next station and catch the train all the way back the following day."

"Wow that sounds like a fun packed day. I'd better keep a tight hold on Scruffy's lead when we walk round the village. He still gets spooked with sheep in the fields when we go to the farm so the fact that they roam freely around the village will probably blow his mind," laughed Sam.

"Yes you are probably right but it will be fun seeing his eyes get bigger with surprise when he sees them just wandering loose in the village eating grass on the village green and things. Off you go and I'll see you in 10 minutes. No later mind or tea will be spoilt."

"Okay Mum, come on Scruffy let's run back down the path and I'll race you across the clearing. Whoever reaches the overgrown path is the leader."

With that both boy and dog set off across the grass towards the path. Good, thought Sam's mum, that showed that Sam still could behave like a boy should despite him changing to become a much more responsible person. She didn't want him growing up too fast but she knew he would change quite a bit over the next year as this was his last year at junior school. She knew once he went to senior school he would change a lot just like her young brother had. There were so many new things to learn and their social world would expand hugely. All that was natural she supposed and she was glad Sam had become a confident and well-adjusted boy but she would miss this close bond they had, although since getting Scruffy that bond had stretched anyway and she supposed it would just stretch further over the next few years until Sam became settled in a job. She often wondered what Sam would eventually choose to do as a career. She wondered if the farming gene had passed from her family to him or would he follow in his father's footsteps and become a city slicker. Only time would tell but at the moment it appeared that like her and Pete, her brother, farming and the countryside were his prominent interest but that might change once he went to senior school in the town and mixed with other young people from all walks of life. For a time she had lived the city life but found after a time her artistic talent faded. Once Sam's father died there was nothing to hold her in the city so she gave up her city job as a graphic designer, found the cottage they lived in now to rent and decided to work from home as a children's illustrator. At first it had been very hard work getting commissions but now she was not having to chase work down and could, in fact, choose which commissions to take. She could actually choose which illustration packages to bid for instead of bidding for everything that was advertised. In fact now several publishers were actually approaching her with offers of work like the one she was about to start. Sam's mum decided she had better go and check the tea or it might get burnt and get organised. She thought she might suggest to Sam that they wander down to the station after tea and catch up with old friends there and introduce them to Scruffy and introduce Scruffy to steam trains as she knew he wouldn't have even heard them let alone see them at close range. Then they could come back and light the camp fire and have a chill out before bedtime. Di, that was Sam's mum's name, thought she might even be able to do some sketches that she could use on her next commission as this place had always had a magical effect on her creative juices.

Just then Sam and Scruffy emerged from the path from the other clearing Scruffy actually dragging the biggest branch ever. Scruffy wasn't a small dog but the branch was nearly three times his size and only just fitted his mouth at the smallest diameter.

"Goodness Scruffy that is a massive branch you have found. How on earth did you manage to drag that home for us?"

"I know," laughed Sam. "I told him he wouldn't manage but he was determined he was going to bring it.

72

He found it himself and pulled it out of the undergrowth although I had to give him a bit of a helping hand to pull the last bit free from the grass and weeds. I was surprised how strong Scruffy had now become since he came to live with us."

"Well I suppose it is because of all the exercise he gets and the fact most days you have a tug of war with something even if it is just the 'goal posts' when you are playing football. He wouldn't get any of that exercise in the kennels. One or maybe two walks a day, and that was likely on the lead, would be all he would get whereas now you are both busy all day long so it is not surprising he is getting stronger all the time. Well done Scruffy take your prize over to the pile of sticks Sam and you collected before and I promise as a reward you can have extra tea tonight. I think you deserve it you have been such a clever dog."

Scruffy dragged his stick over to the pile of stones and sticks then looked over at Sam and his mum as if to say 'anything else I can do for you?' He was so proud of himself and the fact that both Sam and his mum thought he was clever made him prouder still.

"Okay Sam wash your hands quickly tea is ready. I just have to put it on our plates and put a bit of extra chicken I had left over on to Scruffy's tea as I think he deserves a treat. After we have washed up the tea pots I thought we might have a wander down to the station to see if there is anybody we know there. We should just about catch the last train going through if the timetable is normal one and we can introduce Scruffy to the sight and sound of them before we take a trip on it on Thursday."

"Brilliant that is a fantastic idea Mum. Two minutes and I'll be ready and I'll do the washing up for you while you sit and enjoy your coffee after tea if you want," answered Sam.

"What now I know I'm dreaming! Are you really offering to wash up Sam? Now that is a first even on holiday!"

"Yes I know but I've been thinking lately that I should be helping you around the house a bit more Mum now I am growing up and Steve agreed when I mentioned it the other day too so I thought this would be a good day to start. Is that okay?"

"More than okay Sam, you really are changing and growing up. I think Scruffy has been good for you. It has made you take a bit more responsibility and now it is spilling over into home too. Thank you Sam now you get your tea. Scruffy you come and get your tea too. I'm sure you are both hungry."

"Thanks Mum I know I am and the amount of energy that Scruffy must have used dragging that branch out of the undergrowth and back home will have left him hungry too. Come on Mum you sit down too and have your tea. Leave the kettle, we will boil it when we have finished eating."

"My, what a thoughtful boy you are becoming. Okay we will eat together then boil the kettle for my coffee and the washing up water and I'll enjoy my coffee while you wash and dry the pots. Scruffy can watch you and chill with me as there is not really anything he can do to help you."

Sam, his mum and Scruffy all ate their tea then Sam's mum put the kettle on to boil while Sam piled up the dirty dishes and got the washing up bowl ready for the hot water once the kettle boiled. Scruffy laid and watched the activity but realised he couldn't help so he was content to watch. He knew now that Sam and his mum would include him whenever they could and to be honest he was ready for a bit of a rest because that last branch had been rather heavy but he wanted to show Sam he could be a big help too.

Soon the kettle boiled and Sam made his mum her coffee then poured boiling water into the washing up bowl. He added enough cold water until the water was cool enough for his hands and then washed the pots, dried them and put them away. He then went over and arranged the stones he had brought into a circle. He placed some dried grass and little twigs in the bottom with another layer of grass and bigger twigs on top then sorted the twigs into piles of same size twigs. Scruffy wandered over to see what Sam was actually doing. He peered into the stone circle that Sam had created with the twigs and grass. In an act of mischief he grabbed the top twig and ran off with it like he did at home with the sticks they used as goal posts when they were playing football. As he expected Sam gave chase and wrestled him to the ground.

"Scruffy, you beast you have stolen my twig," laughed Sam as the pair chased round the clearing then round the car. "Come on give it up it is my stick. I carried them home and I need it for the fire."

Scruffy knew by Sam's voice he wasn't really cross with him as this was a game they often played at home. Eventually Scruffy was caught and brought down in a rugby tackle and the pair rolled over and over in a tangle of arms and legs. Unfortunately the twig didn't survive this activity and it broke into tiny bits under the two wrestling bodies but neither heard. Sam's mum laughed at the pair and their boisterous fun.

"Crickey Sam, it is like watching your Uncle Pete and his dog, lots of years ago the way you two go on. I really can't believe that you still get up to the same antics as he did. I wonder if your Uncle Pete and Aunty Jan's baby will someday do the same."

"Oh is Aunty Jan having a baby? That is so cool because I'll be able to be like a big brother and teach it all the things I have learnt from you and Uncle Pete. Actually Steve was telling me some of the things him and Max his dog got up to and it sounds as though a lot of it was similar to Uncle Pete because he also grew up on a farm like you and Uncle Pete."

"Yes the baby is not due until after Christmas just before the lambing season gets properly underway at the end of March or early April so that is a bit of time yet and of course it will be a few years before it is old enough for you to teach it how to get into mischief. You will be a teenager yourself by then and will have other interests and Scruffy won't be a young dog either but I'm sure between Uncle Pete and you poor Aunty Jan is not going to know what has hit her. Please remember she wasn't brought up on a farm so there will be times when she just doesn't understand our way of doing things."

"Well I'm sure Granny and Grandad will help all they can and you can always give her tips as the baby gets older. Oh Scruffy that will be something else I will have to teach you how to be gentle around the baby. Also as it begins to learn to walk you will have to learn to keep real still if it uses you to hold on to learn to balance. I know these things Mum because Ben was telling me about his baby sister's antics just before we finished school for the holidays and I got Scruffy. They have a dog too and she uses his tail to hang on to when she is trying to walk and uses his neck or head to pull herself up with."

"Oh I forgot that Ben had a little sister. Yes that is the sort of thing they do but I don't think we will see enough of them all for Uncle Pete's baby to use Scruffy in that way. That usually happens when both baby and dog live together but we will wait and see. Uncle Pete and Aunty Jan are coming for a few days at half term while Granny and Grandad see to everything at the farm then I'm going to see if they want to come and stay after Uncle Pete gets home. It would be nice to have them to stay here for a few days before all the cows go into the buildings for the winter and they start to have their babies. Aunty Jan will probably be too big herself by then to help much so Granny and Grandad will still be helping Uncle Pete around that busy time then after the new baby is born and Aunty Jan gets her strength back and the baby settled. I don't think Granny and Grandad will get over again until Easter but I hope we might go and visit them all and meet the new baby sometime during the half term holiday."

"Wow that sounds a great plan Mum. Okay Scruffy the twig you stole appears to have got broken and disappeared and Mum has finished her coffee so I will go and find your lead so we can go down to the station with Mum. Is that okay Mum are you ready too?"

"Yes I'm ready, you go and find Scruffy's lead and I'll close the cooking tent flap to stop anything blowing in and we will go down and have a wander. I reckon that the timetable has not actually changed and in that case there should be two trains crossing in about 15 minutes providing they are running on time but that is doubtful by this time of day," laughed Sam's mum.

"Yes usually by the end of the day the timetable is merely a guide isn't it Mum," laughed Sam? "But it doesn't matter because we can just wait until they arrive. I think I will need to hang on to Scruffy real tight especially if they release the steam valve and let the steam off because it is such a loud noise poor Scruffy will be scared witless."

"Good idea Sam I remember bringing you to watch the trains when you were quite little and both when they let off the steam and blew the whistle you screamed at the top of your lungs."

"Did I Mum, well I'm not scared now because Ricky explained the noise and why they did it one day when I visited the engine didn't he Mum?"

"Yes you are a lucky boy, let us hope it is Helen in the signal box today and then you can take Scruffy actually into the box to see all the levers before the trains arrive or after they have left."

"Oh brilliant I never thought of that but if it isn't Helen or Mike, because either will let me in, then we can just watch from the platform. Come on Mum, here Scruffy come and have your lead on because the station is a dangerous place especially if trains are coming or going."

Scruffy bounded over to Sam to have his lead on knowing full well that whatever they were going to do would be lots of fun just as they had experienced already today. Oh he was so glad he had such a wonderful life now with Sam and his mum and he desperately hoped it would never change.

Scruffy and the Train

Scruffy, Sam and Sam's mum walked back along the road they had drove on only a few short hours ago. Was it only a few hours since as it felt like days since they had done so much? Scruffy had watched Sam and his mum unload the car and put the tents up before Scruffy and Sam made their beds in the tent and went to look for things for the camp fire. Scruffy was so proud that it was him that had found the path linking the two clearings although he hadn't confessed to the fact that he had actually been following a scent when he had accidently found the path. He knew now that one of the scents he had been following was probably what Sam called a fox. He encountered the smell a lot in 'their' forest. Sam said a fox was like a dog but a red-brown colour with a bushy tail. Sam admitted that Scruffy might never see one in real life although he had shown him pictures of one in a book. Scruffy wasn't too sure why they only came out at night although Sam had said this was usually because they were afraid of people and that when it was dark there was no people about. Sam had also explained that they might be able to find more food among the forest animals when it was dusk. Steve and Sam had explained that it was to keep the hens and geese safe that they were shut up in their houses at night and that the ducks spent their night in their hut in the middle of the pond. Steve had explained to Sam and him that usually foxes wouldn't cross water but even if they were desperately hungry and did the ducks had a chance to fly away. Scruffy had actually picked up another smell, one he hadn't ever smelt in 'their forest when he found he start of the path and decided to explore. He was as surprised to find himself next to his and Sam's tent as Sam had been when he emerged out of the path. It was nice to feel that both Sam and his mum thought he was clever to find the path so he decided he wouldn't tell Sam that it had been an accident. After Sam had carried the stones into 'their' camp site then he and Sam had gone exploring to find wood. Now that had been fun tugging the branches out of the long grass and especially when he, Scruffy, had found the last huge branch and with Sam's help had tugged it out then he, Scruffy, had carried it, no in actual fact if he was honest, dragged it back to the camp site. What a lovely tea Sam's mum had made him too then he had thankfully been able to have a rest while Sam washed up the pots. That last game of steal and chase with the twig had been fun too. There wasn't quite as much space in the clearing as they had in the field where they played football but Scruffy still had a great time. Sam had said something about putting up a game called swing ball tomorrow morning before they went to the seaside. Now as usual Scruffy had never heard of this game but he was quite sure it would be fun anyway as all the games him and Sam played were fun. Now they were going to the station to see the trains. Now what trains looked like Scruffy had no idea but he was willing to go and see. Soon they arrived back to where the car had sort of bumped a bit as they went over what Sam had called railway lines. There were two, no three houses that Scruffy could see and then another tall building that looked a bit like a house but there was no windows on the bottom floor. Oh my goodness there was a woman hanging out of the large window upstairs. Scruffy hoped she wasn't going to fall out!

"Hi Sam, hi Di, great to see you, I didn't know you were coming. I know you usually make it over sometime in the school holidays but I thought I must have missed you this year as they are nearly finished."

"Hi Helen," Sam's mum shouted back. "I've been really busy, also Sam got a dog at the beginning of the holidays so we have been busy getting him settled before we had a camping trip. When is the next train or trains due in?"

"Should be here in about 10-15 mins. Well the one from Pickering should but I think the one from the other way might be a bit later so I think we will be holding one here for a bit so they can pass. That should give you a bit of time to let your dog have a close look at the engine won't it Sam? Do you want to cross over Sam and bring your dog to meet me properly, I'll come down to say hello then you can bring him up to have a look from up here?"

With that the woman disappeared from the window and Sam, Scruffy and Sam's mum walked over the railway lines and round the house to a door. Out of the door emerged the woman from the window upstairs.

"Hi Helen," Sam said. "This is Scruffy and he is my best friend and we do everything together. Now Scruffy be good and say hello to Helen nicely."

"Hello Scruffy well I can tell why you are called that but the best dogs in the world are scruffy mutts. I know mine is anyway and I wouldn't be without her."

"Oh I didn't know you had a dog Helen. What is her name and what breed is she?"

"Her name is really Maisie but she gets Stinky if she has been rolling in dirt which is frequent with her. As to her breed I'm not sure, she has a long curly coat but also loves chasing rabbits so I daren't bring her here as she would be gone in a flash as soon as my back was turned. Despite this, or maybe because of it, I love her to bits. I've always had a dog for as long as I remember as my parents had Jack Russell Terriers but I wanted something different when I left home and found a home where I could have a dog. Like your Mum I work a lot from home so Maisie isn't left on her own much. That is important if you have a dog. We have a dog flap so when I am away like today she can come and go as she pleases in and out of the garden which has a secure fence around it and of course I only volunteer here an odd day a week at most."

"I didn't realise you worked from home Helen. What do you do?" asked Sam's Mum.

"I write mainly short stories although I have written a novel and I am busy with my second. The short stories are really my bread and butter with the novels offering me a bit of extra. I also write the odd non-fiction feature on walks in the countryside that Maisie and I explore. I love country walks and so does Maisie so we always take the camera with us and then afterwards when we get home I have a look at the pictures and decide if I can write an interesting feature then offer it to the local magazine in the area where we have been walking. It gives me a chance to write something different."

"How lovely I didn't realise you were a writer Helen. All these years we have been coming here and you never said anything," exclaimed Sam's Mum.

"Well to be honest I have only been doing it full time for about three years, before that I wrote in my spare time. I had a full time job in social care but all the emotional pressure and travelling that came with the job became too much. I had a few short stories published and I realised that I could produce more if I had more time to devote to it so I took the plunge. I sold my city flat and found a lovely little cottage out in the country, got myself a dog and settled down to write full time. Unfortunately I found that the ideas soon dried up as I missed meeting people so I decided to become a volunteer on this railway, that I had spent as much of my time as I could in the past. It had always provided me with the opportunity to unwind from my stressful job. I became interested in the signal work so I did the training and have found it very inspirational as I am meeting lots of different people when I am here that I can weave into stories."

"So in a way we are really in the same line of business," laughed Sam's Mum.

"Not really," replied Helen. "You are much more creative than me. You have to interpret the writer's vision into illustrations and that takes skill. I just invent the stories in my head and write them down."

By this time Scruffy and Sam had become bored by the adult's conversation and wandered down the platform to see if there was anything interesting to look at. Sam poked his head into an old railway carriage that had an open door and was amazed to see that it had been done out with lots of pictures and articles on the walls and bits of engine parts and other interesting objects sat on tables or in display cabinets. Sam stepped into the carriage but Scruffy held back. Sam tugged at Scruffy's lead but Scruffy just dug his heels in more. Sam turned around to see what the problem was to see Scruffy peering down the hole between the platform and carriage.

"Oh Scruffy, sorry are you frightened of the gap. It is okay you just need to take a bigger step and you will be fine. Come on, have a try!"

Scruffy was having none of it, he didn't want to fall down the hole in front of him. Sam stepped back out on to the platform to encourage his dog to have a go but as soon as Scruffy's lead went slack he took a further step back.

"No Scruffy don't go backwards or you will fall off the platform down on to the rails at the other side."

Scruffy turned and looked behind him and yes there was another edge like the one he was trying to avoid behind him. He looked around in a panic but no it was okay as long as he stayed where he was. There was the long piece of concrete they had just walked on although it appeared that it was almost finished where Sam and he were as it wasn't too far to the end. Scruffy turned around to face the way they had come and tugged at the lead in Sam's hand. He must have tugged harder than he intended as he pulled it out of Sam's hand.

"Now look what you have done Scruffy," Sam exclaimed as he grabbed the end of the lead off the platform.

"Are you okay young man?" asked a voice emerging from the side of the carriage.

"Yes thank you, it is just I cannot persuade my dog to step off the platform into the carriage and I wanted to have a look inside. This wasn't here last year when we were here."

"No I have been working on putting this display together over the winter and early spring since I retired and joined this station group as a volunteer. Gives visitors a bit of something else to do while they are here. We also have an art gallery over the other side that local artists can display their paintings to sell too. Here, I tell you what, give me your dog's lead and I'll sit on this bench and mind him while you go and have a look inside. We don't want your dog getting stressed and I don't suppose he will be that interested in the history of the station either."

"Oh would you, thank you so much," replied Sam. "Now Scruffy be a good boy and stay with this kind man while I go and have a look inside. It might be best as you and I together can be a bit clumsy. Don't worry I won't be long and you can see Mum talking to Helen down there at the other end of the platform."

"Oh is that your Mum and what is your name young man? I deduce that Scruffy is your dog's name."

"Yes this is Scruffy and my name is Sam," answered Sam politely.

"Well now Sam you go and have a look in our history carriage and Scruffy and me will chill on the platform. You have a few more minutes before the train comes in."

"Yes I know Helen said so before her and Mum got talking. Scruffy and I were going up into the signal box but this looks more interesting. I have often been in the signal box before and I shouldn't imagine it has changed since last year but this is something new," replied Sam.

The man laughed,

"No the signal box doesn't change but hopefully this will change every winter. Well at least until I run out of different things to put in it but that won't be for a while yet as I have found enough stuff to change the display every year for at least three years maybe even four. Even if you come every year it will be worth coming to have a look each time you are here. Now off you pop and then when you come back out you can tell me what you think and if you feel I could change it at all to make it more interesting."

"Cool thanks sir I will," breathed Sam as he jumped nimbly into the carriage. Scruffy laid down on the platform with his head on his paws. He was now confident that Sam would come back and collect him when he was finished.

"Well Scruffy, aren't you a good dog laying there quietly while your master goes and has a look at my history carriage. I am sure when I was a boy my dog wouldn't have been so good. He would have whinged and whined all the time I was out of his sight."

Scruffy looked up at the man before laying back down on his paws. He couldn't believe it, here was another adult telling him how good he was. He wasn't sure exactly what was happening, in the past everyone had told him how bad he was and now since coming to live with Sam and his mum he was constantly been told how good and clever he was! He was beginning to think that maybe it hadn't been always his fault and that maybe, just maybe, it was that those other people had expected far too much of him. Just then he heard footsteps coming down the platform.

"Goodness Scruffy where has Sam gone? He shouldn't just abandon you but it looks as if you are being a very good boy laying there waiting for him. You've both come a long way since those first few days."

"It is okay I offered to watch Scruffy as he didn't want to step into the carriage but Sam wanted to go and look at my history of the station in the carriage. Scruffy was no bother he just quietly laid down to wait for his master. I was just telling him how good he was. I used to have a dog when I was a young boy and he wouldn't have been half as good. Not only was Scruffy left with a stranger but he never said a word when he saw his master disappear either."

"Yes I am very proud of him. Like you I am sure my young brother's dog wouldn't have waited so patiently either when he had one at the same age as Sam. It is even more impressive when you realise that Scruffy hasn't been with Sam for 6 weeks yet and that he wasn't a puppy when he joined us."

"My goodness I would never have believed that," replied the man. "I thought they had been together since Scruffy had been a puppy. All credit to them both then. I don't know how Sam has done such a good job in such a short time."

"Well I must admit they have never been apart in all the 6 weeks and Sam has really given Scruffy so much of his attention and they have had so much fun together. Even earlier today Scruffy was helping Sam to gather wood for the camp fire and brought the biggest branch you ever saw. Sam said he had needed to help Scruffy tug it out of the undergrowth but then Scruffy carried it to our clearing where we are camping."

"It just goes to show that with love, work and attention you can train all dogs to be a credit to their family. For a young boy to achieve that is even more surprising. Well done to both boy and dog."

Just at that moment Sam emerged from the carriage and Scruffy jumped up to greet his master.

"Hi Scruffy, have you been a good dog while I was looking at the exhibits? Thank you sir for looking after Scruffy. I have been coming here camping for years and didn't realise the area had such a lot of history. Mum you should go and have a look in the carriage. This gentleman has been responsible for putting together an exhibition of local history. It is really good, very interesting. I will take over looking after Scruffy now. I won't go into the signal box but I will take Scruffy off the platform at least until the train has come in. We can come back and have a look at the engine once it is safe in case Scruffy gets spooked and tries to run off. If we are over in the car park then it is not as important as he won't be in any danger from the moving train."

"What a responsible boy you are. Yes I think you might have the right idea. As you say providing you watch for cars coming in and out of the car park you should have more space if Scruffy jerks the lead from your hand when the train comes in. Once it has stopped moving then you

85

can bring him back onto the platform because Helen says the train from Pickering will be here about 10 minutes before the other one gets in and they can pass because as you know the line is single track only between the stations so they have to pass at the stations. I will go and have a look in the carriage. I did know there was quite a bit of history in this area but there might be things I didn't know either. If you are interested there is, or was, another good museum in Pickering but that used to feature the farming history more. That was why I was so interested in it. Maybe now as you are becoming more interested in farming and spending time with Steve and his dad it might interest you too. We can see if it is still there on Thursday before we have our picnic at the castle if you want," answered his mum.

"Sorry to interrupt but yes the museum you are talking about is still there and if you haven't been for a few years then you will find it has grown and developed a lot."

"That sounds good Mum," replied Sam. "I would be interested in having a look especially as I am going to help at the farm next week."

"Right that is what we will do then. Now you and Scruffy go into the car park because I think I can hear the train in the distance. Listen closely you should be able to hear it now. You have been coming to this station long enough. I'll go and have a look in the history carriage."

"Okay Mum, thank you again sir for minding Scruffy but I'll take over now."

"It was a pleasure. Scruffy was as good as gold and you are a very polite young man. I hope to see you again sometime. Enjoy your visit to the museum on Thursday too. Now off you go as the train will be here in about 5 minutes and I surmise from your conversation that Scruffy has never been this close to a train before."

"No this is his first visit here and as we only arrived this afternoon he hasn't had chance to see any yet. We are hoping to actually ride on one on Thursday so Mum and me thought it best if he had a little preview first. It looks as if we might have a few problems persuading Scruffy to get on the train to begin with after he was so nervous of the gap between platform and carriage. It might take a joint effort between Mum and me especially as it will be more noisy and busy at Pickering."

"Yes," laughed the man. "You might have a difficult task ahead but I'm sure he won't want to let you down and the promise of an adventure at the other end of the ride might help spur him on. I remember my dog could be bribed by the promise of a fun adventure when I was your age."

"Yes," laughed Sam, "Scruffy is the same aren't you Scruffy? We have lots of fun every day."

Sam bent down and put his arms around Scruffy's neck and Scruffy reached out and gave him a big lick over Sam's ear and knocked off Sam's baseball cap as usual. Sam was so used to it he caught the cap in mid-air and plonked it back on his head.

"Right Scruffy let's get off this platform because I can hear the train getting closer. See you Mum, enjoy the exhibition. This gentleman also says there is an art gallery on the other platform that is new since we were here last year."

"Helen was telling me about that too. I might be tempted to have a look in. Probably not a good place for you and Scruffy though," laughed Sam's mum. "Knowing you two you would even manage to knock the paintings off the wall."

"I am not interested in it anyway Mum. Once the train has come in and stopped I'll take Scruffy on to the platform and see if I know any of the staff like the driver or conductor. If it is anyone I know I might even see if I can get Scruffy up close to the engine or even in a carriage. It depends on how many passengers are getting on and off or if there are any empty carriages. In any case it will be good for Scruffy to get a feel of the sound even if we are not able to get on board. Don't worry Mum I'll make sure I get off the train before it leaves the station."

"Good I'm pleased you are aware you need to get off again before it moves on," laughed his Mum.

Sam picked up Scruffy's lead holding it tight and the pair ambled off down the platform. Just at that moment there was a loud whistle just behind Scruffy and Sam and Scruffy leapt into the air. Luckily Sam was ready for this reaction and kept a tight hold on to Scruffy's lead.

"It is okay Scruffy don't panic it is just the train telling us it is about to come into the station. It won't hurt you it stays on the rail track and doesn't come up here on to the platform. Can you hear the chugging of the engine? Come on now let's pop behind this fence. Look Helen is closing the railway gates. That is to stop any cars going over the railway lines while the trains are in the station. I imagine the engine will let off steam while it is stopped. I'm sorry but that is a very loud hissing noise, a bit like the geese at the farm but much louder."

Scruffy didn't think he liked the sound of that. The loud whistle was bad enough, then the clanging of the gates as they went down. Now he could hear the chugging noise getting louder and Sam was telling him that there would a loud hissing too! He thought he would like to go back to the tent and hide his head until all these loud noises had stopped but then when he looked he realised they couldn't go back to the tent because the gates were closed over the road they needed to be on. Suddenly he looked up and saw the biggest, blackest monster coming down the side of the platform where he and Sam had just walked down. Oh dear where was Sam's mum, was she safe, they had left her on her own and now this great black brute was spilling dirty black smoke out and Scruffy couldn't see anything. Suddenly he sneezed.

"Oh dear Scruffy have you got smoke and soot up your nose. Sometimes when you aren't used to the smell it can make your nose itch. It's okay nothing to worry about. Look can you see inside the engine where the fire is?"

By this time the engine had slowed down and stopped and several doors along the carriages opened and a few people jumped out and headed for the tea hut just behind Sam and Scruffy. The engine driver also jumped out of the dirty black cab.

"Hello Sam, it is a long time since I saw you, are you okay? What is this, have you got a dog now?"

"Hi Ted, yes this is Scruffy. He is feeling a bit scared because I don't think he has ever seen a train before and definitely not as close as this. It scared him half to death when the whistle went as we were just walking down the platform. I tried to warn him that there would be a lot of strange noises but I don't think he believed me. Come out Scruffy and say hello to Ted"

Scruffy was still busy trying to hide behind Sam's legs but was also worried about Sam's mum who they had left down the platform. He certainly didn't want to meet this black faced, dirty looking man who had just jumped off the great black monster.

"Hi Scruffy, stop looking so scared, I'm not going to hurt your master neither is the train. It won't move until I get back on and that won't be for a while yet. I'm actually going to get an ice cream for myself and my firewoman. Do you want one too Sam? If you can persuade Scruffy to come out from behind your legs, go and have a close up view of the inside of the engine. I don't think it is a good idea yet to try to take Scruffy actually into the cab, it is too dangerous but why don't you go to the engine shed while you are here and try to get him to go into the cab of one that isn't working that day. I assume you are camping in the forest as usual?"

"Yes we only arrived this afternoon though so everything is still very new to Scruffy. He has only been living with Mum and me since the beginning of the school holidays and I'm not sure, but I don't think he has done much before he came to us. I have had to teach him so many different things. He hadn't ever played football, built dens or anything. Farm machinery and farm animals nearly gave him heart failure and now he is viewing a steam train close up or will be when he finally plucks up the courage to come out from behind me," laughed Sam.

"Oh dear sounds like the poor dog will be scarred for life if he hasn't had chance to grow up with you and your Mum. You are both such active, crazy people it will take him months if not years to adapt."

"Well tomorrow we are going to the seaside, another first for him I imagine, then on Thursday a trip to the farming museum in Pickering, a picnic at the castle then we are catching the train. Well hopefully we are taking a train ride, but as I've just tried to get him into the history carriage down there on the platform and he refused to budge as he could see the gap between the carriage and the platform so Mum and I might have a bit of difficulty," replied Sam. "As to next week, we are going to help our neighbour Steve in the harvest field collecting straw so if Scruffy isn't traumatised now he could well be by the time I go back to school."

"Oh the poor dog, even my mind boggles at all those new experiences and I'm an adult," laughed Ted. "Why don't you go and see Dave while I get the ice creams in and get him to put the wheelchair ramp down for him to get into the guard van then go down into a carriage and come out of the door. If he does it that way the first time he might do better on Thursday because he will know exactly what the inside of the carriage is like so it might not be as scary to him."

"Wow that is a good idea I never thought of that. Right come on Scruffy get your bum out here from behind me and we will go down the platform and ask Dave the guard to put the ramp down for you so you can have a look inside the carriage. Don't get too used to that method though because I can't promise that the guard on duty on the train we are catching on Thursday will be a good friend like Dave is, we will just have to wait and see."

"Well to be honest Sam you have been hanging around this railway and station for so many years it will be a wonder if neither the guard, the fireperson or driver isn't someone you know well and can get a favour granted if you need it but go and give Scruffy a new adventure up the ramp into the guard van then through as many carriages as you can get him and out of a door back on to the platform and I'll meet you with an ice cream. Has Scruffy ever had an ice cream if not I'll treat him to one for being such a brave dog and taking you and your Mum on!"

"Cheeky I'll tell Mum what you said Ted," Sam laughed pretending to be offended. "Come on Scruffy let us run down the platform and catch Dave before he disappears back inside the train. Dave, wait don't disappear," shouted Sam.

Ted gave a huge whistle to attract Dave's attention then pointed at Sam and Scruffy haring down the platform. Dave gave a thumbs up to Ted and waited until Sam slid to a stop in front of him. Unfortunately Scruffy was too busy trying to look at the train as he was hauled along after Sam to realise that Sam had in fact stopped so ploughed into the back of Sam's legs who was then propelled into Dave.

"Whoa there Sam," Dave laughed. "No need to knock me over. Who have we here then? Is this your dog, I didn't know you had a dog?"

"Yes this is Scruffy, my dog, he has only been with me and Mum since the beginning of the school holidays so everything is a bit strange to him. Ted suggested we ask if you could put the ramp down into the guard van like you do for wheelchairs as Scruffy here won't jump over the gap between the platform and carriage and we are planning on having a ride on the train on Thursday and don't know who will be on duty on the train we want to catch. Ted suggested we went into the guard van and down into a carriage and out of the door back onto the platform while you are stuck here so he might be happier jumping in on Thursday."

"No problem. There is no-one in the carriage next to the guard van so why don't you have a few goes one way then try to do it the other way. If you make a game of it he should be having so much fun he doesn't have time to think about the gap. After all we won't be moving from here for at least 10 minutes that should give you quite a few times both ways. That is the way we trained our dog to hop on and off the train. He was a rescue dog and scared of his own shadow but he quickly learnt that being on the train was usually followed by a good long walk in the country so he associated the two activities together. Now after two years he gets so excited when he sees the train you can't keep him off it."

"Oh thanks Dave that sounds a good plan. Ted has gone to get us ice creams as a treat for Scruffy for being brave too so hopefully he will also connect getting on and off trains as something enjoyable. Oh hi Mum, Dave here is just going to get the wheelchair ramp out so Scruffy and me can practise getting in and out of the train. We are going to start with the ramp and stepping out for a few times then the other way round. Hopefully then we won't have so much trouble on Thursday."

"Hey that is a good idea, did you think of that?" asked Sam's mum.

"No," laughed Sam. "Ted suggested using the ramp but it was Dave's idea to run up the ramp into the next carriage as it is empty and out of the door back onto the platform a few times before doing it the other way round jumping into the carriage and out down the ramp. He said that was how they began training their dog who was terrified of their own shadow. Now two years on he is ready to ride on the train any time he is near it. Scruffy is usually quick to learn new tricks especially if we make a game of it so it shouldn't take long for him to gain his confidence and jump into the carriage."

"No," replied Sam's Mum, "He has certainly picked up things quickly and usually trusts you when you are doing something new so I don't suppose you will need to practise for very long. Thanks Dave, here Sam give me Scruffy's lead and you help Dave get the ramp in place."

"Okay Mum thanks I will."

Soon the ramp was secure and Dave opened the carriage door in the next carriage so the pair could just keep going and not stop to open the door. Sam took Scruffy's lead back off his Mum and with a tug and a 'Come on Scruffy follow me' instruction he ran up the ramp into the guard van.

"Well," exclaimed Sam's Mum, "that worked and here they come back out of the door."

Sam jumped down on to the platform and Scruffy followed without ever noticing the gap and off down the platform they raced and back into the guard van again. They did this 4 or 5 times before Sam bypassed the ramp and ran back to the door into the carriage. With a quick 'Come on Scruffy jump' as he jumped into the carriage Scruffy followed him. Although Scruffy briefly hesitated he quickly followed his master and the pair soon emerged from the guard van. Just then Ted wandered up the platform with two ice cream cones in one hand and licking a third.

"Goodness," laughed Dave, "How many ice creams Ted?"

"One for Sam and one for Scruffy when they finish practising jumping on and off the train," replied Ted.

"Oh you shouldn't have bought them an ice cream Ted," exclaimed Sam's Mum. "That is spoiling them both."

"Not at all, they deserve them. Both Sam and Scruffy are doing well. Sam must have worked tirelessly to get Scruffy so settled and confident in 6 weeks and I can see Scruffy is really enjoying his game of chasing Sam."

"I'm not sure who is enjoying the game the most actually Ted," laughed Sam's Mum. "It is certainly getting rid of any pent up energy they might have had left. After carrying stones and sticks for the camp fire and pitching tents and now playing in and out of the train they will certainly sleep tonight. Tomorrow we are having a full day on the beach playing cricket, football and Frisbee, chasing in and out of the sea and rock pooling so that will be another highly active day too I think."

"Sounds like it," laughed Ted.

"It makes me feel exhausted just thinking about it," offered Dave.

Just then Sam and Scruffy came hurtling down the platform both puffing and panting heavily.

"Thank you Dave I think that will do for today. Do you mind if we just walk up to the carriage door and try and get in normally like we need to do on Thursday then I'll help you put the ramp back into the guard van."

"Not at all Sam off you go and keep nice and calm and I'm sure Scruffy will follow you without any bother."

"You go and give Scruffy a try using the step into the carriage and I'll help Dave with the ramp," instructed Sam's Mum. "Then you and Scruffy sit on the bench and have your ice creams that Ted has bought you."

"Cool thanks Mum. Come on Scruffy let us go and do this properly now."

Sam and Scruffy walked down the platform and Sam jumped into the carriage.

"Come on Scruffy you can do it. No don't look at the gap just look at me and jump up here beside me."

Scruffy looked up at his master hesitating slightly before taking a huge leap into the carriage. Unfortunately Sam didn't have time to get out of the way and as usual both boy and dog ended up in a tangled heap. Just at that moment Sam's Mum and Dave were passing the open door.

"Oh normal activity has been resumed," laughed Sam's Mum. "This pair seem to be constantly in a tangled heap in the floor or even sometimes the middle of a stream. I imagine tomorrow they will end up at some point in a tangled heap in the sea! Are you okay Sam?"

"Yes Mum I'm okay but maybe we need to ensure we find an empty carriage on Thursday though. Other passengers might not find our way of getting in the carriage amusing."

"Yes you might be right Sam. Up you both get and go and get your ice creams as I think Ted will soon need to be making his way back to the engine."

"Okay Mum no problem. Scruffy get off me so I can get up and we will try getting off the train in a bit more dignified manner."

Scruffy moved off Sam and suddenly caught sight of the gap between the platform and the train and with a yelp hurtled himself away from it.

"Now Scruffy no need for that," scolded Sam. "It is the same gap you have been jumping over at least 10 times earlier. Now come on I'm going first and you follow me and please be careful, don't knock me over as the platform is a bit hard and will hurt me."

Sam jumped out of the train and turned around giving the lead a slight pull. Scruffy remembered it wasn't that scary jumping down on to the platform so with a little leap he landed next to Sam.

"Good boy now let us go and have our ice creams. Thanks Ted for everything, you and Dave have helped me and Scruffy conquer Scruffy's fear of jumping on and off the train and you have got us ice creams. What a brilliant day this has been."

"That is okay Sam keep up the good work, you are doing a great job with Scruffy but just to warn you when I go back into the engine I will be letting some of the steam off so hold on tight to Scruffy because he is likely to be startled."

"Okay thanks Ted. Right Scruffy lay down here under this seat and eat your ice cream. You deserve it you have worked so hard."

Scruffy did as Sam told him and quickly scoffed down his ice cream. He was just swallowing the last mouthful when there was a huge blast of hissing noise coming from the big black monster. Scruffy was so startled he shot his head up forgetting he was under a seat and banged his head. He yelped out just as Dave and Sam's Mum arrived back at the pair. Scruffy could actually see stars and he scrabbled wildly out from under the seat and was about to take off when Sam gave him a quick tug of the lead.

"No Scruffy settle down it is just Ted letting off the steam. Remember I told you it was loud so it is okay nothing to be afraid of. Listen I can hear the whistle of the next train coming so sit quietly while it comes into the station then Ted and Dave will take this train out of the station and the other one will stop for a few minutes. Once both trains have left the station we can wander on to the other platform and wait for Mum to have a look in the art gallery before heading back to our camp. Does that sound okay to you Mum?"

"Yes fine by me. Are you giving the signal box a miss tonight?"

"Yes I think Scruffy has managed enough new things today. He is not that good at getting up and downstairs yet and as I have been in the signal box loads of times and I don't think looking at a load of levers will be very interesting to Scruffy we will give it a miss. I'll explain to Helen as we go past the signal box once the trains have left."

"Okay Sam I understand completely. We will all cross over to the other platform once the trains have both left the station. You and Scruffy can have a few minutes while I check out the art gallery. If I want to spend longer then I can always have a wander down tomorrow night or even Thursday. Right here comes the other train so keep a tight hold on to Scruffy while Ted gets steam up to get the train moving."

Suddenly the other train shuddered to a stop and with a mighty clanking and clunking slowly Ted's engine pulled away from the station. Dave waved to Sam, Scruffy and Sam's Mum as the train pulled away and Sam, Scruffy and his mum slowly made their way down the platform towards the signal box. They waited until Helen had set off the other train towards Pickering before Sam explained to her why him and Scruffy wouldn't be coming up into the signal box.

"Okay Sam I understand. I had a good laugh watching you and Scruffy chasing in and out of the guard van. What was that all about?" asked Helen.

"Scruffy wouldn't jump into the history carriage as he took fright of the gap between platform and carriage and as we are planning on having a ride on the train on Thursday. I thought we might have problems. It was Ted who suggested we use the wheelchair ramp into the guard van and come out through a carriage door. Dave took the suggestion to the next stage as he knew there were no passengers in the carriage next door to the guard van so he suggested we make it into a game going into the guard van and out of the carriage for a few times then changing direction and doing it the other way round. Scruffy was having so much fun he forgot to be nervous of the gap. We then just made sure he had gained enough confidence to just enter the carriage normally although he just had to take it a step further and knock me over when he jumped in. He made such a big leap that he landed on top of me but hopefully we might be able to do it in a more dignified fashion on Thursday."

"Oh Di your son and his dog are priceless. I'll have to find out who is on duty on Thursday at Pickering to find out if they managed to get on the train successfully or even have a trip out with Maisie that day."

"Well we are going to have a look at the farming museum late morning before we head to the castle for the boys to have some fun in the ruins and a picnic lunch before coming back down to the station to catch the train, probably the 2 o' clock one, to the next station after this then a wander round the village, walk to the next station and catch the train back to Pickering If you want to join the fun and you think Maisie will cope with two mad young males you are welcome to join us," answered Sam's Mum.

"Do you know Di, I think we just might give it a whirl. If Maisie is reluctant to play we will have to give her some female support," laughed Helen. "Shall I meet you at the castle, what time do you suggest?"

"Say 12 or 12.30?" queried Sam's Mum.

"Yes sounds fine to me see you Thursday," replied Helen.

"Okay Helen, come on Sam a quick visit to the art gallery for me then back to the camp and get the camp fire going. I bought some marshmallows to toast tonight as a treat and after all your hard work and training fun you have done I think you both thoroughly deserve a treat. We can always get more tomorrow if we need some for tomorrow night."

"Mum that is fabulous. This trip is turning out better than usual. Having Scruffy with us is more than doubling the fun and now we are having Helen and Maisie joining us on Thursday too. Scruffy we will have to teach Maisie some mischievous antics while she is with us won't we?"

"Oh no you don't," laughed Helen. "She can think up enough mischief on her own without you two giving her ideas."

"Sorry Helen if anyone can teach her tricks it will be these two so watch out!"

"Oh dear what have I let myself in for," groaned Helen laughing. "Ah well I guess it will teach me not to make daft suggestions."

"Go on," laughed Sam's Mum, "you know you are game, just think it will give you lots of ideas for more stories!"

"Hey Di, I never thought about that. I could always write a story featuring all the antics Sam and Scruffy get up to. We will have to exchange e mail addresses so you can keep me posted on their adventures on Thursday."

"Brilliant you are on we will do that on Thursday. Where do you live if it isn't too far from us you could always come and visit us. We live near Ripon is that anywhere near you?"

"Wow yes I live just outside Harrogate towards Ripon. We will exchange addresses and phone numbers on

Thursday. Sounds as though we both live out in the country too," answered Helen.

"Sounds great," replied Sam's Mum, "see you Thursday Helen."

"Looking forward to it already Di. Bye Sam, bye Scruffy see you both on Thursday."

"Bye Helen, see you Thursday. We are looking forward to meeting Maisie too."

With a final wave to Helen, Sam, Scruffy and Sam's Mum crossed the railway line on to the other platform where Sam and Scruffy sat down on a bench and Sam's Mum popped into the art gallery.

"Well Scruffy what a wonderful day this has turned out to be and tomorrow morning I'll set up the swing ball game and teach you how to play it while Mum gets organised. We can always set it up at home in the field where we play football if we enjoy it like I think we will. It will be a good game to play with Maisie when her and Helen come to visit us too. Then when Mum is ready we will head to the beach. Mum and I know a secret little cove that doesn't ever get any other people visiting because there is nothing there but sea, sand and rocks so we can run in and out of the sea, play cricket, make sandcastles, explore rock pools and lots of other things without getting in other people's way. I promise we will have such fun again."

Scruffy lay down at the side of Sam to wait for Sam's Mum. If he was honest he was ready for a rest before they walked back to the camp. All these new adventures had tired him out and listening to Sam just now it sounded as if tomorrow was going to be full of lots of other new adventures.

Scruffy's Scary Night

Sam's Mum was soon back from the art gallery.

"Have you seen enough Mum, was it any good?" asked Sam

"Yes I had a quick look and there are some interesting pieces. There is a mixture of watercolours, sketches in black and white and some stunning photographs. I might have a wander back down tomorrow night after tea because you and Scruffy will be tired so you can chill at the camp site. I know you will be safe as you have been coming here since you were little. There was a few watercolours that I can adapt the ideas to fit around this new commission I am starting next week as I feel the story, or rather stories, could have been set in and around this area."

"Cool Mum, you are so clever. Do you always draw and paint using a real place as inspiration. I always thought you just used your imagination."

"Well I suppose it is a mixture of both really but now that I am in a position to pick and choose which work I take on I usually loosely base my bid using a place that I have lived or visited regularly at some point in my life. For example the last commission I did, the one I have just finished, was based around the Northumberland coast where I spent much of my spare time exploring when we lived in Newcastle. I always felt the need to get out of the city as often as possible into the wildness of the country. The area around Alnwick, Amble, Beadnell Bay, Seahouses and even as far as Bamburgh always drew me to recharge my batteries. I never really settled in the city if I am honest unlike your Dad who loved the bright lights and thrived on the fast paced life of the city. As a young girl I felt I ought to head to the city so took a place at Newcastle University and although I enjoyed my studies but in my heart never really left this area or my country roots. I don't think I would have stayed long in the city if I hadn't met your Dad. He, on the other hand, was soon bored in the country so didn't often go with me when I headed off to the country or coast. We would begin our holiday or even a weekend in the same place and join together again in the evening but he would quickly meet up with people like him who thrived on the cut and thrust of big business, large contemporary art etc. whereas I needed the quiet and solitude and yes wildness, of the open countryside or the coast. Please don't get me wrong I loved your Dad and he loved me it was just we were complete opposites. We quickly established that providing we accepted and embraced that difference we could both be fulfilled in our marriage. I guess we were a bit like two halves of a whole, what the Chinese call yin and yang. Unfortunately after your Dad died and I was left alone I found I couldn't cope in the city I needed the space of the countryside to feed my soul and reignite my imagination and fantasy. A sort of healing and moving on. My work as a graphic designer felt too cold and kind of clinical without your Dad around to bounce ideas off. It was a huge step though to move away at that time and forge a new life for us both but we were lucky finding our cottage that we live in and access to some beautiful countryside all around us."

"Oh Mum where we live is just perfect for us both. I think I am more like you than my Dad. I vaguely remember living in a house that was surrounded by other houses. We used to walk to the park occasionally but seemed to just stay in the house most of the time except when you and Dad went to work and I stayed with Debbie but still always in the house or garden. I don't remember ever going on holiday or anything until there was just us two."

"Well you were only 2 nearly 3 when your Dad died in that terrible accident and I don't think we did ever go on holiday or even away for a weekend after you were born. It seemed too much trouble to take a small baby or toddler away, money was tight as your Dad's firm was going through a complete restructure and moving away from corporate design to a more bespoke service. To be honest I don't think, if he had lived, your Dad would have stayed with the firm long as I think he thrived on the more corporate work. Looking back I don't think he had much imagination as most of the stuff he designed followed a similar pattern with just a few tweaks. That was why I was bored by my job because my firm that I worked for did the same but we couldn't afford our lifestyle if I didn't work. After your Dad was killed I sold the house we lived in and took the life insurance pay out to live on while I established myself and moved away. Your grandparents and Uncle Pete wanted me to move back to the area where I had grown up but I felt you and me had to establish ourselves as a team, just the two of us, but be close enough to visit. As you know we usually go and spend a few days with them in the school holidays but haven't been this holiday due to getting Scruffy. I felt it was more important to get him settled first before introducing him to another set of new people. It has also given both Granny and Grandad and Uncle Pete and Aunty Jan the time to make the change over that they have done. It will seem strange to me to visit what I regard as my old home as Uncle Pete and Aunty Jan's and the cottage in the village as where my own Mum and Dad now live. I know things have to change and in some ways it isn't a strange cottage because I used to visit it as a child because my grandparents lived there until they died when I was away at university. Mum and Dad rented it out until Uncle Pete grew up and met Aunty Jan and they moved in."

"Oh I hadn't realised your Granny and Grandad had lived in that cottage you never said! Was that Granny's Mum and Dad or Grandad's?"

"It was Grandad's Mum and Dad. My Mum had lived and worked in York all her life until she met my Dad," answered Sam's Mum. "She was a real town girl, loved the nightlife, dancing, going to the theatre and things. It must have been a real shock to her after she married Dad but she never said anything to either Uncle Pete or me. In fact now I think about it that might be why she has been able to give Aunty Jan time to settle and ease into the role of farmer's wife because I think my Granny and Grandad moved out of the farmhouse as soon as Mum and Dad got married and she immediately took on the role of Dad's partner in a world that she had no experience of or any real knowledge. I think those early years were a steep learning curve and in many ways she also lost any relationship she had with her own parents too. I remember very occasionally visiting them but they were such busy successful people with a beautiful house it was like visiting strangers. In fact I think Mum felt like that too as she had moved on from their world. Don't get me wrong they were not unkind people just very different. Mum's Dad was a high flying barrister and her Mum a university lecturer. My Mum was training to be a journalist working for the local newspaper and expected to go far but met and fell in love with Dad when she was reporting on the local agricultural show and Dad had just won best in show with his bull. She wrote her report and followed it up with a feature on him as he was taking the same bull to the big show in Harrogate and in fact did very well again but not getting best in show there. She often laughed and said that the bull was the cause of blowing her off her expected career path because a year on she was firmly established as a farmer's wife and expecting me."

"Wow, I never really thought about my grandparents as people before they have just been Granny and Grandad but I guess they were young once too," laughed Sam.

"Oh yes we were all young once like you, even Granny and Grandad. When they come and stay you can maybe get them to talk about the past to you. None of us have ever told you much, partly because you never asked and I guess partly because we thought you were too young to be interested."

"I will Mum, maybe they will have photographs that I can look at too when we go at Christmas."

"They might, as with moving house they will have unearthed a lot of things they would have forgotten about. When I talk to them next on the telephone, when we get back, I will mention you and me have been talking about the past and you are interested in knowing more."

"I am supposed to do a project at school next year which we design and implement individually. I wasn't sure what I was going to do but now I do. I'm going to put together a living history of my family. I didn't know there were so many interesting characters in our family and especially with Aunty Jan continuing the tradition as she was like Granny but a successful estate agent before she married Uncle Pete and now like Granny she is taking on the new role of full farmer's wife and producing the next generation."

"Don't forget you have another branch of the family on your Dad's side though."

"Well to be honest Mum I don't remember Dad much and I've never really felt I knew or had anything in common with those grandparents. I hardly ever speak to them on the telephone anymore. They seem sort of remote and I never feel part of their world. When was the last time I saw them? I was about 7 years old I think, that is nearly 4 years ago. Yes they remember my birthday by sending me a card and money, the same as Christmas, but they don't actually know me as me. Imagine if they came to see us or we went to them and we took Scruffy. It would be a disaster and yet Scruffy is so perfect for us and he will be fine at both Granny and Grandad's and up at the farmhouse at Uncle Pete's so that must tell you that we have nothing in common with that branch of the family."

"Oh dear I'm so sorry Sam I hadn't realised it was so many years since we saw those grandparents. Mind you like you say they could have contacted us and asked to see us and I wouldn't have stopped them."

"I know Mum but honestly I haven't missed them. Remember I was only 2 when Dad died and even after that we never saw them more than once a year. Now if I didn't speak to Granny and Grandad at least every week I would miss them as they are always interested in what I am doing or rather now what Scruffy and I are doing or have done and both Grandad and Uncle Pete have given me lots of advice on how to train Scruffy like lots of other people have, Steve, his Dad and now Ted and Dave. Could my other grandparents support and help me like that?"

"Oh my goodness no, those grandparents have never had any pet, not even a goldfish. Your Dad never understood our way of life at the farm and although occasionally he would visit in the early days of our marriage towards the end he always made an excuse not to go with me. I remember his horror when I wanted to take you to the farm when you would be about 2 or 3 months old saying you would get some nasty infection in the 'dirty' farmhouse surrounded by dogs and cats and whatever young animal needed round the clock attention. We had our first real fight about it and I still took you anyway. I never told him that on the first morning you were joined on the floor by 2 dogs, a kitten and a baby lamb who was tottering about and you were gurgling and kicking your legs in excitement."

"You see Mum my love of animals was always there," laughed Sam. "That is why as I have been growing up I have enjoyed spending time at Steve's place as a sort of substitute for my real family. Do you think I will be able to farm myself when I grow up?"

"I don't see why you shouldn't if that is what you want to do although at the moment I'm not sure how because there are not many farms to rent and unless Uncle Pete expands his farm it won't make enough profit to keep you, Uncle Pete and Granny and Grandad but we have quite a few years yet before we need worry about it. You haven't even started senior school yet so your ambitions may change when you meet other people. At the moment you have no other role models that are not involved in the world of farming."

"I might be able to work for Steve and take over from him you know Mum. That is another idea."

"What if Steve meets a woman and gets married that will scupper that plan," laughed Sam's Mum. "Steve is not that old you know."

"I know why don't you and Steve get married then you can become a farmer's wife, you would be real good at it you know, and then as his stepson I would be in line to inherit the farm."

"Oh Sam whatever makes you think Steve and me would ever love each other enough to get married?" asked Sam's Mum blushing.

"I don't know, just a feeling I have. Steve certainly loves to spend time with us and slowly he is starting to feel a bit like a Dad to me and you seem to enjoy his company. Yes the more I think about it that would be an ideal solution."

"Well you can just shelve the thought and get that camp fire started," instructed his Mum.

"I notice I didn't get a proper answer nor an outright no so I will have to just work on my plan," laughed Sam. "Come on Scruffy let us go and find the matches and light the fire. Who knows maybe next year we can get Steve here to join our little band."

"You are impossible Sam," laughed his Mum as she chased after Sam and Scruffy. "Don't you dare try your hand at match making concentrate on school, your school project and your dog and leave the grown-ups to work on their own futures please."

"Okay Mum I promise," laughed Sam.

"And somehow I don't believe you Sam," muttered his Mum. She wondered how much Sam had picked up and how much was in his imagination. I had better warn Steve where Sam's ideas and plans are heading she thought when we get back. In the meantime she was determined to enjoy this camping trip. By this time they had all reached the camp fire and Sam had found the matches and him and Scruffy were intent on starting the fire. Di looked at them both so intent on their job before filling the kettle to make a nice hot chocolate for Sam and find the bag of marshmallows she had brought.

"Sam have you a couple of longish sticks that we can use to toast the marshmallows with?"

"Yes Mum I kept two back that I think will work and have told Scruffy not to run off with them. I brought my pen knife so I'll make them have a good point on the end to skewer the marshmallows too when I get this fire going properly."

"Brilliant Sam that is a good idea. I'm putting the kettle on for a hot chocolate too, is that okay?"

"Wow more than all right thanks Mum."

Soon Sam had the fire blazing well so he loaded it with the big branches and a few logs he had found and ran back to his tent. As usual Scruffy was intent on watching his master and quickly followed Sam to the tent. Sam disappeared inside and Scruffy stuck his head through the door.

"It is okay Scruffy you don't need to come in I'm just looking for my pen knife and then I'm coming back out. Ah here it is, right get out of the way Scruffy and let me out again. We will just go and move the chairs to near the fire then I'll fashion those sticks I kept back into skewers. I wonder if dogs can have marshmallows or are bad for them. I'm sure Mum will let you have at least one even if like chocolate they are bad for you. Hey Mum can dogs have marshmallows or are they bad for them like chocolate?"

"I don't know Sam I don't think I have read anything about marshmallows but I'm sure we can allow Scruffy at least one," replied Sam's Mum. "But you will have to make sure it is not too hot as we can't have him burning his mouth."

"I was actually thinking of giving him an uncooked one first to see if he likes it then if he does maybe only one that has been toasted very lightly."

"Sounds like a plan Sam. That seems fair as he is still sharing your full adventure but on his own level."

Sam picked up a chair and moved it near to the fire which was burning well before collecting the second chair and putting it opposite the first. Sam then sat down on the chair and instructed Scruffy to lay down next to it. Sam picked up the first stick and began whittling one end to make a point. Scruffy was intrigued so sat up to get a better look at what Sam was doing. He still couldn't see so stood up and poked his nose right next to the bit that Sam was working on.

"Scruffy get back or I'll cut your nose if this knife slips. Anyhow I can't see what I am doing either. I know you want to see but you don't need to be so close."

Scruffy did as he was told and moved to the side a bit so he could see what Sam was doing but not in Sam's way. Soon the stick had a good point on that Sam was happy with and he laid it on the ground next to his chair on the other side from where Scruffy was. Scruffy thought he had better have a good look to actually see what Sam had made and tried to go in front of Sam's chair until he realised there wasn't room between Sam and the fire so he turned round to go the other way. Unfortunately he didn't think about his tail and the fire and if it hadn't been for Sam grabbing his tail and pushing his bum away from the fire Scruffy might have returned home with a badly singed tail. In the end only a few stray wisps actually got near the fire.

"Scruffy you fool, you need to be careful around a camp fire, you nearly got your tail on fire. Where are you going? Oh I see you wanted to see the finished skewer did you? Right turn around again and lay down and I'll show you what I have done."

With another quick push on Scruffy's bottom with one hand and a pull on his head with the other Scruffy was back in his position next to Sam's chair facing the fire.

"Now lay down and I'll show you what I made."

With that Sam bent down and picked up the stick.

"See here Scruffy I have made a point at this end which we push through the marshmallow then we hold on to this end and hang the marshmallow over the fire to toast. No Scruffy don't get up again you will see what I mean when Mum brings the marshmallows over. Meanwhile let me get to work on this other stick or Mum won't have a skewer for her marshmallows."

Sam's Mum arrived soon after this conversation between Sam and Scruffy bearing a bag of marshmallows and two cups of hot chocolate.

"Looks as though the fire is perfect for toasting marshmallows Sam. Well done to you both."

"Yes the fire is just about right and I've just finished the last skewer. It took me a bit longer as Scruffy was determined to have a close look at what I was doing and got his head in the way with the first one then when I had finished it he wanted to see it so tried to go between me and the fire then realised there was no room so turned round and nearly waved his tail in the fire. A bit of instinctive reaction was needed to ensure he didn't go home with a singed tail."

"Oh dear Scruffy that was another near miss was it? I have always been afraid your tail will get you into bother one day," laughed Sam's Mum. "Sounds as though Sam saved the day though. Right Sam here is the bag of marshmallows, you go first and let Scruffy try an uncooked one. I will take my skewer and a few in my hand over to my chair."

"Great Mum. Here Scruffy have a marshmallow and see if you like it. It is okay this one is not warm. Take it gently now you need to practise taking food from my hand gently ready for the time Uncle Pete's baby is born. Do we know yet if it is a boy or girl because Ben seemed to know he was getting a baby sister for ages before it was born."

"No Sam we don't know nor will we until the baby is born as Uncle Pete and Aunty Jan have decided they don't want to know they just want it to be a surprise."

"Oh right well it doesn't matter really because girls can be as much fun as boys, well some girls are anyway, and I'm sure Uncle Pete and Aunty Jan will not encourage any baby of theirs to be a wimp whatever it is."

"No," laughed Sam's Mum. "Neither of them will be an over protective parent, both are too down to earth and practical."

"Very like you then Mum," laughed Sam.

"I suppose so I never really thought about it. I just used my instincts and what I knew from watching my mum with Uncle Pete and also rearing a mixture of baby animals as I felt that all babies need love, warmth and food in no particular order. You seem to have turned out okay anyway," laughed his Mum. "So I must have done something right!"

"Yes Mum you have done a good job and are still doing one. Oh have you eaten that Scruffy, did you like it?"

Scruffy sat up and stared intently at the marshmallow on the skewer that Sam was holding over the fire.

"No Scruffy don't be greedy this is mine. I will cook you one in a minute when I have eaten mine."

Scruffy got up and wandered round to Sam's Mum to see if he could get one of her marshmallows.

"No Scruffy," laughed Sam's Mum. "You are not having mine either you can be patient and wait until Sam toasts your own. I promise you we will share with you so don't worry."

Sam finished toasting his marshmallow and popped it into his mouth. Scruffy padded back to his master's side and sat down as much as to say 'me next'.

"Yes Scruffy I will toast you one next I promise just wait," answered Sam.

Sam stuck another marshmallow on to his skewer and had to move it out of Scruffy's reach quickly or Scruffy would have been helping himself to another before it was toasted.

"I think we can safely assume Scruffy likes marshmallows," observed Sam's Mum. "You were in danger of losing that one then Sam."

"Yes he nearly managed another cold one," laughed Sam. "But I was quicker than him. I am beginning to be able to second guess him better now than when he first came to live with us."

"Well so you should you have spent a lot of hours together," replied Sam's Mum.

"It has been a great few weeks Mum I am so pleased we chose Scruffy. We have had so many adventures and have so many more to come. I thought I would put the swing ball game up in the morning and try to teach Scruffy how to play. I imagine we could have some fun as Scruffy will probably try to run off with the ball. Here you are Scruffy your marshmallow is cooked. Now be gentle, yes that is right have a nibble first and make sure it is not too hot and you like it like this. Oh my goodness you wolfed that down so fast I'm sure you never had chance to taste it. That is it, no more, the next one is mine then I think I'll just drink my hot chocolate. Do you want any more marshmallows Mum?" asked Sam.

"No thank you Sam. Is there some left for tomorrow night?"

"Yes plenty left, in fact if we don't eat too many tomorrow night probably enough for Thursday too."

"Good, like you Sam, I am just going to drink my hot chocolate now and listen to the sounds of the forest."

"Yes that sounds like a plan Mum we will just sit over the fire until it burns down then I think me and Scruffy will wander off to bed. We have had a busy day but it has been fun too."

"You do seem to have had a lot of fun today and I'm sure you will have even more tomorrow. We will aim to set off from here about 10.30 in the morning because it only takes about 30 minutes to get to our favourite cove and we can stay as long as we want as I made a stew yesterday which only needs warming up so we can soon

111

get tea ready quickly when we get back. Will you and Scruffy need to collect more wood tomorrow?"

"No I don't think we will need any more as we haven't used even half of what we collected today so there should be enough for tomorrow night. Listen Scruffy can you hear the owl hooting he is probably going out hunting and saying goodbye to his wife."

"Well done Sam you are starting to have an imagination I see and entering into the spirit of the trip a bit."

"After living with you all these years is there any wonder?" laughed Sam.

"No I suppose not. Right have you finished with your mug? If so I will just go and give them both a quick rinse out. I think the fire is almost finished too."

"Yes I will just spread it out a bit in the pit so it cools down quicker then Scruffy and me will go and get ready for bed as I am suddenly feeling very tired. It might take us a while to get settled too as there will be all kinds of unusual sounds as the forest settles for the night and the night animals emerge to look for food."

"Yes you may have to reassure him about what he is hearing although looking at him he looks very sleepy to me."

Sam's Mum collected the mugs and picked up the chair she had been sitting on and took them over to the cooking tent. Sam got out of his chair and raked over the ash to spread it out. Scruffy jumped up to see what was happening and knocked over the chair Sam had been sitting in.

"Good job I wasn't still sitting in that Scruffy or I would have been tipped out. Okay come on we will take the chair back to the cooking tent too. The fire is almost out and as there is no wind it should be safe to leave now. We will go and get comfortable in our beds and listen to the sounds of the forest. Everything all okay Mum? Scruffy and me are off into our tent see you in the morning."

"Goodnight Sam," answered his mum as she zipped up the opening of the cooking tent. "See you both in the morning."

Sam and Scruffy ambled across to their tent and Sam unzipped the door.

"Come on Scruffy let us both get in. Now where did I put the torch? Oh here it is come on Scruffy you can't stay out there all night."

Scruffy didn't need telling twice and he squeezed himself in through the door and over to the bed Sam had made for him this afternoon. He lay down on it while he watched Sam zip the opening of the tent closed and unzip his sleeping bag.

"You will need to get inside your sleeping bag under your blankets Scruffy as it gets cold in the middle of the night. Here move off your bed a minute while I hold it open for you. Yes that is right now crawl in and I'll cover you up before I take off my outer clothes and get snuggled into my sleeping bag. I will turn off the torch then and we can have a listen to the night sounds and relax. I don't think either of us will be long before we are asleep tonight though as we have had such a busy day."

Sam quickly undressed and settled in his sleeping bag then turned off the torch. At first they felt surrounded by dense blackness but as their eyes adjusted it appeared less dense. Scruffy wasn't sure what he was supposed to be listening for, what were these night sounds Sam kept prattling on about? He began to dose, as like Sam said, it had been a long and busy day with so many new adventures Scruffy's head was reeling. Suddenly Sam said,

"There did you hear that Scruffy, there is a fox barking and now he is howling too?"

Scruffy woke up with a start and tried to concentrate on what Sam was saying. Was it time to get up already? No it couldn't be, it was still dark. Scruffy suddenly heard a dog bark then the eerie sound of a howl or had sleep befuddled his brain? He thought it was a dog and he could feel the cold, hard ground beneath him so he must be back in his kennel at the rescue centre! He listened again then heard Sam say,

"That is another owl answering it's mate," before finally becoming fully awake and remembering they were in fact camping in a wood and sleeping in a tent which was why, he Scruffy, could feel a cold hard floor underneath his bed.

Sam said, "Did you hear the fox Scruffy or were you asleep? Actually to be honest Scruffy I don't blame you if you were asleep I think I might have dosed too. In fact I am going to snuggle down and go to sleep as there doesn't seem to be many sounds in the forest, not even a breeze to stir the leaves. Goodnight Scruffy sweet dreams and I will see you in the morning."

With that Scruffy heard a bit of scrabbling as Sam got comfortable then silence. Now he was awake he couldn't get comfortable. He wriggled a bit, tried to turn around but found he couldn't so wriggled a bit more. Now how did he get to sleep the first time? Oh yes he remembered now he was supposed to have been listening for night sounds but fell asleep. Now if he lay still and listened for night sounds, whatever they were, he might drift off to sleep again. Scruffy lay still and listened intently but he couldn't hear a thing. He listened harder, no not a sound. Suddenly Sam let out a huge snore and Scruffy nearly jumped out of his skin. With a yelp he struggled out of his bed and hurled himself at Sam. Poor Sam ended up with a large hairy monster on top of him.

"What on earth are you doing Scruffy you woke me up? Why are you laying on top of me and not in your own bed? It is no good we can't share the same bed, there isn't room! Now go back into your own bed at the bottom of my feet."

Scruffy wasn't moving, he was protecting his master from 'night sounds' and things that went crash.

"Scruffy listen, it is okay there is nothing to be afraid of honest! Let us move my bed round so our beds are side by side, maybe I should have placed them like that in the first place but I didn't think, then we can have a cuddle and I will explain what you can hear."

With a bit of scrabbling about and pushing things out of the way Sam managed to turn his bed around so the beds were side by side instead of in a 'T' shape.

"There now Scruffy, is that better, come on back under your covers snuggled up tight to my side. Now let us listen and see if I can identify what frightened you. If I tell you exactly what each sound is you will realise that they are just everyday sounds but sound louder because we are only in a tent not a stone built house. Most of these noises are happening every night at home but we just never hear them through the thick walls. Now listen, ah the wind is getting up a bit, listen you can hear the leaves rustling. Now that tiny crack was maybe a branch breaking off a tree. It might have been the wind or a squirrel that broke it off or it might have been a rabbit or a fox that stood on a twig in the forest. It is not necessarily happening just outside the tent either because sound carries more in the forest. Now I think that is the fox again but listen that was a different bark, a deeper, harsher sound so that is probably a deer. We don't have deer in our forest so if you pick up a different smell from them at home it might be a deer smell or even a squirrel as we don't have them either. That loud fluttering is a bird flying through the trees and you can hear the cawing of the crows and rooks as they settle for the night. They are saying goodnight to each other. Listen, can you hear the stream gurgling away. Now the stream is not in our clearing or the one next door because we have explored both so you see what I mean about sound carrying. Now is there anything else going on in the forest that I haven't explained? No I don't think so and you are much calmer now aren't you Scruffy as you have stopped trembling."

Now that Scruffy was nice and warm wrapped up in his blankets right next to Sam he felt much better. It meant he felt he could protect Sam much better too and now Sam had explained all the sounds that he could hear and had never heard in his life before he began to feel sleepy again. He wriggled one last time then promptly fell asleep. Sam was soon fast asleep by his side and the pair never moved again until morning.

Scruffy and the Seaside

Scruffy woke up and for a minute wondered where he was until he remembered that him, Sam and Sam's Mum were away on a camping trip and that Sam had promised more fun and adventures today at something called the seaside. Scruffy opened his eyes to find himself looking right at Sam's face. Oh yes that was it, they had moved Sam's bed next to his sometime in the middle of the night because to Scruffy's embarrassment he, Scruffy, had been frightened of all the strange noises. He told himself he wanted to protect Sam from the noises but in reality it was the other way round! Scruffy reached over and gave Sam a great big sloppy kiss to say he was sorry about last night. Sam woke with a start then started laughing.

"Good morning to you too Scruffy and yes I love you too. Now that was a fun day yesterday and even moving my bed in the middle of the night didn't cause too many problems. I wonder what time it is and if it is time to get up?"

Sam managed to get his arm out from underneath Scruffy who had crept closer to Sam during the night and was half sharing Sam's mattress and looked at his watch.

"Goodness Scruffy it is no wonder the sun is up we have slept in longer than I expected. It is nearly 8 o' clock, right move over, back onto your own bed and let me get up. Oh no just look at the tent and where are my clothes? I left them handy, ready for today but now they are squandered all over. Oh yes I remember sort of shoving everything aside when I was trying to get my bed alongside yours because I thought it was easier to move mine rather than your. Also there wasn't room for two beds side by side without one us being too close to the door. Actually putting them this way made it warmer because my feet are the only bit of me next to the door opening and with our heads closer together and at the back of the tent it keeps us warm but now I need to find my clothes. Ah here are my jeans and I can see my jumper over in that corner but I think I might put a clean T- shirt on. On second thoughts maybe not, I will just take a clean one with us to the seaside in case I get this one wet which is pretty likely. I usually manage to get wet and sandy at the seaside on my own but with you there too Scruffy it will be much worse. Now where are my trainers? Scruffy can you see my trainers, they are somewhere in this tent, but where?"

Sam picked up his bag that had got tipped up when they were moving the bed and repacked it, taking out some clean underwear, socks and a T- shirt to take to the beach. He looked under his mattress and sleeping bag but his trainers were nowhere to be found.

"Scruffy you are going to have to move because my trainers must have somehow got under your bed because that is the only place I haven't looked."

Scruffy looked at Sam as much as to say 'what do you want me to do?'

"Scruffy move off your bed onto mine so I can find my trainers. We can't leave the tent without something on my feet as the grass might be damp but in any case there are lots of prickly plants and tiny stones that would hurt my feet."

Scruffy scrabbled off his bed over on to Sam's.

"Oh there they are Scruffy under your blankets, how on earth did they get there? Never mind I have found them now. I will just tidy your bed ready for tonight then unzip the door and you can go outside while I tidy my bed and put my clean clothes on top ready to take to the beach. Mum will be packing a picnic for us for lunchtime and we usually put our clean dry clothes on top as we have to walk quite a way from where we park the car. We go over the sand dunes to the sheltered cove that we found one year. I think Mum had an idea where it was but we did accidently stumble on it when I was quite little and Mum wanted somewhere that she could keep a close eye on me where there were no other people. She said the year before she had spent the entire day saying sorry to people because I was like whirlwind managing to send sand flying in all directions and she didn't want a repeat that year. Ever since then we have gone back every year and each year Mum lets me explore further and further playing in the sea and scrambling over the rocks. It will be even more fun this year as I can show you how to look for crabs and shells in the rock pools. Last year I found a cave opening just before we came home but Mum wouldn't let me explore inside as she said the tide was coming in too fast for it to be safe. She promised I could explore more this year as I now knew it was there and could go when the tide was fully out. She said she thought it might be an old smugglers cave from the olden days and that she might take a look herself. Mum is always game for some exploring herself as she isn't just a mum who just sits on the sand reading a book like some of my friends' mums do. She always has a few games of cricket too and other years has played Frisbee with me but as I have you this year she might not join in so much although knowing Mum I imagine she will. As she sits still all day when she is working she enjoys the opportunity to do different things when we go out for days away or on holiday like this. Okay Scruffy that is my shoes on and your bed made so move over and I will unzip our door."

Sam unzipped the door and poked his head out.

"Good morning Mum, did you sleep okay last night?"

"Yes thank you Sam, how about you and Scruffy, any problems?"

"Only one. Scruffy got a bit frightened in the middle of the night and I had to move my bed next to his so he could cuddle up to me. After that we both slept right through."

"How did you put the beds in the first place" enquired his Mum.

"In a 'T' shape with Scruffy's bed along the right hand side of the tent and mine down the middle with my feet towards the middle of his bed. I have always slept that way and never thought about doing anything different even though I now have Scruffy. What I did in the middle of the night was move my head towards the back of the tent and my feet towards the door. Now this morning looking at it in daylight I realise that is in fact better because it gives me all the left side of the tent to keep my bag and leave my shoes and clothes there so they don't get lost like they have done this morning."

"Oh goodness what did you lose Sam?"

"Only my trainers, somehow they managed to get into Scruffy's bed and I searched everywhere else first before getting Scruffy to move off his bed and there under his blankets were my trainers."

"He must have been looking after them for you," laughed Sam's Mum. "Right are you two organised and about ready for breakfast."

"Yes I'm just going to tidy my bed once Scruffy gets out of the tent then we are ready when you are."

"Good I'll put the bacon on to fry then. Do you want your bacon and eggs as normal?"

"Yes please Mum it keeps me going and saves us taking such a big picnic lunch like normal. Is Scruffy having biscuits like he does at home?"

"Well I brought some extra bacon because I thought he could have a rasher of cooked bacon mixed in while we are on holiday. After all this is his holiday too."

"Oh Mum you are ace, you treat Scruffy just like another son," exclaimed Sam.

"Well he is, you and him are like brothers, always up to mischief, so that makes him my son too. I have always believed pets, and especially dogs, are part of the family. We take them on for the rest of their lives and are responsible for their health and wellbeing during that time. That is why I insisted we wait until you were old enough to be responsible for him and give him the attention he deserves. I am real proud how well you stepped up to the mark and have taken your responsibilities seriously. Good morning Scruffy, come here and give me a cuddle while your master sorts out his bed and gets you some biscuits for breakfast."

Scruffy bounded over to Sam's Mum for his normal early morning cuddle, a routine they had begun on his second morning with the family. The first morning had been a bit of a muddle when Scruffy had caused so much havoc but since then, now he knew exactly what the routine was, he was quite happy to wait in his bed until Sam and his mum came into the kitchen. After his cuddle he popped into the bushes to go to the toilet like he did every morning before coming back to sit beside his bowl ready for breakfast. By this time Sam had finished sorting out their tent and Sam's Mum had finished cooking the bacon and was about to pop the eggs in the pan. Sam picked up Scruffy's bowl and took it into the cooking tent to put some biscuits in before coming back to his mum at the stove.

"Well done Sam, here put this piece of bacon in Scruffy's bowl. You should be able to tear it up because I have had it out of the pan a while to cool down then refill his water bowl. By then our eggs will be cooked and we can have our breakfast too."

Sam popped Scruffy's biscuits down on the floor, tipped out the old water and put some fresh in.

"What are we going to do about taking Scruffy a drink to the beach with us Mum?" asked Sam.

"I brought an old juice bottle with us that we can fill and a new lightweight, unbreakable bowl I got last week. I thought the bowl could stay in the car all the time then we just have to remember to take him a bottle of water with us if we go out for the day."

"Great, well remembering water shouldn't be a problem," laughed Sam. "You always seem to have at least one bottle of water in the car whenever we go out."

"True," answered his mum, "but I drink fizzy water and he might not be too keen on that it will send bubbles up his nose."

"Oh I never thought about that Mum so we need to always make sure we take water for Scruffy, juice for me and fizzy water for you then when we go out."

"Yes you got it Sam. Right get this breakfast down you then I can get washed up and the picnic packed. Did you say last night you were going to set up the swing ball this morning?"

"Yes I'll get it set up and Scruffy and I can have a few goes before we head off to the beach. It will then be ready for us when we come back tonight. You can leave the washing up to me after tea and go and have a good look in the art gallery. Scruffy and I will wash up then have a few games of swing ball before we light the camp fire again. Tomorrow night I thought we might all go for a walk the other way after tea and do a bit of exploring. Scruffy and me could hear the stream last night and if I remember right it is a bit further on than this clearing after the next bend."

"Yes you are right. We found the stream the year when we had to go right into the forest as there were other people camping in all these clearings."

"Oh yes, I wonder why we were able to get in this first clearing this year," mused Sam.

"I imagine because we are much later coming this year, at least 3 or 4 weeks later. We normally come at the beginning of the holidays, often the first week and I assume everyone else is taking advantage of the school holidays then. This year it is the last full week of the holidays when we have come as we were getting Scruffy settled. I imagine there probably won't be many people travelling on the train tomorrow either so we might get a carriage to ourselves. Dave thought that too when we were watching you and Scruffy practising getting in and out of the train. At least you know you can do it if there are more people than we think and with having Helen and Maisie too we probably do need a carriage to ourselves. Not everyone would want to share a carriage with 2 dogs," laughed Sam's Mum.

By this time everyone had finished their breakfasts, including Scruffy, so while Sam's Mum cleared away and washed the pots Sam and Scruffy got the swing ball game from the car. Sam made sure the cricket set, Frisbee and football were all together in a bag so he could carry them to the beach before setting up the swing ball. Scruffy laid and watched proceedings with interest. He wasn't quite sure how you would play a game that had a ball on a string attached to an upright pole but he trusted Sam would show him when he was ready.

"Okay Scruffy this is what we do. It is really a game for two humans where we have to hit the ball alternatively but we will have to improvise. I'll hit the ball and you chase it and try to catch it as quick as you can. Right let us have a go and see how we go."

Sam hit the ball with the bat and Scruffy just lay there looking on.

"Scruffy don't just lay there you are supposed to get the ball!"

Scruffy just looked at Sam and wondered what on earth Sam was talking about. Surely Sam could see the ball it was still on the string stuck to the pole.

"Scruffy look let us try again. I will hit the ball and you try to catch it as it swings round the pole."

Oh thought Scruffy that is what Sam wants me to do. He stood up and gave a little shake. Just then Sam hit the ball hard and it swung round the pole catching Scruffy on his bottom. With a yelp he shot off down the clearing well away from the swinging ball.

"Scruffy come back, don't go near the road," shouted Sam. "Come back."

Scruffy came back but skirted round the game. He decided he didn't like this game much, Scruffy came up to Sam still eyeing the swinging ball. He wasn't going to get caught again! Sam laid down the bat.

"Well it appears that isn't a game that you and me can play. You just don't get what to do with it, do you Scruffy?"

Sam sat down on the grass to give his dog a cuddle. Scruffy sidled up to Sam and allowed Sam to give him a pat and cuddle Suddenly Scruffy bounded over and grabbed the ball and took off with it. The only problem was it was still attached to the pole by the elastic. Scruffy got as far as the elastic would let him then let go of the ball. The ball shot round the post and hit Sam in the back before ricocheting off in the opposite direction with both Scruffy and Sam in hot pursuit. The ball swung as far as it could then began to swing back again. Both Sam and Scruffy dived to catch the ball but both missed and ended up in their normal position tangled together. Meanwhile the ball had lost its momentum and swing back towards the pole to its resting position. Unfortunately it hit the two miscreants on its way back when it gave it more propulsion so it set off swinging in another direction.

"Quick Scruffy, race you to get the ball," laughed Sam.

Both boy and dog picked themselves up and set off after the ball. Sam was just about to get the ball when Scruffy bowled into the back of Sam's legs, sent Sam flying who then missed the ball with his hands but hit it with his head. The ball shot off round the pole and landed a direct hit on Scruffy's bottom. Scruffy yelped and by trying to get out of the way ended up trampling over the top of Sam just as he was trying to get up. Sam ended up face down in the grass with Scruffy trying to put his brakes on to go and see to his master. Neither boy nor dog thought about the swinging ball until it hit Scruffy on the back of the head before hitting Sam's forehead. Sam's Mum was stood watching these antics and bent double laughing. Eventually when she managed to stop laughing and Sam and Scruffy had rolled out of reach of the ball all legs and arms tangled together she said,

"You thought the swing ball would be fun with Scruffy but I don't think you quite envisaged it like that!"

"No Mum, I didn't but I guess that is the only way we will now ever play it," laughed Sam.

Sam and Scruffy scrabbled to their feet and Sam's Mum said,

"Well I have made the picnic and tidied up so we just need to load the car and we can get off. Well only if you and Scruffy have finished playing swing ball of course."

"Yes Mum I think that will do for this morning or I will be black and blue either from the ball or Scruffy or maybe both!"

"I could see that you were having difficulty keeping out of the way of both things," laughed his Mum. "Now did you sort clean dry clothes to take to the beach?"

"Yes Mum they are just inside the tent on my bed."

"Good I brought an extra two bath towels to take to the beach but can you check that we have at least a couple of old towels for Scruffy too?"

"Okay Mum, do you think it might be a good idea to take one of his blankets to wrap him in on the way home as he might be a bit cold after he has got wet in the sea? We can't change his clothes like we can ours."

"What a good idea Sam, do you want to get one off his bed when you get your clothes?"

"Will do Mum and don't forget water for us all."

"No it is already packed and just needs putting in the car."

Sam raced across to the tent, Scruffy as usual, hard on his heels. Sam unzipped the opening and reached inside for his clean clothes and a blanket off Scruffy's bed before zipping the opening back up and taking the bundle to his mum.

"There isn't room in the picnic bag for both. We can put your clothes in but not the blanket."

"Well the blanket is for wrapping Scruffy in after we get back to the car for the journey home so it doesn't want to be in the picnic bag," pointed out Sam.

"Oh my goodness, yes you are right Sam, silly me!"

Eventually everything was packed into the car and Sam had checked they had towels for Scruffy and they left the clearing. When they arrived at the crossing the train was just pulling out of the station so they didn't have long to wait until the gates opened and they were off on their first seaside trip as a family. Sam kept up a running commentary at first but was soon content to sit in the car, his dog stretched out along the seat beside him with his head on Sam's knee and listen to the radio that his mum had turned on. If he was truthful he actually felt a bit sleepy. It was lovely and warm in the car and all the fun of yesterday and then having to move his bed in the middle of the night had taken its toll. He knew as soon as they got to the seaside he would be full of energy again but right at this moment he wanted to close his eyes and have a nap just like Scruffy was doing. In fact Sam must have dosed off because the next thing he knew they were pulling into the car park and his mum was stopping the car.

"Right Sam, put Scruffy's lead on while I go and get a parking ticket to display in the car then we can meet at the boot of the car and decide who is carrying what."

"Okay Mum, now where did I put your lead Scruffy? Ah here it is in the door pocket of the car. Come here and let me fasten it to your collar. Right now let me get out of the car first then you follow. Gently now as we need to watch where we are going as this is a public car park so cars are coming in and out all the time. Good boy that is right slide along the seat and jump down gently. Well done now we walk quietly round to the back of the car. Here comes Mum with the ticket. Did you see how good Scruffy got out of the car? He stayed real close to the car."

"Yes I did I am real proud of you both. Scruffy is really listening to your instructions now Sam and realises that there is a reason why we ask him to do things. Right if you take the bag of toys, here Scruffy's towels will fit in the top, and I will bring the picnic, blankets to sit on and the towels. Oh Sam, did you remember your swimming trunks?"

"Yes I put them on this morning under my jeans and brought dry underwear to change into when Scruffy and me have finished getting wet, probably just before home time."

"Knowing you two and water I imagine you could be right," she laughed. "Right all set, then off we go."

Scruffy walked quietly by Sam's side out of the car park, across the road to a path that appeared to lead into a field. He was puzzled he thought they were going to the seaside whatever that was but Sam had said there was lots of sand and Scruffy couldn't see any sand at all.

"It is okay Scruffy," said Sam. "We go through this field first then up through that long grass to the top of the hill then down the other side through the sand dunes and onto the beach. Honest Mum and I know the way we come here every year. When we drop over the hill you will feel how different it is on the pads of your feet as although it is long harsh grass it is growing out of the sand, hence the name sand dunes. Mum once we get to the top of the hill do you think it will be safe to let Scruffy off the lead so we can run down the sand dunes together?"

"I don't see why not," answered his Mum. "I shouldn't imagine there will be anyone on the beach for you to scatter sand over. Drop the bag of toys on the beach and go and have a run on the sand. Then come back to me and get rid of your socks, shoes and jeans at least. If you want to leave your T-shirt on and have brought another with you that will be fine. It will stop you getting sunburn on your shoulders at first while the sun is at its height. Later on, if you want, you can take your T-shirt off when the sun has lost a bit of its heat."

"Yes Mum I brought a clean T-shirt and thanks, Scruffy and me will go for a chase on the sand first, like you suggest. There Scruffy we have got to the top of the hill, come here and let me take off your lead then we can have a race to the bottom of the hill and along the sand."

Sam put the bag of toys and towels, well if he were honest he dropped them down, while he released Scruffy's lead then picked up the bag again and the pair disappeared over the top of the hill. Sam's Mum paused at the top of

127

the hill and smiled as she watched her young son and his dog hurtle down the sand dunes. Scruffy seemed to lose his footing and stumbled over a hillock of grass before righting himself and continuing on his downward sprint. Sam was doing real well until he stumbled on the last bit before the pair hit the beach. The bag went flying into the air spilling out towels and toys all over. The football made a bid for escape and bounced off down the beach and the Frisbee went hurtling into the air. Sam picked himself up, located the bag stuffed the towels in grabbed the cricket set and proceeded on to the beach. He dropped the bag and cricket set, left the ball and Frisbee on the beach and the pair raced across the sand at top speed before Sam dropped to his knees to regain his breath before setting off back to Sam's Mum. By the time they had arrived back Sam's Mum had spread the blankets and towels on the sand and sat down to wait for the boys to arrive back. Both Sam and Scruffy were panting so Sam's Mum pored some water into the bowl she had bought for Scruffy before handing Sam his bottle of juice.

"Thanks Mum it was good to have a run. Here Scruffy get a drink while I take off my shoes, socks and jeans then we will go down to the sea and have a splash about. Are you coming too Mum?"

"No not yet I'll let you and Scruffy get a bit more tired before I join you. I didn't bring my swimsuit so it will just be a gentle paddle for me today although I can unzip the bottom off these trousers to make shorts if I want. Whichever way I'm not coming in yet as I know exactly what you two are like when there is water about. You can manage to get wet in a trickle of water in the stream so goodness knows what you will be like with the whole sea to go at!"

"True Mum, right Scruffy let us go down to the sea and have some fun."

Sam took off down the beach with Scruffy in hot pursuit. They hit the wet sand and Scruffy stopped dead.

Oh goodness it felt as if the ground beneath his feet was shifting.

"Come on Scruffy don't just stand there like a stuffed dummy. Come on down to the sea."

Sam ran laughing into the sea then back out again.

"Oh Scruffy it is cold. Come on, you will be okay, you have a thick fluffy coat on."

By this time Scruffy had got used to the feel of the wet sand on his paws so padded a bit nearer to the sea. Each time he took a step the sand seemed to move a bit more. Slowly he crept further towards Sam who was now back in the water. He knew he should be looking after his master really but he was a bit scared of the huge vast piece of water he was looking at. He couldn't even see any end to it, it stretched for miles. Eventually he arrived at the edge of the water. He placed a front paw into the water but quickly brought it back out. It was so cold. He took several paces back then tried again. This time he managed to get both front paws in the water before backing out.

"Oh for goodness sake Scruffy you ended up sat in the stream at home on your first day, don't be such a coward, come and join me."

Scruffy wasn't having any of it, he sat down on the sand, but then his bottom got cold and wet too, so he stood up again. Sam ran out of the water splashing Scruffy as he bounded up to him.

"Look Scruffy, the sooner you get in the sooner you will get used to the water. Come on we are wasting valuable fun time. Oh okay let me get the football then. We will have to play on the wet sand though because the ball doesn't run very well on dry sand."

Sam ran up the beach to get the ball where it had stopped in the sand when it escaped from the bag. Scruffy tried to run after Sam but found his feet sort of slipped in the dry sand. Sam grabbed the ball and set off back towards the water. Scruffy turned round and gave chase totally intent on catching Sam who had a ball which usually signified fun. He wasn't looking where he was going so didn't realise how close to the sea he was. Suddenly he was knee deep in water before he knew it and Sam had stopped to let him catch up.

"Fooled you Scruffy, you were so intent on catching me with the ball you splashed right into the sea."

Scruffy gave a yelp then realised that even though the water was nearly touching his tummy he could still feel the bottom. He paddled out a bit further, yes he was still walking on the ground although the funny sensation of the ground moving underneath him was still there. He lunged at Sam knocking the ball out of Sam's hands and hurtled off with it between his paws like he did at home although it was more difficult as the ball kept bobbing away in the sea.

"Oh I see, now you have got a taste of the sea you think you can steal my ball do you?" laughed Sam. "Okay we will see about that."

Sam splashed after Scruffy and the ball and reached the ball as Scruffy ploughed into him knocking Sam into the water and losing his foothold and crashing into the water himself. The ball just kept bobbing along until a wave came up and sent it on top of both Scruffy and Sam. Both boy and dog sat up, shook the water out of their eyes and plunged back into the sea after their ball. This game continued, everyone getting completely wet, for quite a while before both boy and dog emerged from the sea like sea urchins and crashed on to the sand to regain their breath.

"Now Scruffy that was fun wasn't it? It was nothing to be frightened of, are we going in again?"

Scruffy scrambled to his feet and shot off back towards the sea. Sam picked up the ball and the pair were off again. Eventually after several repeats of this game both boy and dog were tired so wandered back up the beach towards Sam's Mum.

"Well you two seemed to be having fun down there but I am glad I didn't join you it was a bit too boisterous for me," laughed Sam's Mum. "And I would have ended up wet through. Now Sam are you going to strip off that wet T-shirt and spread it on that rock to dry off a bit? Are you ready for lunch yet or are you ready for a game of cricket? I will play that with you as we will be playing up here on the dry sand."

"I think we need a few minutes before we play cricket. Well I do anyway," laughed Sam. "Maybe a sandwich first and I certainly need a drink. Is that okay Mum?"

"Of course, have a sandwich and a drink and get your breath back, we have all day here so plenty of time to play all the games you want."

With that Sam's Mum dug into the picnic bag and came out with a plastic tub of sandwiches and passed it to Sam. Scruffy had been flopped onto the warm sand, steaming gently but sat up to see what Sam was doing.

"Can Scruffy have a bit of sandwich Mum?" asked Sam.

"Yes of course he can, he has had a busy time too. Do you realise you were frolicking in the sea for over two hours?"

"Goodness Mum, as long as that? We were having so much fun we didn't realise how long we had been in there. No wonder we are both feeling a bit tired then. After my sandwich I think I will make a sandcastle for a bit or rather try as I imagine Scruffy will decide to get in on the act and squander it as fast as I build it."

"Probably but you can have fun trying anyway."

Sam broke off a piece of his sandwich for his dog before eating the rest then reaching for another. Both he and Scruffy lay on the warm sand then Sam had a drink before offering Scruffy one too. Eventually Sam dug into the bag that had the toys in and came out with a bucket and spade and wandered over to a piece of sand away from Sam's Mum in case Scruffy decided to help dig and send sand everywhere. As Sam expected, Scruffy got to his feet to see what Sam was going to do next.

"I am going to try to build a sandcastle Scruffy, but first I will dig out a circle to make a moat then we will have to go and find some wet sand to make the walls of the castle unless, when we dig down we find wet sand."

Scruffy lay down again to watch his master but didn't stay like that for long as he thought digging looked fun. Unfortunately he didn't dig in the right place at first and filled in what Sam had just dug out. Sam had to 'persuade' his dog to dig in the right place, which often resulted in a rugby tackle then a cuddle, so progress on the castle was very slow. Eventually they managed to finish the moat and quite a bit of the walls before Scruffy decided to chase off a seagull that had landed on the beach and ploughed through the masterpiece.

"Oh Scruffy, and we were doing so well too," moaned Sam. "What made you think you could catch the seagull, you know you can't catch birds, you have tried several times at home. Oh well I guess it is time for that game of cricket Mum as Scruffy has demolished my sandcastle."

"Well knowing you both I somehow didn't think you would manage to keep a sandcastle in tact but at least you had a go. Okay get the stumps and bat out. Did you remember a ball?"

"Yes but I actually brought a soft ball so Scruffy wouldn't hurt his mouth if he caught the ball."

"Good thinking Sam. I guess Scruffy will always be fielding and you and me take it in turns to bat."

"Yes Mum, at least this year we have an extra fielder as we normally have to bowl and field together."

"True but we might have problems with our fielder as he might run off with the ball!"

"Oh I never thought about that, it might mean we get a lot more runs though," laughed Sam.

"Who knows but let us have a go and see how we do. Whatever happens it will be lots of fun."

Sam stuck the stumps in the sand where it was just a bit damp so they could run a bit easier and knocked them in a bit further with the bat. He then measured out a 'reasonable' run and stuck the second set of stumps in. Scruffy watched this new game with interest. Sam's Mum took off her shoes and socks and unzipped the bottom off her trousers before rolling the rest up nice and high as she was sure at some point the ball, Scruffy or Sam would end up in the sea and she would get wet somehow. She had no illusions about this pair of hers but she didn't mind. She was looking forward now to having some fun with them even if it meant getting wet.

"Are you ready Mum?" called Sam

"Yes just coming," answered his Mum running off down the sand. "Who is batting first? Do you want to start Sam?"

"Okay. Right Scruffy when I hit the ball you run and pick it up and bring it back to Mum. Okay Mum let us have a practise and see if Scruffy has understood."

Sam's Mum threw the ball ready for Sam to hit but Scruffy shot forward and caught it before it landed anywhere near Sam's bat and ran off back with it to Sam's Mum.

"Well he got one bit right," laughed Sam's Mum. "He brought it back to me."

"No Scruffy you let me hit the ball first then take it back to Mum. We will try again."

This time Scruffy stayed where he was even after Sam had hit the ball.

"Scruffy go and get the ball and take it back to Mum."

Scruffy just stood there and looked first at Sam then at Sam's Mum. Sam was so exasperated he actually went and collected the ball himself without even trying to score a run.

"Now Scruffy listen closely. Mum will bowl the ball to me and I will hit it then you run to where it has landed, pick up the ball and take it back to Mum. Have you got that? Here Mum at this rate it will be night before Scruffy gets this right."

"Well," laughed Sam's Mum, "you have to remember he has never played cricket before so it will seem strange to him. Maybe we should have had a practise at home first when there were more of us. We can maybe organise a game when your Uncle Pete and Aunty Jan come at half term and maybe Steve will come down too."

"Now that is a brilliant suggestion. Maybe Steve's parents could join us too but for now let us try again and see what happens this time."

Sam's Mum bowled the ball towards Sam, Sam hit it and Scruffy hurtled after it. Sam was so surprised he forgot to run at first then when he finally set off Scruffy was on his way back with the ball and the pair collided mid-wicket and ended up with Scruffy sat on top of Sam proudly showing off the ball. Sam's Mum couldn't help herself and she just burst out laughing.

"Now is that a run out do you think Sam?"

"Oh Scruffy get off me. Yes I think so Mum, so much for me saying we might get lots of runs today, I haven't even managed one. You have a go at batting Mum and see if you manage better than me."

Sam pushed Scruffy off the top of him and scrambled to his feet. He handed the bat to his Mum and tried to get the ball out of Scruffy's mouth. Scruffy thought this was part of the game so ran off with it so Sam had to chase him. Eventually Sam managed to rugby tackle Scruffy to the floor and get the ball then he ran back to his Mum.

"Right Mum are you ready," asked Sam. "Have you stopped laughing yet?"

"Well you have to admit we are having more fun not playing the game."

"I suppose so now I wonder what will happen this time," replied Sam.

Everyone took up their positions again, Scruffy having been given strict instructions from Sam where to stand and Sam bowled the ball to his Mum. She hit the ball and Scruffy shot off to get it. Sam's Mum managed to get to the other end and back before Scruffy ran up to Sam with the ball.

"Well done Mum and you too Scruffy but you need to get back to me a bit quicker or Mum will end up with too many runs," laughed Sam. "Right let us try again."

Sam's Mum missed the next ball and Scruffy stood and looked as much as to say 'what now?'

"Scruffy the ball is behind Mum go and get it and bring it back please," instructed Sam.

Scruffy ran off and found it bringing it back to his master and wagging his tail as much to say 'aren't I clever'.

"Yes you clever dog," said Sam giving his dog a pat. "Now go back to where you were and I will throw it again for Mum to hit."

This time Sam's Mum hit the ball but straight at Scruffy who jumped up and caught it in his mouth.

"Oh well done Scruffy," shouted Sam. "You clever dog you have just caught Mum out. You see Mum once he got the idea he is a super fielder. Now see if I can do better than last time."

Now that Scruffy had finally got the hang of the game Sam and his Mum were able to have an energetic game of cricket, if not terribly professional. The eventual score was Sam 22 and his Mum 20 after several innings each. They both agreed they had enjoyed themselves but felt it was time to stop. Sam said he and Scruffy were just going to have another paddle in the sea to cool off and Sam's Mum agreed to join them. This time Scruffy had no qualms about plunging straight into the sea with Sam close on his heels. Sam's Mum ran down to join them and was soon up to her knees in the sea. She wished she had brought her swimsuit or even a change of clothes today but she hadn't thought. She hadn't packed her swimsuit but she had brought extra trousers and T-shirt. She hadn't thought she would want to be in the sea but the boys were having so much fun she wanted to join in. She suddenly decided she was going to join in so ran back up the sand and quickly shed the top half of underwear and put her T-shirt back on which was a very long one and took off her trousers. She decided that her tee shirt would likely dry quite quickly but if it was still a bit damp she could drive back to camp in it and change as soon as they got back. If her other underwear wasn't dry she could easily put her trousers on and no one would know any different. She ran back to the sea and joined Scruffy and Sam in a game of rough and tumble and splashing about in the sea until everyone was exhausted and they trooped back up the sand.

"Wow Mum that was great we haven't had as much fun as that for ages."

"It has been a while but to be honest it hasn't been such nice weather the last couple of years we have been here so we haven't spent long in the sea."

"True Mum but you used to always go in the sea when I was little though."

"Yes I was always with you to make sure you were safe but as you got bigger and stronger you didn't need me the same. I just fancied joining in your fun though today."

"I'm so glad you did. I think me and Scruffy will have a quick towel dry and another sandwich then go and explore the rock pools. Can I go and explore that cave I found last year?"

"Of course but if you and Scruffy go and have some fun on the rocks while my T-shirt gets dry I'll come and join you. I would really like to explore the cave you found too."

"Right Mum that sounds like a plan it would be great if we could all do that together. Come on Scruffy I will give you a quick towel down then have a rest while I dry myself. Oh good it looks as though my T-shirt is already dry Mum so yours probably won't take long either."

"It shouldn't as it is only very thin material. Here pass me that towel and I'll exchange my T-shirt for it and see if I can get my underwear dry too although that isn't so important as I can just wear my trousers that are dry."

Sam gave Scruffy a quick towel dry then himself and popped his T-shirt back on before they both sprawled out on a towel and Sam munched on a sandwich. Scruffy was so tired he didn't even bother to ask for a sandwich just fell fast asleep. Sam was equally content to have a sit down too and he soon dosed off in the warm sun. Sam's mum let them rest while she read her book then after about an hour she got up to check on her clothes. Her T-shirt wasn't quite fully dry yet but her underwear was so she got dressed again as much as she could. Sam and Scruffy woke up as soon as Sam's Mum began to move and sat up.

"Sorry Mum I must have dosed off. Come on Scruffy let us go and have a look in the rock pools before Mum joins us to go and look in the cave. We need to go before the tide comes don't we Mum?"

"Yes but I think the tide is still going out or if not has just turned so it will be a few hours yet before it is back to high tide. That leaves us plenty of time to explore both rock pools and the cave."

"Great see you on the rocks near the cave when you are ready. Come on Scruffy time to go and have some more fun."

Sam and Scruffy ran off towards the rocks and soon Sam's Mum could see them peering into crevices and scrambling over the rocks. She settled back and picked up her sketch book and with a few practiced strokes was soon engrossed in capturing the scene before her from lots of angles. At the moment she wasn't too sure when she would use them but knew that the author she was going to work with next had hinted that one of the stories would likely involve the seaside so she was sure she could adapt these sketches to fit in or at least jog her memory if the book was a while before it was written. She had to admit she was really looking forward to this commission as it was just the sort of story she would have written if she had been a writer not an illustrator. It was up to her skills though, to allow the readers to imagine they were actually living in the story, so in a lot of ways her illustrations were equally important to bring the writer's words alive. Meanwhile Sam was showing Scruffy how to turn over small rocks and stones to see what was underneath. In one rock pool Scruffy was having a look on his own when he felt something hard. He poked a bit more but he seemed to have lost the hard bit so wandered over to Sam. His ear felt a bit funny so he shook his head to shake off whatever was stuck to it. At that moment Sam looked up from turning over a rock and laughed when he saw what was dangling from Scruffy's ear.

"Oh Scruffy you have collected an earring. Come here while I take it off you can't keep it you know it needs water to survive. There look that was what was stuck to your ear it is a small crab. Fishermen catch big ones of those for people to eat but that one is so small we will put him back in the rock pool to keep wet until the tide comes back in and takes him out to sea again. Good job it was your ear he latched on to and not your nose."

Sam removed the crab and put it back in the rock pool where it had been until Scruffy had disturbed it and they wandered a bit further up the coast scrabbling among the rocks as they went. Suddenly Sam heard a whistle.

"Looks as though Mum is ready to join us and go and look in the cave. Coming Mum."

Soon Sam's Mum joined the pair and they continued along the rocks but nearer the cliff than Sam and Scruffy had been. Here the rocks were not as slippery and were in fact quite dry so Sam's Mum suspected that the tide never got as near the cliffs as this so it could well be a smugglers cave as they always used ones that were dry and not likely to be flooded. Soon they arrived at the mouth of the cave and Sam's Mum stood and looked around. Yes it had all the hallmarks of a smugglers cave. It was only accessible from the cove they had found, it was well hidden from the top by a rocky piece of cliff which would also shield the view from up there of any activity that was going on here. She suddenly felt quite excited, were her and Sam about to uncover a piece of history that no one knew about? She had been around this area for many years and had never heard any tales about smuggling along this part of the coast either but that didn't mean that there hadn't been any.

"It looks as though it might have been a smugglers cave but we will be able to tell better when we get inside. The location, or rather position, is good. These rocks are dry and look as though they never get wet so that means even at high tide the cave will remain dry. It is only accessible from our cove which if you didn't know was there you would never find it even now. You only stumble on it by accident like we did all those years ago and as there never appears to have any evidence that other people use it I don't actually think anyone else but us has ever found it. That is two ideal conditions for a smugglers cave. Also Sam if you look up you can't actually see the mouth of the cave as it is hidden by that rocky outcrop of cliff that also hides a good deal of the beach right near those rocks so any activity actually down here close to the cliff face would be hidden."

"Wow Mum I never really thought about all those things been relevant but now you have explained I can see and understand why it would make an ideal smugglers cave. Do you think anyone still smuggles things in and if so what? Also what would they be smuggling back in the olden days?

"Well now does anyone smuggle anything now, that I can't really answer, well not in this region anyway, but yes there is smuggling still happening but it is mainly drugs now and appears to be through airports. Smuggling by sea, I think died out many years ago. Also if you think about it this part of the country is a long way from any other land to sail from and the North Sea is treacherous, very stormy and cold so I don't think in this day and age anyone would smuggle anything to here. As to the second part of your question again I am not really sure what they would smuggle here unless it was from a large vessel that was bringing other cargo to and from Europe. I have no proof that there was in fact any smuggling in this area, I certainly have never heard any tales of any, but who knows. In the olden days it was usually barrels of spirits that were smuggled, or it was down in the south anyway, but as you know from geography at school that coastline is much nearer France and Spain than up here. Also this area is not like Scotland, it didn't play any real part in any rebellions against their rulers so I shouldn't imagine there was any people trafficking either. So to answer your question do I really think it was a smugglers cave I really don't know but let us go and investigate it further and make our decision based on facts and evidence, if there are any, when we have seen everything there is to see then you and I can have a big discussion over the camp fire tonight about it all."

"Yes let us do that. Come on Scruffy you are part of this adventure too."

Scruffy, Sam and his Mum scrambled over the rocks towards the mouth of the cave. Suddenly the rocks stopped and there was a stretch of earth completely surrounded by rocks which was completely dry and then what looked like steps carved into the rock face leading to the mouth of the cave.

"Wow Mum look at this. These steps look as if they have been worn away by many feet trampling up from this piece of ground into the cave."

"Yes it does, doesn't it?" laughed Sam's Mum. "Maybe the smugglers dropped the cargo on the beach then brought each piece onto this piece of ground until it was safe to move it into the cave. That would depend on the moonlight and time of night. If it was early enough I imagine they would get it all on to this hidden piece of ground then transfer it into the cave in case it rained as this little bit of earth would soon be soaking wet as it feels as if it is part of the cliff face, a sort of ledge."

Sam led the way up the steps to the mouth of the cave. It was actually very well hidden with a large opening when the trio got up close and certainly high enough to stand upright, even for Sam's Mum at first. The trio stopped in the entrance and gazed back out to the sea. Looking at it from here, it wasn't that far, although the sea would have to get up very high to actually get over the high rocks. Sam's Mum thought it would have to be an exceptional storm to actually lash this opening and looking at it there

140

was no real evidence of erosion from the elements. The trio went in a bit further and the opening narrowed both in width and height. Scruffy was not too sure about this adventure but sandwiched between Sam and Sam's Mum he had no real choice but to follow Sam. It began to be a lot colder the further in they went until suddenly they found that the tunnel opened out again and suddenly they were in a large open space. It was still very chilly in here but lovely and dry. Sam and his Mum had a close look at the walls of the cave and actually thought that the inside had in fact been carved out by humans not nature. There was a ledge at the back which ran about three quarters of the way round the cave, quite deep but scraped and chipped on the edges as though things had been lifted on and off over a number of years. None of the damage appeared to have been done in recent years so Sam's Mum assumed that whatever it had been used for, and she was sure now that it had been used at some time, it was now not used in that way. There was, however, some evidence of recent use as there were initials carved in places where the stone was soft and in a couple of places, holes quite high up, had been gouged out.

"Here Sam come and look at these markings they feel as though they are initials, fairly recently done, and some candle wax in these holes in the wall."

"Cool Mum, so we can assume that someone does actually come here and bring candles to light the space."

"Well to be honest I think the holes would be for lanterns originally hence the reason they are quite deep but yes in modern times I think they are used to stand candles in."

"But who would actually come here Mum?" asked Sam. "It is quite chilly and gloomy even on a bright sunny day like today."

"I don't know the answer to that I am afraid Sam unless someone uses it to get away, maybe to study in peace if they live in a busy, noisy house or just spend time on their own. It could be the local meeting place for the teenagers

141

although I think if that was it you would see much more evidence of litter and things. What about it being used by couples in love who want a private place to go. It would be ever so romantic in candlelight."

"I don't think it would be very good for any of them suggestions it is too dark and cold. You wouldn't be able to read or study even with lots of candles and there isn't evidence of lots of candles anywhere but in the two holes in the wall so that rules out that theory. As you say I don't think the teenagers meet here in large numbers again no evidence. As for your suggestion of couples coming here I think they would just meet at the pub or somewhere much warmer and easier to get to rather than having to scrambler over rocks to get here."

"Well in that case what do you think it is used for?" asked his Mum

"I don't know let me have some time to think about it."

While Sam and his Mum had been bandying suggestions about as to what the cave was used for now Scruffy had been investigating on his own. He had been having a sniff around the walls and over in a particular dark corner at the end of the bench like ledge he had found another opening. This wasn't level with the ground but you had to climb over a large step. Scruffy couldn't help himself and although it was even darker than where he had left Sam and his Mum, he climbed over the step. He gingerly crept forward until he stumbled over a warm lump that was laying on the floor. This was certainly too much for Scruffy who hurtled back the way he had come over the step and ran slap bang into Sam.

"What on earth is wrong with you Scruffy and where on earth did you come from?" exclaimed Sam. "You were here only a minute ago snuffling around because I could hear you. Now you look as if you have seen a ghost."

"Not a ghost me actually," said a voice out of the gloom. "He stumbled over me and took off like a scalded cat."

The owner of the voice emerged from the dark corner wrapped in a blanket or rather several blankets. Scruffy dived behind his master and Sam's Mum for protection. No way was he going to play the big brave dog in this situation.

"Oh sorry sir if my dog disturbed you. I'm not sure where he actually came from as he was travelling so fast."

"He came from that dark corner, there is another smaller opening that leads off from this chamber, and I think he stumbled on it by mistake. I was just having a nap as I use that as my bedroom. Please don't be afraid of me I won't harm you I live here because I have nowhere else to live. Well I spend my summers here to be precise, I usually head more inland in winter as it can get a bit cold here," laughed the man.

"You mean you have no other home?" exclaimed Sam shocked. "Are you a tramp, is that the right word Mum?"

"Yes that is one word or sometimes they are called travellers and they chose to travel around the country," answered his Mum.

"Yes it is my choice to live like this now. I used to be a successful business man once with a home and family but gave it all up to travel around the country. I have my own places that I can pick up casual work if I want some and places that I know like this that I can use in summer. I often don't stop as long as I have this year but it has been such a lovely summer that I stayed on a bit longer. My name is Tom, could I ask what all your names are please as it is nice to know?"

"I'm Sam and this is my Mum and my dog Scruffy."

"Pleased to meet you Sam and Sam's Mum and you too Scruffy. Sorry I frightened you I didn't mean to. I could hear your master and his Mum talking and thought I would stay still as I didn't want to frighten them and never expected anyone would actually find the opening. I didn't bank on an inquisitive dog like you but I am real pleased you did. It can sometimes get a bit lonely and it is nice to occasionally meet people."

"Hi Tom I am actually Di, not just Sam's Mum," she said, "and I'm real sorry we disturbed your peace. We were wondering who used this place now as it had evidence of some modern usage like the candle wax but no litter or anything. Now you have answered our question. I am not sure if either of us would have come up with the real explanation though. The other question that we were pondering was if it was a former smugglers cave, do you know?"

"Actually yes you are right it was a smugglers cave originally but not in the way that is normally the case as it was used to store contraband that was leaving the country not entering it."

"How unusual like what?" asked Sam's Mum.

"Mead," replied the man. "They were excellent at making mead as the spring water mixed with the honey made by the bees in this area was second to none and highly prized on the continent before it found fame here in its own country. Once it found a market at home the smuggling business dwindled."

"How fascinating a little bit of history that has actually passed me by," answered Sam's Mum. "Now if you don't mind I think I will take my family back to the beach and get packed up before the tide comes in as I know once it begins to come in it doesn't take long."

"You are quite right Di, do I assume you know this area well as normally no one ever comes near this place. I imagine you are in the little cove to the right of the mouth of the cave aren't you?"

"Yes we have been coming here a number of years now. I got fed up of receiving black looks and muttered comments when my son managed to scatter sand over people on the bigger beaches, my son is not the most co-ordinated person and never has been even when he was little, so we looked for something more remote and private where he could have fun. We accidently stumbled on it on one of our rambles to let off some steam and thought it was perfect for us. As there is never any evidence, no

144

matter when we come, and we are the latest this year we have ever been, that other people have used it, I assume no one else has stumbled on it yet."

"No I have never seen anyone in that cove before, not that I go down that much myself as I don't want people finding this cave either, so we both have a vested interest in keeping our knowledge to ourselves have we not?"

"Oh don't worry about us both the cove and now this cave will remain Sam, Scruffy and my secret so no one will be disturbing your summer I promise. If you are about and notice us in the cove another year please come down and say hello."

"I most certainly will and Sam when you come back next year come and see if I am in residence maybe next time Scruffy won't get such a fright. Now I will say goodbye and please be careful as you go down the steps I haven't quite got them perfect yet," he laughed.

"Goodbye Tom," Sam and his Mum replied. "You take care of yourself too." With a final wave Sam, his Mum and Scruffy set off out of the chamber towards the tunnel that led to the entrance to the cave. Suddenly Scruffy turned around and bounded back up to man. With a yelp he sat down on his hunches and held up a paw. The man bent down to shake his paw and Scruffy reached forward and gave the man a great sloppy kiss as much as to say 'goodbye from me too'

"Goodbye Scruffy I will treasure that kiss throughout the dark days of winter and I hope I will see you all next year."

Scruffy bounded back to Sam and his Mum and they soon reached the mouth of the cave and tumbled out into the sunshine again.

"I will head back to the beach now while you and Scruffy finish rock pooling. I want to make some sketches of the inside of the cave while it is still fresh in my mind. I am not sure when I will use the but they will be there for future reference"

"Well actually Mum I think we have finished so we will head back with you. We haven't found anything interesting either although Scruffy found an earring."

"Scruffy found an earring, what sort of earring?" asked Sam's Mum in surprise.

"A tiny crab earring in a rock pool, it stuck itself on to Scruffy's ear."

"Oh I see," chuckled his Mum. "You are so clever Scruffy to find a crab and get it stuck on your ear too."

Scruffy wasn't too sure why he was clever this time but he accepted the praise anyway. By this time they had arrived back to where the towels and things were.

"What are you two going to do now," asked Sam's Mum.

"I think we might just finish with a bit of football then I will go and rinse the sand off my body before getting dressed again. Is that okay?"

"Yes fine by me. Do you want anything more to eat?"

"No but I wouldn't mind a drink please. All that cave exploring has made me thirsty."

"Here you are then," answered his Mum passing him his bottle of juice.

Sam had a quick drink then picked up the football for a last game of football while his mum did the sketches she wanted to do. After she had finished she packed her sketch book into the front pocket of her bag and packed the food away into the main body of the bag. She picked up the cricket set and packet it away before replacing it into the toy bag along with the Frisbee. The football would go in last then Scruffy's towels on top. Soon Scruffy and Sam returned from their game and Sam put the football in the bag with the towels on top. He collected a large towel and wandered down to the sea. Dropping the towel on the dry sand he instructed Scruffy to look after it while he rinsed all the sand off his body and trunks. Scruffy sat there wondering what Sam was doing but was proud to have been given the job of looking after Sam's towel. Sam was soon back and picked up the towel, shook the sand out of it, and placed it round his middle. He stepped out of his swimming trunks and both Sam and Scruffy wandered back up the sand to Sam's Mum.

"All done?" asked Sam's Mum.

"Yes I will just dry myself and get dressed then we can head back to the car. What a fantastic day it has been. I always enjoy my days at the seaside but with Scruffy to play with it has been even better. I think Scruffy has had a good time too, haven't you Scruffy?"

Scruffy wagged his tail and sat down by Sam's side while Sam got dried and dressed then Sam and his mother shook the sand out of the towels and blankets before heading back up the sand dunes. At the top Sam clipped on Scruffy's lead, although to be honest Scruffy was so tired he wasn't moving away from Sam, and Sam, Scruffy and Sam's Mum made their way to the car. They soon loaded the car and Sam spread the blanket he had brought for Scruffy on the back seat of the car. With a quick 'up you get' Scruffy Sam and Scruffy were soon settled on the back seat and Sam wrapped the blanket around Scruffy. Before the car even left the car park Scruffy was snoring, worn out by such a fantastic adventure.

Scruffy and Maisie

Sam equally didn't remember much of the drive home either but roused himself when his Mum pulled into the clearing.

"If you want to go and start tea Mum, Scruffy and I will unload the car for you."

"Okay thanks Sam but there is not too much we need bring out anyway."

"No just the picnic bag and Scruffy's blanket for tonight. Do you want the towels bringing in Mum?"

"No I don't think you need bother as we will not need them tomorrow. Even you and Scruffy cannot get wet at the castle as there is absolutely no water anywhere in the grounds."

"True," laughed Sam. "In that case I will just pack both Scruffy's towels and ours neatly in the back of the car along with the beach toys."

All three of them jumped out of the car. Sam gathered up Scruffy's blanket from the back seat and took it into their tent. Sam's Mum made her way to the cooking tent to start getting the stew warm and Scruffy followed Sam making a detour via his water bowl first. After Sam had put Scruffy's blanket back on his bed and put his dirty clothes in the carrier bag next to his other bag, he went back to the car to collect the picnic bag and pile the dirty towels neatly in the back of the car. He carried the picnic bag over to his Mum and began to empty it. He looked in the sandwich box to see if there were any left, only one, so asked his Mum what she wanted him to do with it.

"Oh pop it into Scruffy's bowl. If you pass his bowl I will put him a spoonful of stew in before it gets too hot then you can put his meat and biscuits in and give him his tea if you want. Our tea should be warm in about 5 minutes."

"Great Mum, another treat for Scruffy's tea, you are spoiling him Mum," laughed Sam.

"No I am not but after all he has done today I imagine he will be very hungry so an extra spoonful of stew will go down a treat."

Sam finished emptying the picnic bag and put the empty containers next to the washing up bowl ready to be washed up after tea and put Scruffy's tea down next to his water bowl.

"Can you just give the stew a stir while I pop into my tent and put some clean clothes on," she asked Sam. "Then if you want to get us both a bowl out and some spoons and I will cut us some bread when I come back."

"Okay Mum, no problem. Oh good boy you have eaten all your tea up. Was it nice?"

Scruffy wagged his tail then disappeared into the bushes.

"Don't go too far Scruffy, I don't want you getting lost."

"It is okay Sam he will have just gone to the toilet. It is where he went this morning," answered his Mum as she emerged from her tent.

"Oh probably, I never thought about that. Scruffy has had his tea and the stew is bubbling so I assume it is warm enough now."

"Good well done Sam, oh here comes Scruffy now. Good boy Scruffy now lay down while Sam and me have our tea too."

Sam's Mum put stew in the bowls for her and Sam and cut some chunky slices of bread to eat with it and carried it over to the seats where Sam and Scruffy were sat. Soon they had finished and Sam collected the dirty pots. His Mum had already boiled the kettle so Sam poured water in the washing up bowl and started to wash up.

"Off you go and have a better look in the art gallery Mum. Scruffy and me are fine here on our own. If Scruffy manages to wake up we will have another go at swing ball but if not I will just light the camp fire instead," instructed Sam.

"Okay thanks Sam I know you will both be fine although I don't imagine I will be that long. I will do some sketches when I get back before the light fades using inspiration from what I have seen in the gallery."

Sam's Mum walked off and Sam finished washing up and drying the pots before putting them away.

"Right Scruffy, are you up for another go at swing ball? I will not bother with the bat this time as I liked the way you stretched the elastic then let go. That way neither of us knows where the ball will go."

Scruffy sat up then followed Sam to the game they tried, with limited success, this morning. He was willing to give it another go although he had doubts they would get it to work any better tonight than they had this morning.

"We will start gently this time Scruffy. Here you try and catch the ball as it comes towards you."

Sam let go of the ball but it whizzed past Scruffy's nose so quick Scruffy missed it. He turned around just in time to see it coming back at him at the speed of light. He lurched at the ball but didn't catch it clean so it shot off in another direction. Scruffy was having none of this so he chased after it. Suddenly the ball changed direction and began to come back again. Right thought Scruffy I will catch it this time no problem. He lurched at it and actually caught the ball but then couldn't stop so stretched out the elastic which tugged at the ball dislodging it out of Scruffy's mouth. The ball shot off, hit the pole and sent it straight at Sam. Sam had to duck quickly or it would have hit him in the face. The ball shot off past Sam to a spot close to Scruffy who was on his way back after the ball. This time he caught it clean and was able to keep going in the same direction as the ball. Round the pole ran the dog with the ball in its mouth, colliding into Sam. Scruffy was so surprised he dropped the ball and the ball shot off back in the direction it had just come from catching both Sam and Scruffy as it passed them. This again altered its direction so both Sam and Scruffy gave chase. Eventually Sam managed to catch the ball before setting it off again in another direction. The pair had great fun, trying to catch the ball in Sam's case, and catching but letting it go in Scruffy's case until they were both completely out of breath. Scruffy ran off at one point to grab a drink before returning to play some more. When Sam's Mum returned they were both still playing the game so Sam's Mum was able to do quite a few sketches of ideas that she was sure she could use in her next commission.

Eventually the pair were completely tired out so Sam lit the camp fire and set the chairs close to it like he had last night. He found the bag of marshmallows and the sticks from last night that they had used as toasting forks, so he was ready when the fire burnt up a bit. Soon the fire was ready and Sam's Mum had finished her sketching so joined Sam and Scruffy next to the fire. Sam toasted himself and then Scruffy a marshmallow while his Mum toasted her own. They sat munching their toasted sweets for a while until Sam's Mum said,

"I have had enough marshmallows but I would love a hot chocolate. Do you want one making Sam too?"

"Yes please, like you I think both Scruffy and me have had enough marshmallows but a drink would be good while the fire dies down then I think it is bed for us."

"Yes I imagine you are both tired as you have done so much today and Scruffy has learnt so many new games. I will just go and make us all some hot chocolate, I think I might make a bit extra and put a little in Scruffy's dish, not too much as it is bad for him, but give him a little treat too. It always helps us to sleep Sam so it might do the same for Scruffy."

"To be honest Mum, I don't think he will need much to help him sleep tonight," laughed Sam. "He is falling asleep as we speak."

"So he is Sam but he has had a busy day," she replied.

Sam's Mum went over to the stove and soon came back with a mug of hot chocolate for Sam, and Scruffy's food bowl with a little bit of very milky hot chocolate in for Scruffy. She went back for her own mug and they sat around the dying fire while they finished their drinks. As soon as they were finished Sam spread the dying embers of the fire out while his Mum rinsed their mugs and they moved the chairs away from the fire. Scruffy lay and watched this activity until Sam said.

"Come on Scruffy, time for bed."

Scruffy slowly got up and padded over to Sam as he was so tired. Sam unzipped the opening of the tent and crawled in.

"Come on Scruffy, in you come so I can zip the door closed. Right climb inside your sleeping bag and I will cover you up before I get ready for bed. I don't think we will be listening to many forest night sounds tonight I am far too tired and I suspect you are too."

Sam was soon tucked inside his sleeping bag but even still Scruffy was asleep and snoring first. Sam snuggled down and was soon fast asleep too. Neither woke nor stirred before the sun woke them up. They could hear Sam's Mum putting the kettle on so Sam opened the tent flap to let Scruffy out before dressing and tidying the tent. As he emerged he found his Mum just putting his breakfast on a plate and Scruffy already tucking into his breakfast.

"Good morning Sam, did you and Scruffy sleep better last night?"

"Yes Scruffy was asleep before I even got in my sleeping bag and we slept all night. In fact we just woke up when we heard you putting the kettle on."

"Good that meant you were tired out but it was really no wonder as we had such a busy but fun day yesterday."

"Yes and today will be fun too meeting Maisie and Helen and I am really looking forward to visiting the museum you were telling me about Mum."

"Yes it is so many years since I was there I am looking forward to it too. We will have to leave Scruffy in the car while we go to it because even if they allow dogs in, which I doubt, Scruffy is too clumsy to manage a museum. Don't get me wrong I love him to bits just the way he is but him in a museum would be a disaster."

"I agree Mum and I am sure Scruffy will not mind having a snooze in the car while we have a look especially as we are heading to the castle after the museum to let off steam."

"Well it is also quite a way to walk from the car park as I will park in the railway car park for the day. The museum is also just next to the station so it is perfect for all we have to do today."

"Well done Mum and thanks for breakfast. We need a bit more wood for our camp fire tonight as we used it all up last night so Scruffy and me will go and collect some."

"Good idea Sam, I will tidy up after breakfast then make us our picnic while you do that then I imagine we will be about ready to set off."

"Perfect Mum. Come on Scruffy we need more wood so we had better go and find some."

Scruffy didn't need telling twice, he was up and heading for the path before Sam had finished speaking.

"Looks like he knows what we are going to do Mum. See you soon."

"Yes Scruffy does not need showing anything more than once," laughed Sam's Mum. "See you two soon."

Sam ran after his dog down the path into the next clearing then across to the other path. Sam thought they may have to go a bit further into the forest as he thought Scruffy and him had exhausted the pile they had found on Tuesday. They soon arrived where they had found their first haul but as Sam thought there was no more just there so they veered off right along another path. Soon they came across another tree that had fallen down the only problem was that it had been a much larger tree so the branches were far too big for the pair to carry. Sam bent down to see if there were any smaller branches underneath when Scruffy decided to try his hand, or rather mouth, to pull on the big branch.

"It is no good Scruffy, that branch is far too big for us to carry so you might as well leave it alone."

At that there was a huge crack as the branch splintered away from the main body of the fallen tree.

"Oh Scruffy you clever dog I never thought it might break off. It must have been there a while and gone dry. Let us see if we can break it down a bit further."

With a lot of tugging the pair pulled the broken off piece out of the undergrowth and immediately Sam could see that there was several smaller branches he could probably break off which he proceeded to do. Then he tried to break up the larger piece. It didn't take much bending before it snapped and then Sam could break them down into smaller pieces. Sam continued to break up the branches until he had enough for an armful for himself to carry.

"Okay Scruffy I think that will do as we only have tonight as we go home tomorrow. We are then going to work at the farm until I go back to school next week."

Sam gathered up his armful of sticks and began down the path when he became aware of a rustling behind him. When he turned around he was astonished to see Scruffy coming down the path dragging the remains of the broken branch.

"Oh Scruffy I didn't think we needed it and anyway it is far too big for the fire like that."

Scruffy laid down his prize and looked so forlorn at Sam as much as to say 'I tried' that Sam relented and said,

"Okay Scruffy bring it along and I will see if Mum and me together can manage to break it up into small enough pieces to burn it on the camp fire. Come on then you will have to manage on your own as I have my arms full."

Scruffy picked up his branch again and with a super effort managed to drag it back to their own clearing.

"Goodness Scruffy another even bigger branch than before. Now how are we going to get that to fit the camp fire I wonder? Any ideas Sam?"

"Well it breaks quite easily but I wasn't able to break that one on my own. I was going to leave it but Scruffy had other ideas and looked so upset when I told him we couldn't use it I had to let him bring it. I wondered, if you helped me Mum, we could maybe break it down together."

"Well let us have a go as it was so good of Scruffy to bring it we ought to try real hard before we disappoint him. Move over Scruffy let me and Sam see if we can break it up. Ah here Sam look it has cracked across here so let us break it there to begin with."

"That must have cracked as Scruffy dragged it across the ground. That makes it look more promising because if it cracked purely by being dragged it should yield to us working together."

Sam held on to one side of the branch while his Mum bent the other and the branch soon splintered across the crack and another crack appeared. Sam and his Mum soon had the branch broken into small enough pieces for the fire and Sam, Scruffy and Sam's Mum piled it all near the camp fire ready for the evening.

"Right," said Sam's Mum. "We are all ready now. I have already put the picnic bag in the car so let us have you two in the car and get set off on today's adventure."

Sam and Scruffy didn't need telling twice and they raced off to the car. Their Mum followed and they were soon driving out of the clearing. There was no train at the station today to hamper their progress and as the town was much closer than the seaside they soon arrived at their destination.

"Shall we have a wander up the town first before we go to the museum Sam?" asked his Mum. "It would give Scruffy a walk before he was shut in the car."

"Good idea Mum. Come here Scruffy you need your lead on in town and in any case we have to cross over the railway lines using a bridge before we reach town and it looks as though there is a train in so I need to make sure you stay safe."

Sam clipped Scruffy's lead on while his Mum went and got a parking ticket for the day.

"We don't need a bag or anything do we Mum just yet?" asked Sam.

"No I will just take my purse in case we see anything that we want to buy," answered his Mum.

The trio soon left the car park and walked into the station and crossed over a bridge, Scruffy could see another, or maybe the same black monster, that Sam had called an engine below them, but now he wasn't quite so frightened of it, and down the other side.

"I will just pick up a timetable so we can work out which trains we are catching later," said Sam's Mum.

"Okay Mum but surely Helen will know the train times anyway won't she?"

"Oh gosh yes clever boy I never thought about that but I will pick one up in any case."

As the family left the station Dave gave them a wave and called,

"See you all later, which train are you catching?"

"Not exactly sure but I should imagine the 2 o'clock," called back Sam's Mum.

"Great I will be guard on that one so if we have any problems I can help," laughed Dave.

"Well you never know but probably not, as we are joining Helen and Maisie and I am sure Scruffy will not want to show himself up in front of a lady."

"That Maisie is no lady I can assure you Scruffy. She will probably make your hair curl with her antics. She will teach you a thing or two," laughed Dave. "See you later."

"See you later," chorused both Sam and his Mum as they wandered out of the station and crossed the road. They wandered up the town looking into shop windows until Sam's Mum said,

"Did we finish the marshmallows last night Sam?"

"Yes or nearly anyway, there are not many left," answered Sam.

"Right I will pop in here and get some more then. Anything else you want?"

"No I don't think so. Scruffy and I will stay here and wait for you."

Sam's Mum popped into the shop and was not too long before she joined Sam and Scruffy again. They continued to amble along, Sam being very proud of the way Scruffy behaved. He showed how far he had come as he was not fazed at all by the traffic on the road and was happy to stand and wait whenever Sam or his Mum stopped to look in a shop window. Eventually they had finished looking at the shops and returned to the station, back over the bridge and into the car park. Although it was a dry day it was not too warm and Sam's Mum had parked the car in the shade of the trees so Scruffy would not be too warm in the car while they visited the museum. Sam's Mum left all the windows down a little bit so there was plenty of air for him and with the instruction of 'look after the car Scruffy' Sam and his Mum made their way to the museum. The museum certainly measured up to their expectations and both were soon in discussion about the various exhibits they were looking at. Sam was even more fascinated when he saw the exhibits in the farm machinery section. Sam's Mum was able to tell him that his great grandad had probably used some of the implements as she believed he had in fact done some work with horses. There were a few that she could remember them using when she was real young but not many. She suggested Sam ask his grandad more about them when they came to stay. Sam's Mum took some photographs on her telephone of the things she vaguely remembered and said they might bring her parents to see the museum if they came at Easter. It was no good planning a trip earlier because the museum closed for the winter. Sam thought this an excellent idea and picked up any free leaflets he could. They bought a book in the museum that showed pictures of some of the things they had been looking at and quite a bit of history about the museum and area that Sam was interested in reading when

157

they got home. He also thought Steve's dad might have some interest in what they had seen.

Soon they arrived back at the car and after putting Scruffy's lead back on and his Mum collecting the picnic they left the car park again but this time going away from the station as the castle was more accessible from that side. They crossed the railway lines and over the road before attacking the steep hill up towards the castle. About halfway up they stopped at a bench to regain their breath before carrying on up the hill. As they crested the hill just about to head into the castle grounds they were hailed by a shout. There coming from the opposite direction was Helen.

"Now that was good timing," said Helen. "I forgot to bring Maisie and me a drink so had to go up town. I thought you might have already gone in."

"Well to be honest we went to visit the museum and stayed a bit longer than planned so I was worried you might have got here before us. Never mind we have both arrived at the same time. So this is Maisie, hello Maisie."

Maisie was feeling a little bit shy she had never met these people before and she was looking at Scruffy in amazement. He was so big, much bigger than her. Sam bent down and urged Scruffy to sit down so he was not towering over Maisie so much and gave her a pat and a cuddle.

"Hi Maisie, I am Sam and this is Scruffy. Scruffy say hello to Maisie, gently now."

Scruffy picked up his paw and placed it on top of Maisie's head. Maisie yelped in fright and shot back and then sidled back up to Scruffy's face as much as to say 'hi Scruffy' then stood by his side. Scruffy was very proud to have been accepted by this very beautiful girl that he wagged his tail furiously.

"Oh Maisie are you flirting with Scruffy? You usually do not like big dogs but he appears to have won you over straight away."

By this time the group were entering the castle grounds. Sam took Maisie's lead from Helen and shot off across the grass. Sam's Mum and Helen followed them. As soon as Sam was sure they were all safe from traffic he bent down and unclipped both dogs leads then hurtled across the grass towards the ruins. Despite the fact that Maisie was much smaller than Scruffy she gave chase to the boys yapping loudly. Every so often Scruffy glanced back to make sure she was managing to keep up before resuming the chase. Eventually the trio reached the ruins and balanced on low walls, scrambled over broken down walls and played hide and seek among the ruins. After about half an hour the trio came back to the adults who had found a flat stone to sit on and set out the picnic. Sam poured Scruffy and Maisie a drink then flopped down on the stone reaching out for a sandwich.

"Maisie did real well balancing on the walls but Scruffy could not get the hang of it and kept falling off," laughed Sam. "Maisie was not very good at hide and seek though as she kept giving herself away by barking or darting out as soon as she saw Scruffy. Despite that I think they both had fun and look at them now even drinking out of the bowl together."

"I know I can't believe my eyes. Maisie normally takes ages to make friends with other dogs. She does not hurt them, just will not leave my side unless she gets the scent of a rabbit then she has gone in a shot. Whereas today she went off with you and Scruffy and never looked back. Did you not have any problems Sam in keeping her with you?" asked Helen.

"None at all she never attempted to leave me or Scruffy. In fact she appeared almost glued to Scruffy's side all the time. Occasionally if Scruffy smelt at a rock or anything she would copy him but as soon as he moved off so did she."

"Well I never. I have had her for nearly 2 years and she has never behaved like this. You two must be a good influence," laughed Helen.

"My son and Scruffy, a good influence, that will be the day Helen," exclaimed Sam's Mum. "You have to be joking!"

By this time Scruffy and Maisie had finished having a drink and were laid side by side watching Sam avidly to see if they were going to do anything else. Sam had a few more sandwiches breaking his last in half to give to the dogs then had a chocolate biscuit and a drink.

"Thanks Mum I was hungry. Now come on let us go and do a bit more exploring you two."

Sam raced off both dogs close at his heels and was soon lost among the ruins. Sam's Mum collected up the remains of the picnic leaving Sam's drink and the dog bowl out as she was sure they would soon be back for another drink. Sure enough they all soon wandered back much more slowly and both dogs had a drink.

"Do you want another drink Sam?" asked his Mum.

"Please," answered Sam, "then I think we will call it a day here. We have managed to cover the whole of the ruins and I think both dogs will be happy to quietly walk back to the train."

"Scruffy might but I shouldn't think Maisie will do. She never walks quietly on the lead and always pulls me along. She seems to want to speed on to the next adventure."

"When we walk back I will have a go with both dogs walking together and see if she picks up any tips from Scruffy. He was the same when we first got him but now he behaves himself much better."

"Yes okay Sam," answered Helen, "I am happy to let you have a go or if you like we can swap dogs. Actually that might be better as it will give you all your strength to keep Maisie focused then."

"Yes maybe, we will just give it a go and see how it goes. Right Mum are we ready to set off? We do not want to miss the train. Have you and Helen worked out exactly which train we are catching back? Do not forget we have to walk from one station to the other. How long does it take to do that walk I seem to have forgotten?" asked Sam.

"Helen and I were trying to remember too. Helen thought an hour but I thought it was a bit more."

"Well we haven't done it for the last couple of years because the weather has not been very good and I think it was over an hour Mum but I was younger then and could not walk so fast so I imagine Helen maybe more accurate. Neither of the dogs will slow us down either as they are not puppies."

"No I remember doing it when Maisie was a puppy, I am not sure exactly how old she was but maybe only about 4 months. It took me ages as she kept laying down and we had to have several rests on benches or on rocks on the side of the path. I somehow do not think that will be a problem this time though unless you have managed to tire her out running around the castle grounds which I very much doubt," laughed Helen.

Sam's Mum picked up the picnic bag and Sam clipped on Maisie's lead and passed Scruffy's lead to Helen.

"Now Scruffy you be a good boy for Helen. Do not let me down now I have sung your praises."

Scruffy was a bit perplexed, what was happening, why wasn't Sam holding his lead not Maisie's lead? Did this mean Sam did not love him anymore, was he being sent off to live with Helen? Oh he did not want that, he loved living with Sam and his Mum. He pulled away from Helen and stuck himself tight to Sam's legs.

"Oh look Sam, Scruffy is frightened that you are handing him to Helen. You must remember he was handed back to the kennels a couple of times before he came to us. You must be stirring up bad memories for him," Sam's Mum told Sam.

"Oh Sam I did not realise Scruffy was a rescue dog and of course he has not been with you long. Here give me Maisie's lead and you take Scruffy. If we let both dogs walk side by side in the middle between us maybe Maisie will learn from Scruffy that way."

161

Sam passed Maisie's lead to Helen and took Scruffy's lead off Helen.

"You big softie Scruffy," exclaimed Sam giving his dog a big cuddle. "I will never give you away to anyone you belong to me and Mum now. I was only going to show Maisie how to behave on the lead like I have done you since you came to live with us. I am sorry I did not mean to bring back bad memories No worries come on let us show Maisie how good dogs behave when they are on a lead."

Sam, Scruffy, Helen. Maisie and Sam's Mum set off down the road towards the station. It did not take as long this time as it was all downhill. Maisie behaved well only trying to speed up a couple of times but Scruffy stopped her by taking a bit longer stride and getting his head in front of her and sort of gently pushing her back.

"Oh isn't Scruffy clever he is actually teaching Maisie what to do. I wonder if she will remember though when Scruffy is not there."

"Well if you just give her a little tug on the lead when she begins to pull, not too hard, just enough to remind her to concentrate, she probably will remember her lesson. It is how they learn in the wild. There has to be a leader of the pack and in Maisie's case that is you. I have taken that role with Scruffy. It is not always easy but if you stick at it eventually it will come."

"Oh thank you Sam you have been a real help. I will do as you suggest and let you know how we get on. Oh here we are at the station already. That did not take us long to get here. I will go and get the tickets Di as I travel for free and I can probably get you and Sam discount rates. How old are you Sam in case they ask me?" queried Helen.

"10 almost 11," answered Sam.

"We will meet you on the platform then Helen shall we?" asked Sam's Mum.

"Yes I will not be long," replied Helen.

162

Sam, Scruffy and Sam's Mum wandered on to the platform. The train was in but would not be setting off for a while.

"Do you want to look in the shop Sam? If so give me Scruffy to hold while you have a look."

"Yes thanks Mum I would like a look as I brought my pocket money in case I saw anything I fancied."

"Okay I will hold Scruffy and wait for Helen and Maisie," replied his Mum.

Sam slipped into the shop for a quick look around. His Mum collected fridge magnets and he wondered if there might be something different that he could get to say thank you for getting Scruffy and the wonderful camping trip they were all enjoying. Sam had a look at a few things before heading for the fridge magnets. There he found one that looked almost identical to Scruffy with just a simple 'thank you' sign hanging from the dog's mouth. It was absolutely perfect! Sam quickly paid for it and popped it into the pocket of his jeans. He would give it to his Mum on the very last day of his holiday next week. He emerged from the shop just as Helen and Maisie stopped next to Sam's Mum.

"Oh there you are Sam, was there nothing interesting?"

"No nothing Mum but thanks for looking after Scruffy anyway."

"No problem. Right are we all ready to get on the train?" asked Sam's Mum.

"Yes," answered Sam and Helen and the two dogs wagged their tails.

"Oh there you are," said Dave as he sauntered up to them all. "I have a nice empty carriage just up here where there is plenty of room for the dogs to spread out. Come with me."

He opened the door and produced a step from inside.

"Just in case Scruffy is still unsure," he said.

"Oh that is brilliant," exclaimed Sam. "Come on Scruffy up into the train please."

Sam used the step and entered the carriage Scruffy confidently stepping in just behind him. Next came Maisie as much as to say 'don't leave me Scruffy' then Helen and finally Sam's Mum.

"Wow that was so easy. I have to admit I was a bit apprehensive," Sam said. "Well done Scruffy, oh and you too Maisie," as Maisie's head nudged Sam.

"Well done all of you," laughed Dave. "Have a good journey and enjoy your walk."

"We will," they all chorused and settled down on the seats. As it happened both dogs wanted to be together so Sam sat in a seat where they could lay at his feet and Helen and Sam's Mum sat at the other side of the aisle.

"I am not sure if Maisie is besotted by Scruffy or Sam," she laughed.

"Maybe both," answered Sam's Mum. "They are both a bit special."

After giving both dogs a pat he settled down in his seat to wait for the train to set off. He wondered how Scruffy would react to the motion of the train when it was travelling but was sure between him and Maisie they would be able to reassure him. Meanwhile Scruffy was so happy he was laid at his master's feet with a beautiful lady by his side and Dave had just said 'have a good walk' so he now knew at the end of this train ride was a walk. What could be better he was sure he was in heaven!

Scruffy on the Train

Suddenly there was a slamming of doors then a loud whistle which made Scruffy nearly jump out of his skin but apart from just raising her head Maisie was content to continue to lay there so Scruffy pretended he was not bothered either. Suddenly there was a shudder and then the train began moving. Now this was a step too far. He jumped to his feet dislodging Maisie from his side and attempted to jump up on the seat next to Sam. What on earth was happening, it did not feel a bit like riding in a car?

"It is okay Scruffy we are quite safe it is only the train setting off. No you cannot sit on the seat next to me but if you put your paws on my knee you will be able to see out of the window and watch us leaving the station. Look Maisie is quite happy although she looks a bit unhappy that you are upset. See there we go past the car park along the railway lines that we crossed as we went to the castle and out into the country. Now settle back down on the floor next to Maisie and enjoy your first train ride. You had better get used to it because we have a ride on here every year. Now feel the rhythm of the wheels saying clackety clack. Come on now settle down we have quite a long way to go before we get off so you might as well have a snooze next to Maisie because you will need your energy once we get off because we have a long walk in front of us."

Scruffy gingerly lay down again and Maisie snuggled up close to him to try to reassure him. She had been travelling on steam trains since she was a puppy because Helen adored them. Today was even more special because she had met Sam and Scruffy who she just adored and they were going on her favourite walk over fields, and by the side of the railway lines from one station to the other. Helen and her usually had an ice cream before getting the train back to the car and she rather hoped they would still do that. Scruffy settled down a bit more and laid his head on his paws, Maisie reached out and gave him a lick on his nose which made him sneeze.

"Oh dear Scruffy did that tickle?" asked Sam. "Never mind Maisie is just trying to reassure you everything is all right."

"Well Maisie has been travelling on trains since she was 12 weeks old and could go out after her injections as a puppy so it is now nothing special or frightening to her and actually seems to be helping to keep Scruffy reassured. I am afraid I think my dog has actually fallen in love with your dog Sam," laughed Helen. "Look at her gazing at him with adoring eyes."

"Oh yuk, do not listen Scruffy we do not want any lovesick girls do we? Although I must admit she is a bit of a tomboy, or rather tomdog. She is no pretty lady afraid to get her feet dirty," replied Sam.

"I can assure you Maisie is no lady you can be sure of that Sam. Trampling through mud, splashing in puddles, chasing seagulls and waves at the seaside and rolling in anything dirty and smelly are her favourite pastimes," Helen replied. "Did you not work that out at the castle?"

"Well there were no puddles, mud, seagulls, waves or anything to roll in so she could not really get into mischief so I will just have to wait and see those antics for myself in time Helen. In the meantime I will reserve judgement on her suitability as a girlfriend for Scruffy. He is far too young to even consider such an idea yet," exclaimed Sam.

"It is okay Sam her love interest will remain in her head yet for a while as I have no intention of her having puppies for a long time, if ever," assured Helen.

"Good I am glad we have far too many new adventures as boys together before we begin to be interested in girls."

"Oh Sam," laughed his Mum. "Scruffy will not stop being happy to have adventures if he did become a father, it is not like humans. Anyway I think Maisie would make an excellent girlfriend and eventually Mum. Watching you all together though I fear for the sanity of anyone having a

166

puppy born to Scruffy and Maisie. With those two as parents life would be mayhem."

"Mum they would be beautiful puppies, so full of fun with these two as parents. Do not be so cruel. Maisie is so beautiful and Scruffy adores her. They could teach their children so much not that I agree to them having babies you understand," answered Sam in a shocked voice.

"I was not being cruel to either Scruffy or Maisie but you have to admit they both have boundless energy and a love of life so I actually think they would make an excellent couple," replied Sam's Mum.

"Like you and Steve would," Sam pointed out slyly.

"Well just to put all your minds at rest, relationships between Maisie and any male will not be resulting in puppies yet for a while but what is this about a Steve Di? Have you got a love interest?" asked Helen.

"No," answered Sam's Mum blushing. "Steve is our landlord, well I suppose to be honest, he is the landlord's son who farms the farm with his parents, our neighbours, and is a very good friend. Sam here thinks he wants to be a farmer and has decided that if Steve and me got together he would be able to realise this ambition. There is absolutely no chance of it ever becoming anything more so you can both just shut up."

"Ah Sam I detect a note of wistfulness in that reply. Is this Steve kind and handsome, if so you will have to introduce us. Maybe I could help with your ambitions if your Mum refuses," laughed Helen. "Although I know nothing about farming unlike your Mum but I could probably learn."

"Well my Aunty Jan who married Mum's young brother did not know anything about farming and she has slowly learnt and my Granny, Mum and Uncle Pete's Mum was also a town girl before she married Grandad so it can work. You live in the country already so I suppose it would not be such a big difference."

"Will the pair of you stop hatching a plan to entrap Steve into marriage, Helen I am surprised at you, and Sam

167

you have too much imagination. Now both of you shut up about Steve and marriage when he is not here to defend himself. For all I know he probably has no interest in getting married and is happy with his life as it is. As for me I have Sam to rear, although if he carries on I might just throttle him, and my career to develop which is a full time occupation thank you. Now drop the subject of boyfriends, girlfriends, marriage and most of all puppies and enjoy our train ride. We are about to pull into the station that we are camping near then it is not far to the next station where we get off."

"Oh dear Sam," laughed Helen. "I think we have rattled your Mum's cage. Di, calm down I have never seen you get so ruffled. You are usually so laid back what has got into you?"

"Wow Mum I am sorry I was only teasing you. Like Helen says, this is so not like you, what is the matter?"

"Sorry both of you I know I have never got so uptight about anything before I can usually see the funny side of most things. Maybe I am worried because if Steve were to get married then I guess him and his wife, or more likely his parents, would want to live in our cottage and I love it there and do not want to leave. It is exactly what happened to the people who rented my grandparents cottage, although to be fair they had decided they were leaving and had given in their notice when our Pete and Jan got married. Pete and Jan took over the cottage but this summer have exchanged with Mum and Dad and have moved into the farmhouse."

"I am sorry Mum but to be honest I do not think Steve even has a girlfriend or goes out anywhere except down to our house so I do not think you need not worry about that happening just yet. Oh here we are at the station and the other train is already in so I guess we will not have long to wait until we leave the station again."

"No," said Helen. "Everything appears to be running on time today up to press. Mind you there is plenty of time for that to all change before we want to come back tonight."

"Yes," laughed Sam's Mum, "These trains are not renowned for running on time but that is the beauty of them."

The train stopped briefly at the station and both Scruffy and Maisie got up for a stretch. Scruffy had a look out of the window and was surprised to see they were at the station they had visited on Tuesday night.

"It is okay Scruffy we are going on further. No need to get worried we are going on a walk like I promised you. Next time the train stops we will be getting off."

"Do not say that Sam," exclaimed Helen, "in case there is anyone waiting at the halt in the forest."

"Oh sorry yes I had forgotten that possible stop, although to be fair all the times I have travelled on this train I only remember stopping there once."

"Yes I know it is very rare but possible all the same," Helen answered.

As there was no-one waiting on the platform to board the train or anyone wanting to get off, the train soon moved out of the station again on its journey. As it happened Helen's fears were unfounded and no-one wanted to take the opportunity to have the train stop at the halt in the forest. The dogs had returned to their snoozing and Sam to gazing out at the passing scenery. Helen and Di were quietly chatting putting down the foundations for a solid friendship for the future. It seemed no time until the train was pulling into the station. Helen clipped Maisie's lead on and Sam did the same for Scruffy. Helen led the way off the train with Maisie hanging back to ensure Scruffy was following.

"It is okay Maisie, do not worry Scruffy is coming too," said Sam.

Soon the little party were assembled on the platform and left the station to walk up into the village. Suddenly Scruffy came face to face with a sheep. What on earth was it doing in the middle of the grass verge and then his eyes widened further. It was not only one sheep but a whole load of them! Some were grazing on the grass at the side

169

of the road, others were laid chewing their cud in the sunshine. There was even one that he could see following a couple walking up the road. What on earth was going on? Sheep were supposed to be in fields behind fences. Well they were at Steve's farm anyway but these sheep were just wandering about in a village. How on earth did they stay in one place with no fences to keep them in? He looked around, no there was no fences as far as he could see anywhere except around people's houses. He hung back a bit, he was not too sure of sheep to begin with behind the fence in the field, but here when they could actually walk right up to you, now that was just plain scary!

"Why are you trying to walk behind me Scruffy?" asked Sam. "Oh I see you have spotted the sheep. It is okay they live here, free to roam in the village. They will not harm you as they are used to people and dogs. As long as we do not bother them they will just stay where they are."

Scruffy was not so sure. They looked very scary to him. They had such big horns on their heads and did not look a bit like the ones on Steve's farm. Sam must have read his mind as he asked,

"Mum why are these sheep so very different from Steve's sheep. I know they are still sheep and they have always looked like this but why are they so different? They are even a different colour with their black faces."

"Well it is all to do with the breed. These are what we call moor sheep or to give them their proper name Swaledale, I think. They are specially bred to capitalise on their homing skills or what we call 'haafing' skill. This is to do with the fact that they have been bred in this area for generations so will remain here and not stray despite there being no fences," answered his Mum.

"Cool that is so clever. You mean they do not stray, ever. What happens if they do?" asked Sam.

"Well if you look at them they have a coloured mark on their back. This denotes who they belong to, in other words, which farmer. Each farmer has their own mark and so even if the sheep do get mixed up when the farmers gather them for shearing or dipping they can sort them out. Have a look around and see if you can spot any sheep with different markings as we walk around the village and then on our walk," suggested Sam's Mum.

"Okay Mum I will in the meantime come on Scruffy keep up."

Scruffy finally came out from behind Sam's legs and walked at his side but he kept a watchful eye on the sheep. Eventually he realised that in fact the sheep were not even glancing his way, never mind going to attack him, so decided to do the same to them and just enjoy the walk with Sam and Maisie and the two grown-ups. The group finally reached the heart of the village passing a pub and then a garage before finally arriving at the shops or rather a few shops as there was only 3 or 4.

"Do you want to have a look in the shops Sam?" asked his Mum, "or you Helen as I am happy to hold the dogs then one of you can take over the dog sitting while I have a look."

"Yes please," answered both Sam and Helen.

They passed Scruffy and Maisie's leads to Sam's Mum before entering the first shop. Sam's Mum sat down on a bench nearby to wait for them enjoying the sunshine and tranquillity of the village. Soon Sam was back having looked at all the shops.

"Off you go Mum I will look after the dogs. Helen is still browsing in the shops so go and join her."

"Okay thanks Sam I will. See you soon."

Sam took his Mum's place on the bench and took the leads off her.

"Okay you two settle down again we are not ready to set off yet. Mum and Helen are still looking in the shops. I am just going to sit here in the sunshine and wait for them."

Just at that moment a couple of sheep ambled past the bench that Sam was sitting on and stopped to see if they were eating anything. Maisie sat up and pressed herself a bit nearer to Sam but with a yelp Scruffy shot under the bench and squashed himself as close to the wall as he could. If he could have made a hole in the wall he would have preferred to have been inside the shop with Helen and Sam's Mum.

"Now Scruffy there is no need to be scared. You are supposed to be looking after me not hiding under the bench. The sheep are just checking us out mainly to see if we have anything to eat because a lot of people actually feed them titbits but also sometimes crumbs and crusts fall off their sandwiches. Now come on Scruffy, you can crawl out a bit and see. Oh that is okay they have moved off now when they have seen we are not eating anything."

Scruffy crawled out a bit from his position tight against the wall but he could not actually see where the sheep were so he crawled a bit further out. He lay flat on his tummy and peered round Sam's legs. No there was still no evidence of any sheep looking at him! He crawled out further and could see the two sheep walking away from where Sam and Maisie were sitting and he was hiding under the bench. He suddenly realised that he had really shown himself up in front of Maisie. There she was calmly sat leaning against Sam's legs and he, Scruffy, was cowering under a bench, hiding. He quickly scrambled out and shook the dust and gravel out of his coat and promptly sat down next to Sam on Sam's other side.

"Oh you want to protect me now the sheep have gone do you Scruffy?" laughed Sam. "Are you afraid that Maisie has shown you up as she sat at my side while you cowered under the bench! It is okay Maisie has been coming here regularly since she was a puppy whereas this is your first time. Both Maisie and I understand, do not worry although next time try and be a bit braver. Now look here comes another sheep to investigate us so try and sit still and see what happens."

Scruffy pressed himself tight to Sam's legs but despite trembling all over he managed to stay where he was. The sheep ambled past and began nibbling the grass at the side of the path.

"There Scruffy, see the sheep really do not take any notice of us at all. Well done you showed how brave you could be."

Just at that moment Sam's Mum and Helen emerged from the shop.

"Everything okay Sam," asked his Mum. "We are finished here shall we head off on our walk?"

"Yes I think that might be a good idea as Scruffy has had a massive fright as two sheep came right up to us sitting on the bench and Scruffy tried to burrow through the wall under the seat into the shop. Maisie just calmly sat there and stared out the sheep. She never said a word."

"Well she is getting much braver now," answered Helen. "She used to hide behind my legs whenever one came by which was fine if I was sitting down or even stood talking to people but could be a bit a bit tricky if we were walking. She will still tend to change sides to be furthest away from the sheep when we are walking down the village which is fine if she crosses behind me but she often crosses in front of me and nearly trips me up. The funniest thing is if there are sheep at equal distance from us as then she does not know where she wants to be and keeps criss crossing from side to side and I have to keep changing the lead from hand to hand. I am real proud of her if she managed to stay by your side. Poor Scruffy though must have had the fright of his life. You have to remember that Maisie has been coming to this village since she was a tiny puppy and we have sheep in the fields all around our cottage so she has been encountering them all her life. She does not see many cows so I am unsure how she would react to them. Have you sheep on the farm next to where you live Sam?"

"Well yes there are sheep at the farm but they are away in the fields away from the farmyard at the moment. Steve will bring them into the fields nearer the house once the grass has grown back after making the hay and silage.

173

Also he was telling me the other day that some of the fields have been planted with kale and other winter crops for the sheep to eat during the winter months. He was also telling me that the sheep stay in the fields close to the farmyard while they have small lambs so Steve and his parents can look after them easier. My Grandad and Uncle Pete do the same," Sam said.

"Oh I see well the area around my cottage is mainly sheep and corn so I guess that is why most of the fields have sheep in. Does Steve have any cows on his farm?" asked Helen.

"Yes he does have some cows but they are like the sheep, away in the far fields at present. He was telling me that they will soon be bringing the cows and their young calves, the ones that were born in the spring, back from the hills as it is time to take the calves away from their mothers and put them in the sheds. Those cows will stay out over winter as they are a hardy breed and do not have their babies again until spring but the other cows who are due to have babies soon will be coming into the sheds as it is easier to look after them inside. He was saying that these cows have babies in October and early November, the sheep have their babies in late January and through February and then the other cows March and early April so we will soon have lots of baby animals around the farm. Steve only has a few pigs, well 5 to be precise, that have babies but that means there are usually baby piglets about and one of the goats had two babies about 3 weeks ago. Steve has another 3 goats who have babies at different times during the summer too. Steve was saying last week that now I am growing up I can soon help him at his busy times and I am going to work for him when we get back aren't I Mum?" asked Sam.

"Yes you start work on Saturday helping to bring in the straw into the sheds ready for the winter then I imagine Steve and his Dad might start ploughing the land or they might leave the ploughing until spring like Grandad and Uncle Pete do. I imagine the land is better around us than

174

where I grew up, although I am not sure," answered his Mum.

"No Steve said they just spread the land with manure in autumn then plough in spring Mum. He said it fed the land better if it was left on over the winter as there was a lot of straw in their manure," Sam explained. "That is why he can have a few days off if he wants around half term and he is looking forward to meeting Uncle Pete and Aunty Jan when they come to stay."

"Oh dear," laughed Sam's Mum. "You, Uncle Pete and Steve together along with Scruffy could be a disaster. What are you all planning on doing?"

"Well football is top of the list of course, then Steve said he would enjoy showing Uncle Pete around the farm. He promised we could all go and look at the land he owns if Uncle Pete was interested. That will be cool as I have only ever seen the farmyard area. Do you think Uncle Pete would be interested Mum?"

"Yes he would, like me and your Grandad, farming is in his blood and he would be real interested to see how Steve farms in contrast to him although to be honest the way you have described it Steve appears to do things in an almost carbon copy of the way we do it. I thought they might have done things different as the land is more flat and fertile around us," Sam's Mum said in a surprised tone.

"Sounds as if you and Steve might have more in common than you thought Di," observed Helen.

"Yes maybe, who knows! I am sure my brother will soon winkle out any information he wants and incorporate new ideas if he thinks they would work at home," laughed Sam's Mum. "He is forever on the lookout for new practises that will either lessen the workload or enhance the profits as all farmers should. It has in the past caused a bit of tension between Dad and him but I think it will be better now that Pete is taking full responsibility for the farm and Dad is semi-retiring."

"I did not think farmers ever retired," exclaimed Helen surprised.

"Well they seldom give up completely and are always on hand to help at busy times but certainly on my Mum's insistence they are going to ease back and give Pete and Jan some space to develop their own methods. Mum and Dad will remain on hand to help them when they need it especially during the latter stages of Jan's pregnancy and in the early days of motherhood. That is why I will suggest Mum and Dad come to stay with us straight after half term when Pete and Jan have gone back. I know Mum would like to spend 2 or 3 weeks with us as she wants to explore the Yorkshire Dales but she has yet to persuade Dad to stay away from his beloved farm that long. Then when they go back it would be time to help Jan to prepare for Christmas and New Year."

"Do you and Sam go to your parents for Christmas?" asked Helen.

"Yes we do or always have done when they lived in the farmhouse but there is only 2 bedrooms at the cottage so Jan suggested Sam, me and Scruffy should stay at the farmhouse as usual with her and Pete. We will have to discuss it a bit more yet but we have plenty of time."

"Wow do you mean we can stay with Uncle Pete and Aunty Jan at Christmas?" asked Sam. "Listen Scruffy that would be fabulous wouldn't it as we will have much more space? We have never stayed with Uncle Pete before Mum have we?"

"Well no because they lived in the small cottage that now Granny and Grandad live in so we stayed at the farmhouse but we used to go to Uncle Pete's too," answered his Mum.

"Yes I know and please do not get me wrong Mum, I love Granny and Grandad, but I was very worried about us staying there with Scruffy, not that Granny and Grandad would have been cross if Scruffy knocked anything over but Scruffy could have got upset. We can still go and spend whole days there over the holidays but it will be much better for me and Scruffy if we have the big farmhouse to spread out in and I am sure Grandad will still be up at the farm a lot."

"It looks as though you are not going to have much say in it Di," laughed Helen. "How will Pete and Jan feel about a young boy and his boisterous dog invading their home?"

"Oh I am sure Pete will be in his element he loves Sam so much and I am sure Scruffy will worm himself into his heart like he has mine and Sam's. The only problem we might have is that Pete might revert back to his childhood and cause as much havoc as Sam and Scruffy. It is Jan I feel most sorry for coping with them all and being pregnant too although when I talked to her just before we came away she said it would be fun and a good learning curve for when she had her own child to cope with. It just worries me that she was not brought up on a farm and that she has not seen first-hand how much havoc my son and his dog can cause at our house let alone in the middle of a working farm. Add the excitement of Christmas into the mix and you can understand my worries."

"Mum, Scruffy and I are not that bad and we are getting better all the time," Sam said horrified that his Mum was worried that he and Scruffy would behave badly at his Uncle's house. "I promise we will try to be good and not play football anywhere near the house. I do not want to frighten Aunty Jan like it did Granny when the football ended up in her washing up bowl!"

"What," exclaimed Helen! "How on earth did the football end up in the washing up bowl?"

"Well the ball broke the kitchen window and ended up in the washing up bowl when my Mum was stood at the sink washing up," laughed Sam's Mum. "Mind you Sam has I think, helped by my brother, broken every pane of glass in the greenhouse over the years too so nothing is really safe to be honest."

"Oh I love the image I am conjuring up in my mind of your Mum stood at the sink and the football landing with a splash in the soapy water amid a shower of glass."

"I suppose it does sound like something out of a cartoon picture," laughed Sam's Mum.

While this conversation had been taking place the group had moved off, away from the shops and headed through the village to the start of the footpath that would take them through fields and woods and along the disused train track that connected the two villages. As soon as it was safe to do so Helen and Sam released the two dogs off their leads so they could explore on their own and Sam followed the dogs to ensure they behaved themselves. Di and Helen continued chatting trusting that Sam would look after the dogs. Periodically Maisie would bound back to check her owner was still close at hand before hurtling back to Sam and Scruffy.

"Maisie is having a wonderful time with Sam and Scruffy. Thank you for asking me to come and join you Di," Helen said at one point.

"No thank you for joining us it has given me the chance to chat with another grown up. As you will have realised I would have been walking along on my own most of the time. I love my work but it can get a bit lonely at times especially as Sam is growing up and now does not need me so much."

"Yes I know," answered Helen. "I also love my job but like you I can sometimes get a bit lonely too. That is why I try to do at least one day a week in summer on the railway. I do not have that luxury in winter though and can often go weeks at a time never having the chance to chat to anyone. You are so lucky having such a good relationship with your parents and brother."

"Do you have any brothers or sisters Helen?" asked Di.

"No I am an only child and my Dad died when I was very young. My mother has suffered with mental illness problems all my life so I have no family to speak off. My Mum now spends her life in and out of different care and although I visit her a few times a year most of the time she has no idea who I am."

"Oh poor you, well you are welcome to come and visit me and Sam whenever you need company and join in with all our crazy family times. My Mum and Dad will just gather you up and treat you like another daughter if I know them and Pete will probably tease you constantly. What do you do for Christmas and New Year then normally?"

"I just stay home and often work all the holidays. The other public holidays are not too bad as the railway is operating then but not at Christmas. It is not quite so lonely since I got Maisie as we can go for walks if the weather is good and curl up together over the fire if it is not."

"Right leave it with me and I will see if I can sort something out. I cannot have you spending the festive season alone. In the meantime come over and meet my brother and his wife when they come to stay with us during Sam's half term and then spend time with us when my Mum and Dad come to stay after they go home. We are planning on having a bonfire party on the 5th November as we hope my parents will be with us and Dad and Sam could build a bonfire and Guy. I will talk to Steve to see if he will be cutting his hedges or has any spare wood about the farm. I thought it might be nice to ask Steve and his parents to join us too. Mum will no doubt help me with the food and Steve's Mum might want to contribute. Scruffy will no doubt be helping Sam and his Grandad and you and Maisie can fit in where you feel most comfortable."

"Oh please let me help you and your Mum in the kitchen. I love to cook but do not do much when there is only me. Maisie, I imagine, will be hanging on to Scruffy's tail if she can but that will be fine as Sam seems well able to cope. As for Christmas though I cannot intrude as Christmas is for families."

"Well as from now on you are my long lost sister that I never knew I had so that cancels out that excuse," laughed

179

Di. "I promise you will just slot into our family, both you and Maisie, although I warn you we are quite crazy. We always have lots of friends round and Mum and Dad have always encouraged me and Pete to bring our friends home too. Unfortunately Sam's Dad discouraged me from doing that and did not even want family around so I slowly lost my friends. After he died and I moved into the cottage all my time was spent bringing up Sam and getting my career off the ground and I had not realised how much I missed the company of friends until today. From now on we are going to spend at least one day a month together maybe more during the winter months when you are not at the railway."

"That suits me fine," laughed Helen. "I never had friends and certainly could not have them come to the house because Mum was never well enough to cope so my childhood was very isolated. Even when I worked as a social worker I never built a relationship with any colleagues so I continued to be a loner. After getting Maisie I think I realised how nice it was to have a friend, even a doggy one, and after today I do not think I want to continue with my isolated life. Thank you and I will look forward to meeting your brother and parents and spending time with you, Sam and Scruffy and Maisie will certainly agree. You 3 are welcome to visit us too when you have time although Sam will soon be back at school now won't he?"

"Yes he is going to work at the farm from Saturday and goes back to school next Thursday. I have a new commission that I need to get my head round for the next couple of weeks but we will stay in touch by telephone and sort something out when we have space in our diaries."

"I have a publication deadline to meet so I cannot take time out for a couple of weeks or so either but after that we can sort out a date to meet up."

The group ambled along content in each other's company until they arrived at the station.

"Maisie and I always have an ice cream here before we get on the train for the return journey. Do you 3 want one too?" asked Helen.

"I will get the ice creams in Helen for us all as you got our train tickets. Sam leave Scruffy with Helen and Maisie and come and help me please."

"Okay Mum, Scruffy stay with Helen and Maisie and then you can have an ice cream."

Sam passed Scruffy's lead to Helen as both dogs had needed to be put on their leads before crossing the road near the station and Scruffy laid down next to Maisie although he kept a close eye on his master to make sure he was not going to be abandoned. Soon Sam and his Mum were back with the ice creams and Helen held Maisie's for her while Sam held Scruffy's in one hand and ate his own using his other hand. The 3 humans were content to rest on the bench and the two dogs on the ground at their feet. Soon all the ice creams were eaten and the train soon pulled into the station. Scruffy showed no sign of nerves this time and confidently jumped on the train without needing a step after Maisie and Helen. The dogs settled down together on the floor without any prompting and Sam joined them on the seat. Sam's Mum and Helen sat opposite each other to continue their conversation. The dogs were soon asleep snoring softly and Sam relaxed into his seat. He had experienced such a fun day today looking after the two dogs and was pleased to see his Mum and Helen chatting so effortlessly. The train chugged out of the station, Scruffy merely opening an eye when they set off, but he soon settled straight back to sleep next to his new best friend and master and dreamed the whole journey long about all the good things that had happened today and every day since he came to live with Sam and his Mum.

Scruffy, Maisie and Sam Go Exploring

It seemed no time at all until the train reached its final destination for the day. Sam passed Maisie's lead to Helen before jumping off the train with Scruffy.

"Are you parked in the station car park Helen?" asked Sam's Mum.

"Yes are you?" answered Helen.

"Yes we are. I think Sam and I will go and get fish and chips for tea as then I do not have to wash up back at the camp."

"What a great idea I think we will do the same," replied Helen.

"Are you in a rush to get home Helen, because if not, do you want to come back to our camp with us? Sam, Scruffy and I are just going for a walk further into the forest tonight so Sam and Scruffy can play in the stream we know as they have not got wet today so they will be feeling sad. You and Maisie can join us and then we will be lighting the camp fire and toasting marshmallows when we get back," suggested Sam's Mum.

"Thank you Di that would be wonderful. No, we are not in a rush to get home and the offer of toasted marshmallows and a camp fire sounds bliss. Maisie will enjoy frolicking in a stream with Sam and Scruffy too and I have a couple of old towels in the car to dry her with after she gets wet. We will follow you to the fish shop first then back to where you are camping."

"Great, okay you two get in the car please," instructed Sam's Mum.

As it happened Helen, unbeknown to her, had in fact parked next to Sam's Mum so both cars left the car park together. They were soon at the fish and chip shop and purchased their tea. Sam's Mum and Helen allowed both dogs to have some fish for their tea too.

"We have plenty of biscuits that both dogs can have when we get back to camp Helen so do not worry about Maisie she can have tea with Scruffy."

"Wow Scruffy this day just gets better and better," breathed Sam. "Maisie is coming back with us. What a wonderful day this will have been."

Sam, his Mum and Helen were just as hungry as the dogs so everyone soon finished their tea and set off back to camp. At the clearing everyone piled out of the cars and Sam raced off to change his jeans for shorts so he, Scruffy and Maisie could splash and paddle in the stream. Maisie was not going to be left behind and her and Scruffy followed Sam. Sam dived into his tent quickly followed by Scruffy then Maisie.

"Blimey," Sam exclaimed. "There is hardly enough room for Scruffy and me in the tent without you joining us Maisie. Okay Maisie lay on Scruffy's bed while I swap my jeans for shorts and get my old trainers on. I cannot paddle in the stream without trainers on as the pebbles hurt my feet."

Both dogs lay on Scruffy's bed while Sam changed then tried to get out of the tent together and got stuck in the doorway. Both Sam's Mum and Helen were watching and burst out laughing.

"Well Helen you were just saying that Maisie, Sam and Scruffy were inseparable. Now you can see just how inseparable Scruffy and Maisie are as they are both trying to get out of the tent together."

"I can see," laughed Helen. "Inseparable twins springs to mind. Okay Sam are you ready? Maisie do you need a drink before we go off exploring?"

Maisie ignored Helen and set off after Sam and Scruffy.

"I guess the answer is no," laughed Helen. "Come on Di or we are going to get left out of this adventure. How do you manage to keep up with Scruffy and Sam, their energy is boundless?"

"Oh I do not even try now. Sam is very sensible and looks after Scruffy well so I just kind of oversee their antics to keep a watchful eye on them."

Helen and Di wandered out of the clearing and could see Sam, Scruffy and Maisie walking down the road. They could hear Sam telling the dogs something and both dogs were listening intently to him but Helen and Di could not actually tell what he was saying. It was not too long before Sam veered off the road and both dogs quickly followed him. By the time Helen and Di had joined them they were all splashing about in a beautiful, clear, clean stream. Both boy and dogs were totally drenched but having a wonderful time. Sam was using his hands to splash water on to the dogs' faces and they were trying to catch it.

"Well I guess that is one way to get the dogs to have a drink," laughed Helen.

Just then Scruffy got a bit too excited and tried to get the water before Sam threw it over him and bumped into Sam's chest. Over went Sam, sitting down in the stream with a huge splash. Scruffy landed on his chest and Maisie followed as she did not want to miss the fun. Sam tried to get up but slipped on the pebbles and fell back down again this time landing full length in the stream. He came up laughing wiping the water from his face with two dogs busy trying to lick him dry. Sam decided he might as well stay sat down so began to splash the dogs again from this position.

"We may as well sit down on the bank of the stream Helen as this game could continue for quite a long while knowing my two and by the looks of things Maisie is quite happy with the game too."

"Yes she is having a super time. Life with just me after today is going to be pretty boring I think."

"No she will be fine once you are home again but she will quickly pick up where she left off whenever she is with Sam and Scruffy. I wonder how Scruffy will manage next week when Sam goes back to school. It will take him a while to settle into a new routine, just me and him during the day especially as I have a large piece of commission work that I will need to concentrate on."

"What is the new work you have booked?" asked Helen.

"Oh a series of books about a fairy and all her adventures. Initially I am working on the first 12 books which are already written but the author is still working on others and thinks there may be as many as 20 in the series. I need to keep the main fairy character throughout the books, changing her clothes to keep her fresh and also changing the background to portray what is happening or where she is in that particular story."

"Wow that is so interesting but will be a huge challenge too. You need to make the illustrations new and fresh without altering the character's features. I really admire your talent and imagination to be able to bring the written word to life."

"Yes it will be a challenge although I cannot change the basic fairy design that I submitted to the author in the first place as that was the one she chose. I actually submitted 5 different designs for her to choose from as she had approached me, through her agent, asking me to design her fairy. She sent me excerpts from each book, just a paragraph, so I could picture the scenes better. I drew 5 different fairies, although the one she chose was in fact my favourite, and then after the contract was signed I got the finished manuscripts to read and digest before I started the work proper. I have managed to do several sketches whilst I have been here which I will use to complete the full illustrations when I get home. If you come to visit you can have a look at some of my completed work."

"Oh that would be fantastic. Like I have said before give me 2 or 3 weeks to get my manuscript to the publishers and Maisie and me will be out to visit you," answered Helen.

Just at that moment a boy and two dripping wet dogs emerged from the stream. Both dogs shook the excess water from their coats and Sam pushed his hair out of his eyes.

"I think we have had enough Mum so can we head back to the tents. If you give me the car keys I will get the towels from the beach out of the car and dry me, Scruffy and Maisie off then put on some dry clothes and light the camp fire."

"That sounds like a good plan Sam. Helen and I will put the kettle on for hot chocolate. Is that alright Helen, you can have tea or coffee if you would prefer?"

"No hot chocolate sounds yummy. It is ages since I sat round a camp fire eating toasted marshmallows and drinking hot chocolate. In fact to be honest I am not sure if I have ever done any of those things."

"What, not done them together or not done any of them?" chorused Sam and his Mum.

"I have never sat round a camp fire nor had toasted marshmallows since I was a child. I cannot actually remember the last time I had hot chocolate," answered Helen.

"Oh my goodness you are in for a treat then," laughed Sam's Mum. "Here is the car keys, make sure you are all well dried off so you do not get cold Sam."

"Yes I will do Mum. Come on you two, back to the car."

Sam, Scruffy and Maisie set off down the road, Sam squelching in his trainers. As Helen and his Mum arrived at the clearing he was just putting the wet towels back into the car.

"I will not be long Mum until I get the fire going. No Scruffy and Maisie stay out of the tent this time as you are both still a bit wet. I will not be long stay with Mum and Helen."

Both dogs wandered over to the dog dishes and Sam's Mum put some clean water down in one dish and filled the other with biscuits. Scruffy and Maisie took it in turns to choose a biscuit out of the dish before eating it. Soon Sam was back from the tent and collected the matches to light the fire. He quickly built up a layer of dry grass, then a layer of small twigs followed by a layer of larger twigs. He lit the dry grass and kept feeding the fire until it was burning nicely. By this time both dogs had finished eating and came and sat down on the grass next to Sam. Helen and Sam's Mum finished making the hot chocolate and brought the drinks, chairs, toasting forks and marshmallows over to the fire. Helen and Di sat on the chairs while Sam was happy to lounge on the grass with the dogs. Helen and Sam's Mum toasted the marshmallows and passed them to Sam. Neither dog woke up to even think about asking for a marshmallow. Once all the sweets were gone and the camp fire burnt to ash Helen got up from her seat and took the empty mugs and chairs back to the table ready to wash.

"We just rinse the mugs Helen in the evening then wash them properly at breakfast. Thanks for your company I have really enjoyed it."

"Thank you Di and Sam and especially you Scruffy for our wonderful day. Maisie and me will have to think real hard to do something as good when you visit us. Come on Maisie time to go home say goodbye to Scruffy and Sam. Do not be sad we will see them again real soon."

Maisie got up and stretched, nuzzled Scruffy's side, gave Sam a lick on his arm and wandered off after her mistress. With a quick look back she jumped into the car and settled down again. With a quick goodbye from Helen the car left the clearing and Sam and Scruffy made their way to the tent.

"Goodnight Mum, see you in the morning."

"Goodnight Sam and you too Scruffy, see you in the morning," answered Sam's Mum.

Sam and Scruffy crawled into the tent, Scruffy burrowing into his sleeping bag and Sam quickly undressing and climbing into his own. Soon the pair were fast asleep.

Home Again

Sam and Scruffy slept through the night without waking up even once. In the morning they emerged to find Sam's Mum just putting the kettle on.

"What do you need me to do first Mum this morning?" asked Sam.

"Well you can pack away the swing ball game and get rid of the stones that we used for the sides of the fire. I imagine they will be cold by now and then if you have time before breakfast pack your clothes up and put your bag and sleeping bag in the car."

"Okay Mum I will do. Come on Scruffy let us take the swing ball game to pieces and put it in the car."

Scruffy laid and watched Sam put the game away and then Sam tested the stones with his hands to ensure they were cold enough to move. They were cold so he picked them up and carried them over to the side of the clearing. He got a stick and spread the heap of ashes about too. By this time his Mum had the breakfast ready so Sam sat up to the table and ate it while it was still hot. Scruffy had his bacon with a few biscuits then laid down again to see what his master was going to do next. Sam and his Mum quickly washed and dried the pots before storing them away with all the left-over food. Sam collapsed the table and chairs whilst his mum dismantled the cooker. The pair worked steadily together until there was just the cooking tent left and then they both went to their tents to pack up their clothes and sleeping bags. Once the clothes and beds were stowed in the car Sam and his Mum took down the tents one by one and packed them into the car.

"Okay Sam we need to check over our camp site to make sure it is completely clean and tidy and then we are ready to set off for home. Have you had a good time?"

"Definitely Mum, this has been the best camping trip ever but it will be nice to get home too. I am looking forward to a nice hot shower before Steve comes for tea. It will be great to tell him all about our trip. It was fun having Helen and Maisie along too wasn't it?"

"Yes it was. Helen is going to come and visit us later next month then she is coming again to meet Uncle Pete and Aunty Jan and to the bonfire party. She has no family as her Mum is very sick and does not even know Helen when she visits so we are going to adopt her into our family."

"Cool so I will have an Aunty Helen too will I?" queried Sam.

"Well maybe not, you can just carry on calling her Helen but I hope she will eventually look on us as family."

"Well we are happy to have Maisie with us aren't we Scruffy?"

Scruffy just wagged his tail. Soon the camp site had been checked and declared clean and tidy and they all piled into the car for the return journey. Scruffy and Sam were so tired they both dozed most of the way home and Sam's Mum listened to the radio as it quietly played in the background. Eventually they turned off the main road and down the lane to their house. Sam undid his seat belt and stretched and Scruffy lifted his head to see why the car had stopped.

"Okay you two sleepy heads we are home. Sam go and unlock the door so we can get the car unloaded. It makes it easier to unpack if we can put things straight into either the house or garage. I will open the garage doors."

"Okay Mum, come on Scruffy let us go and get the door opened. Mum I might as well take my bag in with me as it is here by my feet."

"Good idea Sam," answered his Mum.

Sam was soon back and both him and his Mum worked together to empty the car and store the tents, cooking equipment and games into the garage. The coats and boots were put away in the porch and the sleeping bags, blankets and bags with clothes in brought into the house.

"Put the wet towels from you and Scruffy near the washing machine and any dirty clothes that you can find and then take your bag upstairs Sam and unpack your clothes. I will load the washing machine before we both get ourselves a warm shower and put on some clean clothes. The casserole smells real yummy that Steve's Mum has sent down so I hope Steve is not too long before he comes for tea as it is making me feel very hungry."

"I do not think you will have long to wait Mum," laughed Sam. "I can see him striding down the field now."

"Oh good off you go then and get your shower. No Scruffy, you need not go with Sam this time, get yourself settled in your bed for a bit while Sam and I get showered and some clean clothes on. Oh hi Steve, we have just got the car unloaded and Sam is going for a shower and then I will follow him. That casserole smells fantastic say thanks to your Mum for me later please."

"Well actually I made it under Mum's watchful eye this morning then I popped it down into your Aga. I was hoping to have got the animals fed and back down to help you unload the car but you got back sooner than I expected."

"To be honest Steve, Sam is now getting to be a real help so we got set off at a reasonable time and there was not as much traffic as there usually is. I guess going that bit later in the summer at the end of the holidays instead of, as we usually do, the beginning made a difference. It was not as busy on the train either," commented Sam's Mum.

"Did you have a good time though despite it being later in the holidays," asked Steve.

"Yes we had a great time and the weather stayed fine. Can't you tell as Scruffy is completely zonked out?"

"Oh my goodness so he is. Has he not slept while you have been away?"

"Oh both him and Sam have slept, well to be honest I do not think either slept much the first night, but since then it has been fine but they have done so much over the days while we have been away they are both tired out. A good night's sleep tonight in their own beds and they will be ready for work again tomorrow."

"Good as Dad and I are looking forward to having them with us and Mum is so excited. She says it will be as good as having a grandson to spoil."

"Well Sam is so excited to be having the chance to learn about farming. He has decided he wants to be a farmer when he leaves school so he is looking forward to the experience. I took him to the farming museum while we were away, I had not been there myself for years, so he will no doubt be bombarding your Dad and Mum with questions over the next few days and then my Mum and Dad when they come to stay."

"Oh are your parents coming to stay? I knew your brother and his wife were but I did not know your parents were too. Who is looking after the farm then if they are all coming?" asked Steve.

"Oh no they are not all coming together. Pete and Jan are coming first, Saturday until Tuesday then going home on Wednesday. Mum and Dad will probably arrive on the Friday so that Sam gets a few days with his grandparents before he goes back to school. We are hoping to have a bonfire party on the 5th November too. I know it is a school night but if we start it off earlier Sam can still go to bed at a reasonable time. Is there any chance you might have some spare wood around by then? I thought I would mention it now so you can get organised. Sam's Grandad will be on hand to help him build it."

"I know that Dad and I will be trimming the hedges after we get the harvest in and the cows brought down from the hills for the winter so I am sure we can easily amass enough wood to build a nice big bonfire. I will tell Sam to mention it to my Mum too as she can usually be relied on to find some old clothes to fill with straw for the Guy. She always did for me anyway. Dad and I will help Sam and his Grandad do not worry."

"Oh thanks Steve we would like you and your parents to come down and I have invited my friend Helen to join us. I know that Sam has a couple of friends he wants to invite and I will extend the invitation to the boys' parents too."

"Mum will love to be part of it and I am sure she will want to help with the food too. She always says she misses all the fun things we used to do when I was a boy so she will be in her element. Dad too, but on a more practical level. I will take over the responsibility of buying the fireworks too if you concentrate on the food."

"Fantastic Steve thank you so much now here comes Sam. I will just go and have a shower and put on clean clothes. I will leave Sam to tell you all that we have been doing while we have been away."

"Hi Steve, Mum do you want me and Steve to set the table while you have your shower and shall I give Scruffy his tea?" asked Sam.

"Good idea Sam."

Scruffy pricked up his ears and raised his head at the mention of his tea.

"Yes Scruffy," Sam laughed. "You heard right I will get your tea first I promise."

Sam got Scruffy his tea and refilled his water bowl. He was telling Steve about teaching Scruffy to get on the train, playing with the swing ball, cricket and all the other frightening things he, Scruffy, had encountered during the camping trip. By the time he had finished and the pair had set the table Steve was laughing so much he was doubled over. This was the scene Sam's Mum walked onto after her shower.

"I guess Sam has been telling you about all the antics him and Scruffy, oh and Maisie too, have got up to. Scruffy attracted the adoration of a young female yesterday. Did Sam tell you that?" asked Sam's Mum.

"No he did not Di. Scruffy what is this I am hearing? Was the attraction mutual Sam? Has Scruffy fallen in love?"

"No he has not fallen in love Steve he is far too young for that," exclaimed Sam. "Mind you she was a bit of a beauty wasn't she Scruffy?"

Scruffy wagged his tail vigorously and looked towards the door.

"No Scruffy she is not here although Mum says her and Helen will come to visit in a week or two then we can show her all our walks and teach her to play football."

"Oh dear Di, Scruffy, Maisie and Sam loose with a football sounds like you are going to have fun."

"Well it gets worse as Helen and Maisie are coming when Pete and Jan are staying here so I suggest you stay away. Pete and Sam can cause mayhem so add Scruffy and Maisie into the equation and it goes from bad to worse," answered Sam's Mum.

"No I most certainly will not stay away I want to share some of this fun. You cannot be greedy and keep it all to yourself."

"Well do not say I did not warn you," laughed Sam's Mum. "It could get pretty dangerous around here. Right everyone let us get some tea because I do not know about anyone else but I am starving."

Sam's Mum dished out the casserole and Sam, Steve and her sat down at the table. Just at that moment Scruffy let out a loud snore making them all jump.

"Scruffy has the last word as usual," observed Sam as he tucked into his tea.

Sam and Scruffy Go to Work

Sam was up early the next morning eating his breakfast when his Mum came downstairs.

"Goodness Sam you are up early this morning," she exclaimed.

"Yes Scruffy and I want to get up to Steve's place early because I want to help him feed the animals before we go out into the fields to gather up the bales of straw. Steve was telling me last night about the different rations the calves have depending on their ages and I want to know more," answered Sam. "Scruffy has had his breakfast already and I have nearly finished mine now. The kettle has just boiled for your coffee too Mum."

"My goodness Sam you really are being so helpful at the moment. I only hope this new Sam remains in our life especially next week when we go back to school."

"I am really going to try Mum this year as Steve says education is important to make a success of farming. Come on Scruffy time to go and help Steve."

Scruffy bounded out of the house in front of Sam and Sam's Mum stood and watched them go.

"Well I never, all these years I have been trying to encourage Sam to try harder at school and Steve comes for tea one night and Sam is completely under his spell. It might mean we do not have so many arguments about homework though. I will have to encourage Steve to come for tea more often if this is the result."

Sam's Mum made herself a coffee before going outside to peg the washing out then settling down to work. Meanwhile Sam and Scruffy had arrived at the farm and met Steve just crossing the farmyard.

"Goodness Sam I thought you and Scruffy would be tired this morning and need a lie in."

"No we have come to help you. I want to be a farmer like you and Uncle Pete when I grow up so I thought I would come and help you all day. I was fascinated last night when you were telling me about the different ratio of foodstuffs you give the calves according to their ages. That means a farmer needs to be good at sums then does it?"

"Yes but you need a good all round education. You need reading and writing as there are so many forms to fill in these days. You need to be able to read to find out about different grants you might be able to apply for and the writing ability to actually apply for them. Using the internet is a good skill too as we can use this method to search for information on a particular grant or subsidy. Lastly you need to understand science. You need to be able to understand your land and what needs to be added via fertilizer to correct any imperfections in the soil but also understand the different soil types so you can plant the best crop for that soil. A basic understanding of geology helps too as then you will understand your land better. Although we rotate our crops, certain fields will not grow corn whereas in other fields corn will thrive. Some of the fields that are stony is best suited to grass for the sheep and cows to graze as we would break our machinery if we used those fields for hay or silage. There are so many things to learn and understand about land if you want to be a farmer. I am lucky as I know this land well. I have lived here all my life like my Dad and Grandad before me and have absorbed so much information by just being around them but despite this I am still learning and discovering new ways to make life easier. That is why I suggested that your Uncle Pete and me spend time together as we may both learn things from each other."

"Mum says she is sure Uncle Pete will be interested in looking round the farm and fields as farming is in his blood. To be honest Mum also has a lot of interest and knowledge about farming too. I did not realise how much she knew until we visited the farming museum. She was able to tell me about the machinery and what the tools were used for in a lot of cases. Those she did not know she suggested I ask Grandad. She took a lot of photographs on her telephone and we bought a guide book which showed some of the things she did not know about."

"I will have to get her to show me the pictures. This museum you were telling me about sounds real interesting. We will have to visit sometime as Dad would probably be interested too."

"Oh that would be brilliant. Mum says we might take my Grandad next year when him and Granny come to stay again. She says that it is no good this time as the museum will be closed as it closes for winter."

"Well we will have to organise a full family day out next year then. My Mum and Dad, your grandparents, me, your Mum and you. How does that sound?"

"It sounds a great idea," Sam answered.

By this time Steve, Sam and Scruffy had arrived at the shed that held the calves. Scruffy was staying well away now as he was not going to allow any of these big creatures lick him again!

"Okay Steve what do we do first?" asked Sam.

"Well I have a bucket of food here for the oldest ones at the back of the shed. Here hold up this door whilst I undo the bolts then let it come down slowly moving back out of the way as it comes down. Well done you did well there."

Sam was fascinated because the door made a ramp up into a channel that all the stock could eat across from both sides. All the calves woke up and began to stretch. Down each side of the concrete channel that you could walk down were troughs.

"Right bring those 2 buckets of feed down here," instructed Steve. "The blue bucket is for these here on the right and the black bucket for the ones on the left. The ones on the right are our oldest and will be going to market soon and then we will clean out the pen and move them all round so the youngest ones, the ones coming back from the hills, go in the first pen at the front of the shed on the left hand side."

"How do you get them out of that pen at the back?" asked Sam.

"If you look there is a door out of that pen. The cattle lorry can get round the back of the shed to that door and we load the calves, well to be honest they are no longer calves, so I should say stock, into the wagon. Then after the pen is cleaned out we use the gates to move all the calves round. The tricky bit is getting the calves from this last pen on the left out through the door, round the building to the front pen on the right. When we are moving that pen it is all hands on deck as we do not want them running around the farmyard. It takes me and my Mum and Dad normally but this year we can ask your Mum if we can borrow you too which will make another pair of hands."

"Wow that would be exciting wouldn't it Scruffy helping move calves? I am sure Mum would love to help too Steve if you asked her. Remember she grew up on a farm."

"Good idea Sam I will ask her. It will not be for 2 or 3 weeks yet as we have to get the straw led into the barns before organising the action of sending those last 5 from that pen to market. After that we have to clean out the pen although that is now much easier than it used to be. We can use that yellow tractor to dig the manure out of the pen and load it onto a trailer to take down the field and put it into a heap ready for spreading on the fields where the corn has been."

"That would work fine as Mum says she will have to work hard for the next 2 weeks to perfect her drawing of the fairy in the book before setting her in different locations depending on the story and what adventure the fairy is having. Once she has the basic pattern for the fairy she just needs to change her clothes, settings and positions as she works through the story."

"Your Mum is so clever making the books come to life using her drawings. I am afraid I could never do anything like that but I really admire her talent."

197

"Well to be honest Steve Mum admires you too and the work you do as she knows how hard farming is. I think she was a bit surprised when she found out this week that you actually follow the same pattern as Uncle Pete and Grandad before him. Somehow Mum thought your methods would be different because she said the land was better land or something!"

"She probably thought as we are not situated in the hills like her parent's land was our land would be more productive. I admit some is a bit better but as our land stretches quite a way up those hills behind us, we also have a lot of poorer quality of land. I will have to tell her all about the different levels we have on this farm as she would probably be interested," answered Steve.

"I am sure she would be Steve so that would be great."

By this time Steve had poured the food all along the troughs of both sides of the back pens.

"Now Sam take those empty buckets down the rack as we call this channel and I will follow. We then need to give these 2 pens some wheelbarrow loads of silage before we go back to the shed where the food is kept and prepare the next 2 buckets for the next 2 pens."

Scruffy had been watching his master anxiously while Sam had been down the rack and just as Sam and Steve prepared to come back Scruffy took a chance and ran up the ramp towards them. Unfortunately he was so busy trying to watch the calves at either side of him he bumped into Sam and sent the empty bucket flying into the pen.

"Oh Scruffy look what you have done now, do be careful please!"

"No worries Sam just climb down into the pen and rescue the bucket. It was a good job it was empty."

Sam climbed down into the pen and quickly retrieved the bucket. He handed it to Steve and tried to climb back into the rack. Unfortunately it was harder to climb back up than it had been going down so Steve had to give him a pull up. Soon order was restored and Scruffy was thankful he could scamper down the rack back into the farmyard.

He and Sam watched Steve tip the silage down the centre of the rack before all three made their way back to the food storage shed. Steve showed Sam how to measure out the rations for the next 2 pens before they went back to the calf shed and performed exactly the same procedure as before. Eventually all the calves were fed, the goats fed and led into the orchard where they were put on a long chain each to graze the grass.

"Why do you chain them," asked Sam.

"That is because goats are very naughty and can climb over fences or even open gates. If they got out of the orchard who knows what damage they might do to themselves or to crops or anything. The babies will not leave their mother so we do not have to secure them they will play around their Mum," answered Steve.

"Oh how interesting, I did not realise they were so clever but naughty Steve."

"Believe me they are very naughty animals but also good fun too. When the babies get a bit bigger you can see the mischief they can get up to. They will climb anything, logs, piles of stones, just anything then launch themselves off and run off playing tag around the trees before jumping on to something else."

The pair released the geese and hens from their huts where they had spent the night and the ducks swam across the pond towards the farmyard to be fed too. Sam and Steve fed the pigs and then opened the stable door for Ned, the horse, to come out as and when he wanted to. By this time Steve's Dad had emerged from the farmhouse too.

"Oh good morning Sam and Scruffy it is nice to see you here early and all ready for work I hope?"

"Yes thank you," replied Sam.

"Have you finished feeding the animals Steve?"

"Yes Dad, Sam and Scruffy have been helping but Scruffy was more interested in snuffling about among the straw."

"That was probably because there will be mice about. Wait until be start moving the straw then there will be all kinds of wildlife to smell, chase and try to catch," laughed Steve's Dad. "Now how are we going to work today? Do you think it might be best if you and Sam do the loading on to the trailer and I use the loader to pass them up to you? You will have to teach Sam how to load the bales so they are stable Steve as he has not done it before. If I place the tractor and trailer in the middle of the field and then bring the bales to you on the loader, would that work? It saves me jumping on and off the loader to move the tractor and trailer."

"To be honest Dad it may be easier the other way round. You and Sam on the trailer, me and Scruffy working the field. Otherwise the loader is trundling back and forwards 8 times just for one pile of bales. I can pass 2 piles to you before moving on to the next 2. I think it will be quicker that way too. That was the way I learnt to do it. Grandad and I were loading the bales on to the trailer and you, in them days, walked the fields and forked them up to us. Once Grandad was confident I could do it on my own he then drove the tractor and trailer around the field. Once we get Sam taught what to do I imagine we can follow the same pattern."

"Well it was a bit different for us you were my son so your Mum was happy that you were safe and she knew that farming was your destiny. We have to remember Sam has not grown up on the farm absorbing things from a toddler and we are not his Dad or Grandad so Di might not be as trusting as your Mum was."

"It is okay Dad," Steve said. "Di told me last night she trusts us completely. Remember she grew up on a farm too so understands the way of life like Mum did. You are perfectly capable of taking over the role of Sam's 'surrogate' Grandad and as Sam has been telling me this morning, and Di told me last night, he has decided he wants to be a farmer like his other Grandad and Uncle Pete so he might as well start to learn now. I was about the same age as him when I began to be involved on the work side of the business. Before that I mainly took it all for granted. I maybe helped a bit if Mum was involved too but on the whole left the work to Grandad and you. Who knows maybe one day he will be the next generation to farm this land. He certainly has the credentials and aptitude to do so. It is up to us two to guide him now."

"Now that is interesting. Are you trying to tell me there is a growing attraction between you and Di? If so your Mum will be pleased as she thinks the world of Di and young Sam here. Well in that case let us get going and between us we will mould young Sam into an excellent farmer. Come on Sam and Scruffy let us go and get the tractor and trailer. Steve can you pop your head into the house and tell your Mum that we are away to the fields so she knows where we are?"

"Fine I will do that Dad then I will follow you with the loader."

Neither Steve nor his Dad had realised that Sam had been listening to their conversation with great interest. By the sounds of things Steve was happy to teach him, Sam, all about the farm and how to do things properly and if he was not mistaken maybe interested in spending more time with Sam's Mum. Scruffy had wandered off again across the farmyard while Steve and his Dad had been talking and was busy investigating under a bush that had bright yellow flowers on. He was not interested in the bush but what was underneath it. There was something underneath right in the middle of the bush but he could not see what. He pushed in a bit further trying to reach whatever it was. He was sure it was an animal of some sort but it was making a strange noise, not one he had heard before. As he pushed deeper his coat got snagged on the needles of the bush and then just as he nearly reached the furry creature a leg shot out and a claw caught his nose. With a yelp Scruffy shot back but his coat was tangled in the bush and he could not get back out again fast enough and the leg with the claws on kept stabbing at his nose accompanied by a hissing noise. With another yelp of pain and a more frenzied attack on the bush that was holding him he crashed back out of the bush and ran to his master. His coat was covered in needles from the bush and a few broken bits of branch. Scruffy ran behind Sam and laid down on the ground covering his nose with his paw whimpering.

"What on earth is the matter Scruffy and how have you managed to get covered in gorse bush?" asked Sam.

Scruffy uncovered his nose and looked up at his master with such sorrowful eyes. Sam was looking around the farmyard and spotted the damaged bush and then looked at his dog's nose. There was blood pouring out of a deep scratch on his nose and several smaller ones on each side. Sam knelt down to have a better look and said,

"That looks as though you have been scratched by a cat. Did you disturb one of the farm cats having a snooze in the bush?"

"What is the matter with Scruffy?" asked Steve.

"It looks as though he has got scratched by a cat in that gorse bush over there as he is covered in gorse needles and his nose has a bad scratch on it. It is okay he should not go poking his nose under bushes," answered Sam.

"Well that is a strange place for the cat to sleep because by the looks of things it was deep in the middle. They often lay on the edge in the shade but not as deep as that. Let us go and have a look. Mum was saying she has not seen one of the female cats for a few days and wondered if she had given birth to kittens somewhere."

"Do you mean that Scruffy might have found her with her new born kittens?" asked Sam.

"Well it is possible but they more often go into the barns and sheds. Giving birth under a bush is less common. If that is the case I will need your help as we will need to collect the mum and babies and take them to the house and get my Mum to make her a bed in a box next to the stove where she will be safe. Dad wait a minute we think Scruffy has found Tabby inside the bush over there and she may have kittens. Mum was saying she had not seen her for a few days and then I think we had better treat Scruffy's nose before we head out into the field."

"Oh well done Scruffy if you have found her as we would soon have had to make a search for her. We like to bring the kittens into the house to rear so they get used to people as we cannot keep them all but we can usually find a home for them when they are ready to leave their mum."

"I wonder if Mum would let us have one as it would be company for Scruffy when I was at school and Mum was working."

"Don't you think your Mum has enough with you two madcaps causing mayhem without a kitten too?" laughed Steve. "I guess you can always ask her though tonight if we are correct and have found the kittens. Come on Sam, you come with me and we will leave Scruffy with Dad so he does not get scratched again."

Scruffy was going nowhere near the bush again as his nose still hurt and Sam had not even given him a cuddle to comfort him.

"Poor boy does your nose hurt real bad?" said Steve's Dad reaching down to fondle Scruffy's ears and give him a few pats. "Never mind we will go up to the house and get Jane, Steve's Mum, to bathe it and put some ointment on while Sam and Steve deal with the cat and her kittens. Tabby would not mean to hurt you but you probably startled her. Come on let us go and see Jane and get you mended. Steve, Sam, Scruffy and me are going up to the house to get Scruffy's nose bathed. See you there, have you found anything?"

"Yes," answered Steve. "It is certainly Tabby and the way she is purring I think she has kittens but she is right in the heart of the bush so is going to take some reaching. Warn Mum what Sam and me are coming with please once we have got them all."

"Yes Scruffy and me will sort it. I will leave Scruffy in your Mum's capable hands and make Tabby a bed ready for her."

By this time Steve had managed to prise back the branches of the bush so he could reach into the heart of it

"Yes Sam she definitely has kittens. I will pass them to you one at a time, handle them gently as they are only about a day or maybe two days old."

Sam used his feet and legs to hold back the branches so Steve could pass him the kittens.

"She has 4 kittens Sam and all look healthy. Okay Tabby do not panic it is only me. Come on let me take your babies and give them to Sam and then I will carry you over to the house. Mum will make you a lovely bed near the stove so your babies are safe and you can leave them to have your meals. You know Mum will spoil you rotten now. I think we will keep one of your babies as Bert and Arthur are now getting too old to catch mice and rats so that only leaves you and Mabel so you need some help. Here you are Sam kitten number one coming up."

Steve passed the kittens to Sam who used his T-shirt bottom to make a cradle as he realised he could not hold 4 squirming kittens at once. Soon Steve emerged from the bush carrying the most beautiful cat in his arms.

"This is Tabitha or usually known as Tabby because of the markings on her coat. It is alright Tabby your babies are safe with Sam. Look how clever he has been as he has made a pouch with his tee shirt to carry them in."

Soon the little party arrived at the house. There was a box with an old jumper in ready for the mother cat and her babies and Scruffy was having a fuss made of him by Steve's Mum while she smoothed ointment into the scratches on his nose. Scruffy looked at Sam with reproachable eyes as he had not forgiven him yet for not making a fuss of him when he got his nose scratched. Steve popped Tabby into the box and Sam crouched down and gently transferred the kittens from his T-shirt into the box next to their mum. Tabby gave each kitten a few licks before settling down again to feed them. By this time Steve's Mum had finished putting cream on Scruffy's nose and after giving him a quick cuddle walked over to the box to have a quick look at the kittens.

"How many are there Steve," she asked.

"There are 4 in all Mum and they seem healthy and normal. I was just telling Tabby we would probably keep one ourselves as Bert and Arthur are getting too old now. They are ready for retirement so that just leaves her and Mabel to keep all the vermin down on the farm. Sam here is hoping to persuade Di to let them have one too."

"Yes Bert and Arthur are like me and your Dad, they have earned their retirement but as yet you have not done anything about a family of your own so we have to just keep going. Poor Di, does she really deserve another crazy animal as soon as this after just getting Scruffy?" laughed Steve's Mum.

"Knowing Di she will just take it in her stride. As to your other comment let us just say I am working on it but I am not ready to spill the beans just yet and especially not with little ears about. By the way Mum and Dad while I remember Di was saying she is going to have a bonfire party as her parents will be staying then and asked me if you and Dad would like to contribute and join them. I said we would likely be able to find some wood for the bonfire and you might be able to find some old clothes for the Guy Mum. I promised to be in charge of buying the fireworks and helping Sam and his Grandad build the bonfire," Steve informed his parents.

"Great idea Steve, we will start to stockpile the wood up here and then I will help you, Sam and his Grandad build it in the field between the 2 houses nearer the time. That way if any wildlife have used the wood to make nests in or hibernate they will get disturbed. What about you Jane, can you help with the food?"

"Yes I will Tony but I will talk to Di directly so we do not all make the same things. Di is so busy with her work maybe just me and her own Mum can do the baking and most of the food. I will talk to her about it later. Now off you men go or it will be lunchtime and you will not have even started."

"Cool I did not realise Mum had told you about the bonfire party. Her friend Helen and her dog Maisie are coming too," said Sam.

"Yes she told me last night and she is going to invite a couple of your friends from school and their parents too so we will have a nice little party."

By this time Scruffy had sidled up to Sam and was gingerly peering at the box where the cat and kittens were laying. The mother cat was quite content so Scruffy edged a bit closer. He knew this was the thing that had scratched his nose so he was approaching with caution.

"Oh Scruffy, did you want to see the kittens? Okay creep up slowly, do not frighten the mum. You will not frighten the kittens as their eyes are tightly closed. When do they actually open their eyes Steve?"

"Usually at about a week or 10 days old Sam," answered Steve.

"Oh I will be back at school by then," moaned Sam.

"Well you are not there all day so you can come up to see them every day after school if you want. That would be good if you are having one of them as you could watch it develop and it can get to know you."

"Do not encourage the boy Steve until his Mum has agreed as she has enough work as it is and enough mouths to feed," corrected Steve's Mum. "It is not as if you are there to help her although I must admit you spend a lot of time down there."

"True Mum," laughed Steve. "Okay Dad, Sam and Scruffy back to work. Sam and Scruffy go with Dad and I will follow with the loader. Off you go Scruffy, Mum will look after the mother cat and her kittens."

"Look after the boy you two he is precious to Di," Steve's Mum instructed her husband and son.

"We will," chorused Steve and his Dad as they all left the kitchen Steve following it with, "he is precious to me too."

"Well, well Tabby do we sense there might be more interest than just friendship between Steve and Di? I do hope so she is such a lovely woman. Right I had better get on and get some work done myself as I have two hungry men and a growing young boy to feed," Jane told the cat as she bustled about the kitchen.

Meanwhile Steve's Dad, Sam and Scruffy had arrived at the tractor which was already hooked up to the trailer.

"Up you get Sam and sit on the seat next to the driver's seat and I will give Scruffy a push up to you as he might find it difficult to get into the tractor cab at first."

"Well if it is anything like it was teaching him to get on a train it will take all day but if you give him a push and I will tug from the top we might manage," laughed Sam.

"Oh dear, did you have problems getting him on the train?" asked Steve's Dad.

"Just a bit but luckily Scruffy is a quick learner."

Sam scrambled into the tractor then turned around to pull Scruffy up. Steve's Dad told Scruffy to put his front feet on the step then put his hands under Scruffy's bottom and gave him a push. Before Scruffy knew it he was in the tractor at the side of Sam. He was not too sure how it had happened but it had. Sam scrambled on to the seat and found there was enough room for Scruffy to sit at his feet. Steve's Dad quickly joined them and drove out of the farmyard with Steve following behind with the loading tractor. Scruffy was not too sure about this mode of transport as it was very bumpy and something was sticking into his bottom. He wriggled a bit to try to get comfortable but it was not any better.

"Sit still Scruffy, stop wriggling or you will fall off the ledge you are sitting on down onto the step and that will be an even tighter squeeze for you."

"Do as Sam says Scruffy. I know it is not too comfortable but it is not far to the field and then you can get out and run about while we collect the bales of straw."

Scruffy did not want to disappoint Sam so he tried to sit still but every time the tractor went over a bump whatever it was that was sticking into him jabbed him again. He was very glad when the tractor pulled into the field where the straw was. Steve's Dad jumped down off his seat and said to Sam,

"Stay there and I will open the other door for you."

Sam and Scruffy tumbled out of the tractor cab just as Steve trundled into the field with the loader.

"Right Scruffy you can run around the field if you want or lay and watch us but if you are running about be careful to keep out of the way of the tractor wheels," said Steve. "Sam come on, you and Dad are on the trailer. I brought you some gloves as the baler twine will cut into your hands until they get hardened like mine and Dad's hands have. Follow Dad's instructions and keep away from the edges of the trailer when we are moving across the field."

Soon everyone had got into a routine and the bales of straw slowly got less in the field but the layers on the trailer got higher. Sam had not realised how high up they were until Steve said,

"That will do as I cannot get the loader any higher. We will rope these down then you and Sam will have to slide down the ropes. Show Sam what to do Dad please. How has he done helping you with the first load?"

"Fine he has worked well. He is a quick learner as by the time we had done 5 levels he had a pretty good idea where each bale needed to be put without much help from me. At this rate we will definitely get it all in by the time Sam goes back to school maybe even a day or two before."

"Good I thought he looked to be doing well. Di will be pleased when I tell her because she was worried he would slow us down," remarked Steve. "Scruffy did well down here too as he managed to chase a few rabbits and got startled when a rat shot out from under a bale but did not have time to catch it before it disappeared."

"Actually Steve we will not all fit in the tractor cab to travel back to the farmyard so it might be best if Sam and me ride on top of the load. I have left a space for Sam to put his feet and he can hold on to the rope at one side of the load and I will keep him safe at the other side. You and Scruffy can then travel in the cab. Scruffy might be pleased to sit on the seat as he was sat on the head of a bolt as we came and was a bit uncomfortable," answered Steve's Dad.

"Good thinking Dad. Right are you ready to catch the rope as it is coming up to you now?"

"Yes we are out of its direct way. I will catch it and send it back over the other side."

Sam was fascinated how easily Steve could throw the rope over the trailer and the load was soon secure.

"Right Sam come and sit on this bale of straw and put your feet in this hole and then hold on to the rope at your side and I will sit next to you at this side. You are quite safe because we are sat in the middle of the load and the bales are securely tied on the trailer. Do not worry about Scruffy Steve will look after him. Now it will feel very rocky as we travel across the field but it will be much smoother once we get on the road."

Sam did as Steve's Dad told him and Steve gave Scruffy a hand up into the tractor cab then told him to sit on the seat where Sam had sat on the way to the field. Scruffy was glad to sit on this especially as it meant he could look out of the window where they were going. They were soon back at the farmyard and Steve pulled the tractor and trailer inside the barn. He jumped down and began loosening the ropes. Scruffy wondered if he ought to get out but decided against it. He was nice and comfortable on his seat and he did not want to encounter any more dangerous cats so laid back down on his seat. As soon as the ropes were off the load Sam and Steve's Dad dropped the bales down on to the ground for Steve to stack in the barn. It was not very long before all the bales of straw were off the trailer and stacked neatly in the barn.

"Well done team we will go and get at least one more load before lunch, we might even get two," said Steve. "Are you riding back to the field on the trailer Sam with my Dad or do you want to ride in the tractor?"

"Please may I ride on the trailer with your Dad Steve?" asked Sam.

"Yes of course, Scruffy will be pleased as he likes riding on the seat," laughed Steve.

He jumped into the tractor and set off for the field again. This time Sam had more idea what he was doing and him and Steve's Dad were able to keep up with Steve as he passed the bales up to them. Scruffy got down off the tractor when they arrived in the field and continued to hunt around in the hedge bottoms to see if he could find any wildlife. He soon stumbled on a couple of pheasants who flew off in a rage. He saw a few more rabbits but could not catch them either. He saw another rat shoot out from under a pile of bales but he was not close enough to give chase. Soon the trailer was loaded and securely tied down and Scruffy did not need any encouragement or help to get into the tractor again. As soon as the trailer was empty the 3 humans and Scruffy headed for the farmhouse kitchen where Steve's Mum was waiting for them.

"That was good timing you three, dinner is ready so get your hands washed and sit up to the table. Scruffy come here I have found an old dog water bowl from under the stairs and you can have a sausage as a treat if you have been a good dog."

"He has behaved himself real well Mum," answered Steve. "Sam has also done well I think we will make a farmer of him yet."

Sam glowed with pride and quickly washed his hands and sat down at the table. Scruffy flopped down on the floor next to the box of kittens. Tabby was curled up in the box protecting her kittens but was not bothered about Scruffy being near the box. Scruffy had been busy all morning so he thought he would have a quick snooze. The next thing he knew was Sam shaking him awake.

"Come on Scruffy wake up we have finished our dinner and we are going back to work now."

Scruffy scrambled to his feet and followed Sam out of the door. Steve's Dad and Sam climbed up on to the trailer and Steve opened the tractor cab door. Scruffy bounded up into the tractor and sat on 'his' seat ready to go back to the field. They managed 3 loads more in the afternoon. By this time the layer of bales in the barn was higher than the trailer so they had to use an elevator to get the bales up to Steve. Sam struggled at first to drop the bales on to the elevator correctly and quite a few wobbled off the side. Steve's Dad was very patient with him explaining what he was doing wrong and by the last load Sam managed to get all his bales to stay on the elevator.

"Well done everyone," Steve said. "I am going to feed the animals again Sam. You and Scruffy can either help me and then I will walk you home or you can go home now on your own."

"Please can we help you again Steve?" asked Sam.

"Of course you can, no problem. I think with your help we can do it in record time," answered Steve.

Scruffy and Sam followed Steve across the farmyard and Steve's Dad went into the farmhouse.

"Has Sam and Scruffy gone home?" asked Steve's Mum.

"No they have gone to feed the animals with Steve then Steve said he would walk the pair home. Sam is like Steve's shadow hanging on to his every word," answered Steve's Dad.

"Yes I know I watched them at dinner time, mind you Steve thinks the world of Sam too. Do you think there is more to his friendship with Di than merely friends?" questioned Steve's Mum.

"I do not really know for sure but Steve sort of hinted that he hoped one day Sam and Di might be part of our family this morning."

"Oh I do hope so Di is such a lovely woman. She would fit in so well too as she knows all about farming."

"Yes but she is also a talented artist do not forget. Maybe she would not want to give that up to help Steve on the farm. It is okay at the moment as you and I can help him but eventually the day will come when we want to retire like Di's parents have done," answered Steve's Dad.

211

"Well I think she would be able to do both, after all I do not do much on the farm now apart from feed you and Steve and look after a recurring series of baby animals that need attention," observed Steve's Mum.

"No not now since Steve grew up but you used to help me before that you know."

"Well Sam is not a baby so by the time we are ready to retire he will likely be a man and can take over from you."

"You have it all planned out haven't you." laughed Steve's Dad. "Leave them alone to find their own path. Is there any chance of a cup of tea please?"

"Of course I will just put the kettle on."

Shortly after that Sam, Steve and Scruffy tramped into the kitchen.

"I am just going to walk Sam and Scruffy home Mum. I will be back soon," Steve said.

"Okay Steve, stay as long as you want. Your Dad says you have done so well today you are not going to need to do anymore straw leading until Monday. That is a real shame as I was going to ask Di to come up for Sunday dinner if you were working."

"No the weather forecast is good for all next week and we only need another couple of days to clear it all. Is it Thursday you go back to school Sam?"

"Yes," answered Sam.

"Well that works fine then. We work Monday and Tuesday and then you can use Wednesday to get ready for school on Thursday. If you want Mum I can ask Di to come for dinner anyway even though Sam is not working for us. They could all come as it would save Di cooking and I am sure Sam and me could find something to do along with Scruffy."

"Yes ask her Steve," answered his Mum. "After all I am cooking for us three so another two is no bother. It might give her chance to get a bit more work done in the morning especially if Sam and Scruffy come up here."

"Okay Mum it sounds like a good plan I will ask her for you. Right Sam collect your dog from gazing in awe at the cat and kittens and let us get you home. Scruffy seems completely mesmerised by them."

"Yes he does Steve. Come on Scruffy let us get home and tell Mum all about our day."

Sam whirled out of the kitchen with Scruffy, after another quick peek at the kittens in the box, following tight behind him.

"I had better go or they will be at home before I get halfway down the field," laughed Steve. "See you later Mum and Dad."

"See you later son," they chorused.

Steve quickly caught up with Sam and Scruffy and they ambled down the field towards Sam's house. When they arrived Sam burst into the house saying,

"Hi Mum, we have had a brilliant day. Scruffy found a mummy cat and kittens and we had to rescue them and take them into the house and please can we have one. Scruffy thinks they are wonderful, we got 5 loads of straw in and I fed the animals with Steve."

"Whoa slow down Sam you are not making sense Sam. How did Scruffy find the cat? Start at the beginning please," ordered his Mum. "Oh hi Steve was everything okay today?"

"Hi Di yes both as good as gold. Both Sam and Scruffy are quick learners. Scruffy quickly learnt how to get on and off the tractor and Sam picked up loading bales real quickly. You have a very bright boy there and I am sure he is a farmer in the making."

"Good, now Sam tell me about Scruffy finding a cat please."

"Well after we had fed the animals we were discussing, or rather Steve and his Dad were discussing, how we were going to work together to load the straw. Scruffy wandered off and poked about in a gorse bush and found Tabby and her babies. Tabby actually scratched Scruffy's nose so Steve's Dad took him to the farmhouse while Steve handed me the kittens to carry into the kitchen while Steve brought Tabby. We settled them in a box at the side of the stove. They are so cute please can we have one as Steve's Mum will have to find homes for them as there is 4 in total. Steve says they will keep at least one and I wondered if Helen and Maisie would have one too. Scruffy now just stands gazing into the box so he loves them already."

"Oh Sam how old are they? If we get a kitten now it will be still a baby when we go away at Christmas and it will wreck the Christmas tree. I know we had several when I was young and living at home," answered his Mum.

"Oh please Mum come on they are only one or two days old so it will be ages before they can leave their mum and Scruffy is getting less clumsy all the time now. Please, I could have it for my birthday," cajoled Sam.

"I will think about it now are you ready for tea?"

"Please Mum, I am starving, working makes you hungry."

"Sam, you are always hungry so it has nothing to do with working," laughed his Mum. "Sit down and I will serve it up. Do you want to stay for tea Steve? I am afraid it is only chips, fish fingers and peas, nothing exotic."

"Do you know I have not had fish fingers for years. I would love to join you providing there is enough," answered Steve.

"I always cook more than we need Steve so please do join us. Sam get another plate and some cutlery for Steve please while I finish Scruffy's tea and then I will bring our tea to the table as it is ready."

"Sam you get my plate and Di I will get the tea out of the oven while you see to Scruffy and then we will all finish our jobs together."

"Thank you Steve that would be a great help."

Soon everyone was tucking into their tea and Sam was telling his Mum all about his day. Suddenly Steve remembered his Mum's invitation.

"Di, Mum said would you come to us for Sunday lunch tomorrow as we are not leading straw. Sam and Scruffy can come up to me as soon as they want as I can find some jobs for them and then you can get a few hours work done before joining us for lunch. Dad and I need the boys on Monday and Tuesday as we are leading straw again and then you and Sam can check you have all you need for him going back to school on Wednesday. Does that work for you?"

"Yes perfect as I need to check his uniform still fits as he grows so quickly especially in these long summer holidays."

"I know I can remember my Mum saying that about me too. Are you happy to come for lunch? I think Mum craves some female company sometimes."

"Yes that would be great I can do ever so much if I do not have to stop to cook lunch and I am sure Sam and Scruffy would enjoy another day with you."

When tea was finished and the washing up done Sam and Scruffy went into the sitting room to watch television while Steve and Di enjoyed another cup of coffee. Steve filled Di in about Sam's day but soon other topics of conversation were discussed. Neither noticed the time until Sam and Scruffy wandered back into the kitchen.

"Goodnight Mum, I am so tired I am going to bed. Goodnight Steve, I will see you in the morning."

"Goodnight Sam," they chorused and Scruffy snuggled back into his bed to dream about catching rabbits.

"I must go too Di but thank you for my tea. I have enjoyed my evening and I will look forward to seeing you tomorrow. Lunch is usually about 1pm, does that work for you?"

"Yes that is fine, say thank you to your Mum for asking me. I will see you tomorrow."

The following day after much badgering from Sam his Mum gave in and agreed that they could have one of the kittens so Sam had great fun choosing which one he was going to have. Scruffy was equally interested in each kitten as it was taken out of the box and examined and even managed to give one a kiss.

"I think this is Scruffy's favourite," said Sam. "He always licks this one when I take it out of the box. It looks so cute with its little patch of white under its chin. It looks as though it has a bow tie on so I think I will call it Bows."

"Yes I think that is my favourite too Sam and I love the name so Bows it is. Which are you keeping Steve?" asked Sam's Mum.

"I am not sure yet I normally wait until they are scampering about before I choose."

"I spoke to my friend Hele after you left last night Steve and she wants one too but she cannot get over just yet as she has a publishing deadline to meet," Di told Steve and Sam. "So she suggested Sam choose one for her as, in her words, he makes good choices. So you have to choose one for Helen and Maisie please Sam."

"Oh definitely the little grey one for Helen she will adore that one," Sam told his Mum. "It is perfect for Helen and Maisie so that just leaves you to choose Steve."

"I think the ginger one probably so Mum you only have to find a home for one."

"To be honest we might keep both because as you say Bert and Arthur are ready to retire and Mabel is also getting on a bit. It takes a kitten about 2 years before it can catch a rat and Mabel will be too old to hunt much by then so a farm as big as this needs at least 3 working cats if not 4."

"Wow does that mean that all 4 kittens are staying where I can often see them," exclaimed an excited Sam. "That will be awesome. I have had such a great summer holiday. Thank you Mum and you too Steve for making this the best holiday time I have ever had but best of all was getting Scruffy."

Sam put his arms around Scruffy and gave him a long cuddle. Steve and Di watched the pair before Di said,

"What have I done not only have we got a dog but the household is going to increase further to accommodate a kitten. Oh I must be mad!"

"Yes definitely mad but neither Sam nor Scruffy would want you any different and I am sure Bows will also give you hours of pleasure, maybe some headaches too, who knows. I will be on hand to help you all I can. I am like Sam and Scruffy I would not want you to change."

"Neither would we, would we Tony?" added Sam's Mum. "You are just perfect the way you are."

Sam could not resist another cuddle with his kitten and this time Scruffy was not going to be left out so he laid his face alongside the kitten on Sam's chest. The kitten nuzzled into Scruffy's warm furry face and for the rest of their lives Scruffy and Bows were inseparable.

Lightning Source UK Ltd.
Milton Keynes UK
UKOW02f0640261116
288548UK00002B/22/P